ABDULRAZAK GURNAH is the winner of the Nobel Prize in Literature 2021. He is the author of ten novels: *Memory of Departure*, *Pilgrims Way*, *Dottie*, *Paradise* (shortlisted for the Booker Prize and the Whitbread Award), *Admiring Silence*, *By the Sea* (longlisted for the Booker Prize and shortlisted for the *Los Angeles Times* Book Award), *Desertion* (shortlisted for the Commonwealth Writers' Prize), *The Last Gift*, *Gravel Heart* and *Afterlives* (longlisted for the Walter Scott Prize and shortlisted for the Orwell Prize for Political Fiction). He is Emeritus Professor of English and Postcolonial Literatures at the University of Kent. He lives in Canterbury.

BY THE SAME AUTHOR

Memory of Departure
Dottie
Paradise
Admiring Silence
By the Sea
Desertion
The Last Gift
Gravel Heart
Afterlives

PILGRIMS WAY

ABDULRAZAK
GURNAH

BLOOMSBURY PUBLISHING
LONDON • OXFORD • NEW YORK • NEW DELHI • SYDNEY

BLOOMSBURY PUBLISHING
Bloomsbury Publishing Plc
50 Bedford Square, London, WC1B 3DP, UK
29 Earlsfort Terrace, Dublin 2, Ireland

BLOOMSBURY, BLOOMSBURY PUBLISHING and the Diana logo are trademarks of Bloomsbury Publishing Plc

First published in Great Britain 1988
This edition published 2021

A catalogue record for this book is available from the British Library

ISBN: PB: 978-1-5266-5347-5; eBook: 978-1-4088-8569-7;
ePDF: 978-1-5266-5418-2

2 4 6 8 10 9 7 5 3 1

Typeset by Newgen KnowledgeWorks Pvt. Ltd., Chennai, India
Printed and bound in Great Britain by CPI Group (UK) Ltd, Croydon CR0 4YY

1

It was just after seven and the pub was almost empty. The only other customer apart from Daud was a thin, old man leaning over his drink at a corner of the bar. The barman was talking to him, and nodded at Daud to show that he had seen him and would presently attend to him. It was getting towards the end of the week and money was short, so Daud bought himself the cheapest half-pint of beer and sat in the alcove by the window. The beer tasted watery and sour, but he shut his eyes and gulped it.

He heard the barman chuckling softly at something that the old man had said. They both turned to look at him. The old man grinned as he leant back to stare at Daud over an angle of his shoulder, nodding as if he intended to reassure and calm him. Daud made his face as lugubrious as he could and his eyes glassy and blank, blind to the old man's antics. He thought of the grin as the one that won an empire. It was the pick-pocket's smile, given tongue in cheek and intended to distract and soothe the innocent prey while the thief helped himself to the valuables. It had travelled the seven seas, flashing at unsuspecting wogs the world over. Millions of them succumbed to it, laughing at its transparently conniving intention, and assuming that the mind behind such a ridiculous face must be as idiotic. Daud imagined how embarrassing the sight would have been: half-naked men, skins baked red by the sun, smiling with such complete insincerity. By the time the victims discovered that those bared fangs had every intention of chomping through their comic and woggish world, there was little for them to do but watch with terror as the monsters devoured them. *Never again*, Daud vowed. *Go find yourself another comedy act, you old fool.*

He felt exposed when he sat in a pub alone, and worried that somebody would come to speak to him, and flash yellow teeth at him. When he was new in England, and innocent of the profound antagonism he aroused by his mere presence, he had gone into pubs he should not have gone into. At one he was refused the cigarettes and matches he had gone in to buy. To begin with, he thought that the barman was mad, a *character* who was going to shame him by some act of perversity. Then he saw the grins all around the pub and understood. He had wanted to protest, to make a scene and perhaps hurl a curse on the inn-keeper. Afterwards he had replayed the scene in every detail, except that in these latter versions he was not flustered with surprise and had the perfect riposte to their abuse. He imagined and rehearsed in front of a mirror how he thought his father might protest at such a public indignity. But that first time he had simply stood in the pub, unable to summon the words in the stranger's language, and watched the grins turn him into a clown.

At another pub, the Seven Compasses, he was told that the spaghetti advertised on the menu was finished, when he could see hot, steaming plates being passed over the counter. He had asked to see the landlord, sniffing his pound note ostentatiously to indicate the drift of his case, but he had noticed a few of the beefier patrons getting interested. *No need for alarm. God save the Queen*, he said and ran.

A group of burghers had chased him out of another pub with their stares and angry comments, incensed that he had invaded their gathering and ruined their pleasure. *This could have happened to you*, he cried as he stood at the door. *Fate could have dealt you such a body blow too, and you might have found yourself as unfortunately miscast as I, chased from one haven to another, wretched and despised*. They had turned round and barked their hearty burgher guffaws, their breaths smelling of the burnt fats of animals. *Oh my goodness*, they said. *Oh goodness gracious me*.

The most poignant exclusion was from The Cricketers, where he had gone two or three times and had begun to feel safe. The photographs on the walls were a disappointment, honouring only English and Australian players. There were no Sir Garys and no Three Ws, but he found the cricket paraphernalia on the walls soothing. In the end the landlady had asked him to leave. She told him she could not be sure of restraining her husband from jumping over the bar and cracking him one. So he had gone, saddened and shaken that it was a lover of that noble game who had so misused him.

Daud took as long as he could over his half-pint, but nobody turned up to buy him another one. It was still light outside when he left. He turned into one of the lanes by the cathedral and headed towards the hospital. The route he followed was the same as the one he took in the morning when he went to work. It occurred to him that he could have found something more interesting to do in the evening than that. Had his life become so empty? How would he feel if anyone found out that this was how he spent his hours? He shrugged off the intimations of inadequacy, tossed his head at them, and walked on.

It was a warm June evening, and Daud would not have been surprised to see pavements teeming with frisky teenagers and cocky young men, with a sprinkling of responsible adults taking a stroll and shooting the breeze. Instead the streets were empty and afflicted with gloom. He hurried now, made uncomfortable by the silence and the expectancy of the streets. It was as if the town had been abandoned, its purpose fulfilled, and its inhabitants engaged elsewhere in other pursuits. He avoided the darkest alleys. Who knew what might jump out of them? Who would hear his screams for help?

He imagined a recently returned representative of the greatest empire the world had ever seen walking these streets, after what had seemed like centuries of absence, when the thought of the conviviality of his people would have sustained him while he tortured the silent, sullen peoples under his charge. He would surely have screamed with anguish as he strolled the soulless streets of the evangelical heartland of the old country, and saw the self-deception he had practised in the isolation of his imperial outpost. With what relish he would then recall the hypnotic throbbing of the jungle drums and the scratchings of the shrill cicadas in the tropical night. How fulfilling would seem those endless, dreary afternoons in a tropical hell-hole, where men were still men and knew the potency of rank and power. Surely, surely! But there was very little for him to feel smug about, Daud reminded himself. Shrill cicadas or no, at least the streets were paved and clean, and no scavenging dogs roamed the streets at night, looking for carrion. When he arrives at his house and runs the shower, water will sprinkle out of the rose, instead of dust and the whine of rusted cogs and nuts. His lights worked, his toilet flushed and there were always onions in the shops. He admired the organisation that could make all that function, and pave the paths and make the trains run.

The clock on St George's Tower said twenty minutes past eight. It was always seven minutes slow. He knew this from long experience, but felt it was a small and bearable eccentricity. The tower was the only thing within a radius of hundreds of yards to have survived the wartime bombing. Perhaps, he thought, its heart had stopped for seven minutes. It survived and now stood squat on its arches and colonnades like an old molar. The bombs had been meant for the cathedral, but it had escaped almost untouched, its precious glass long-since secreted away, and its granite walls and spires secure from all but the most direct of hits. Almost by a miracle, the little streets leading to the cathedral had also survived, leaving the monument to Norman piety nestling in its medieval inaccessibility, buffered by a warren of winding alleys.

He looked through the open gate to the cathedral into the floodlit maw of its precincts. He caught a glimpse of the stone massif, with its elegant spires looking even more like fairy-tale towers in the unreal light. For all the years he had lived in the town, he had never been inside the cathedral. He had walked through the grounds hundreds of times, taking a short-cut through the Queens Gate. He had been chased through the cloisters by a group of skinheads: *Gi' us a kiss, nigger*. He gave them a good view of his right royal arse and shouted abuse as he ran. *Go suck a dodo, you fucking pricks*. But he had never been inside the cathedral; which those skinheads probably had.

He took the path across the common to Bishop Street. Most people called it the rec, which had disconcerted him at first. He had thought it was *wreck*, the site of some immemorial foundering. The rec was in a sunken piece of ground surrounded by high banks overgrown with bushes and trees. One path ran alongside the road just below the bank. The one he took cut across the playing pitches and would bring him out by the disused water-mill near Bishop Street. He knew it was a mistake as soon as he had gone far enough to be unable to withdraw without looking scared. He saw a man scrambling down the bank from the road, watched him bend down to take his dog off the lead. He was always wary of dogs, and this one was large and sleek, with a drooling lower jaw that made it look hungry. He glanced away quickly so as not to attract its attention, the way a child might shut its eyes tight to rid itself of a monster that was threatening it. He kept to the path and stretched his legs, aware that with every step he was moving farther from the road and the street-lights, and deeper into the darkness. After a while it became obvious that the couple were after him. From a dozen yards, Daud saw the man start to grin. He threw dignity to the winds and fled, the dog panting and leaping behind him. He heard the man laugh and then whistle for the dog to come back. When he reached the little bridge that straddled the stream, which was the boundary of the rec, Daud stopped and called down a round of curses and plagues on the man. He had not seen him properly, only a glimpse of a skinny figure in an overcoat, with greying hair slicked back like an unfunny parody of a silent-movie star, but he was sure God would have no difficulty identifying him. He had probably come across him before.

He heard the cathedral bells tolling nine as he reached his door. He let himself in, holding his breath and then allowing the air to enter his lungs in small pockets. The landlord believed in piano keys but was very reluctant to have the rotten floor-boards seen to. Daud had even openly questioned his belief: *How can you say you believe in the co-existence of the races, like the black and white keys on a piano, and then exploit me and my people in this way?* He had especially enjoyed that *my people*, and had watched the man squirm with shame and anguish, confident that his floor-boards would be fixed. But the landlord had controlled his pain in some way, and confessed to Daud that he could not get the repairs done unless he received a little more rent.

Daud switched the television on and sat down in front of it. It was more for the noise and distraction that he put it on, to dispel the grip of misery that the silent house had on him. It did not work; and he heard through the strident music on the television the angry grumbles of his mind as it refused to be silenced so easily.

The thought of the letters he needed to write reproached him with its habitual and irresistible force. With it came the memory of what he had left behind, and he felt resolve wobbling, and wondered if the habit of endurance had made him uncritical and self-deluding. Flashes of warm golden beaches appeared in his mind, although he was often unsure if the image were not one he had culled from brochures of other lands. He could not resist the romance and drama of his isolation, and he felt himself giving way. He remembered the walk to school, and felt himself straining for every step, for a picture of the shops and the people he would have passed. Then he knew he had gone too far as the faces of old friends came to chide him with his neglect.

He rarely heard from anybody, and he was happy with that. Letters from old friends were always full of an optimism about England that he found embarrassing. They were so far removed from the humiliating truth of his life that they could be taken for mockery, although he knew that was not so. For they had done a good job, he thought, those who had gone to take the torch of wisdom and learning to the benighted millions of Africa. They had left a whole age group hankering for the land that had produced their teachers. Poor Rabearivelo, the Malagasy poet, had committed suicide when he failed to get to France. *It was enough to make you laugh*, Daud thought, *until you read his poems. And then you wondered how a mind like that could be so easily eaten.* He hated getting letters from his friends, and dreaded having to reply. He found himself cultivating an eccentric style when he wrote to them, in the hope that they would be too embarrassed about his decline to be able to reply. His father's generation was safe. They had been born while the memory of a time without Europeans was still fresh in people's minds, before the grin of empire had filled the rest with the self-despising anxiety of frightened men.

2

Daud leant against the wall in the ophthalmic theatre, counting the seconds as they ticked past him. A few feet from him, two student nurses cowered against the same wall, masked and terrified. This was their first day and they stood exactly where the Sister had told them to stand and did not even whisper to each other. Daud glanced at them, indulged an admiration for their lovely forms, and then returned to the passing seconds. They glanced at him and wondered who he was, wearing a frilly cap and wellington boots, and looking as if he had nothing to do. The surgeon glanced at him too before continuing with his yachting tale, made uneasy by something in the way that Daud stood. Unlike the young nurses, he knew that Daud was a theatre orderly who had a tendency to give himself critical airs. His poses, the surgeon thought, made him look ridiculous. Once or twice he had seen Daud leaning against the wall reading a book, which he thought was a bit much in an ophthalmic theatre.

Sister Wilhelmina Shelton (Jamaica and Brent) was in charge that afternoon. She glowered over her mask, looking for something to do. Her eyes rested on Daud and smiled. He raised his eyebrows at her and pretended to be nodding off to sleep, sliding gently along the tiled wall as if he would end in a heap on the floor. She flashed a warning and glanced quickly at the surgeon. She had had something of a soft spot for him since he had told her that she reminded him of his mother. He enjoyed working with her because she was always provoking the surgeons and laughing at everybody. He had often been tempted to ask her how she came to be where she was, such a long way from home. But she might ask him the same question and then where would he begin? She was a short, plump black woman with a pleasant smile and a combative edge in her voice. When he first met her she looked at him with aloof disdain, warning him to keep his distance and not hurl himself at her just because he was black. At the first opportunity on their own he had called her *Auntie*, just to please her. She snorted with contempt at his brazen flattery but he could see the laughter in her eyes.

She was kind to him in those early weeks and he was grateful. He had needed as much help as he could get then. The sight and smell of bodies being opened up had revolted and sickened him. He had no idea that bodies bled like that, or smelt like that. Most of all he resented that circumstances had forced him to find out, had humbled him to such an extent. His job included cleaning the dirty theatre after use, and scrubbing the pus and whey off the instruments and the furniture. Those were his simplest duties, and the ones he had been started on when he began working there. It was still what he did most of the time, although occasionally he was allowed to hold the surgeon's hand or wipe a Hippocratic brow. His list of tasks also included shaving the patients' pubic hair should he be directed to do so. It was not a fate that had yet befallen him, but one he dreaded. The thought of handling a bunch of decrepit cobblers filled him with revulsion, and he was afraid he would accidentally cut the patient. He did not even know where he would begin if he was asked to shave a woman.

Sister Wilhelmina Shelton cupped her hand to her mask, indicating that she wanted him to go to tea. He stopped counting, having got to three thousand two hundred and twenty, which meant that there were still three thousand seven hundred and eighty seconds to go before he finished work, and levered himself off the wall. The Sister glowered at the two nurses and nodded for them to follow him. He waited for them outside the theatre door, in case they did not know where to go. He did not realise how stiffly he was holding himself, as if expecting a rebuff. The two nurses took their masks off, their eyes bright with embarrassment. They smiled at each other and took deep, exaggerated breaths. They were both wearing the frilly hats that women staff used to cover all their hair. He wore one as well, or sometimes two, because he knew it irritated the Superintendent, Mr Solomon. He wished Student Nurse Mason was not wearing one. He thought her face so beautiful that it made his chest ache.

'Do you know where the rest room is?' he asked her.

She shook her head but it would not have mattered. He did not intend to abandon her yet. He started to walk away slightly ahead of them. As he turned to say something about the ophthalmic theatre, he saw out of the corner of his eye that he was still wearing a mask. He reached up hurriedly to remove it and thought he saw a flash of amusement in her eyes.

'That was typical of the eye theatre,' he said, making cheerful conversation. 'Very little happens and you're lucky if you can stay awake. Have you had a good first day?' This time she smiled and nodded slightly, discouraging his interest. She turned to her companion, and exchanged the briefest look with her. Daud thought he recognised it. It was a look that asked for commiseration, that flashed a warning about the creature in their midst. He felt himself stiffening with resentment. They darted away from him as soon as they reached the rest room, joining other students who were starting in other theatres on the same day. He saw her take her cap off, and noticed that her hair was coiled up and tied at the back of her head in a bun. She sat quietly among her animated companions, seeming older than most of them, he thought. She seemed uncomfortable. Nobody looked in his direction. He left quickly, embarrassed by the way they all ignored him. She followed him out into the corridor, thinking that the break was over. 'No, you have fifteen minutes,' he said. 'Can you find your own way back?' He saw a flicker of uncertainty in her eyes, then she shook her head and followed him.

He saw her around in the next few days, and saw how quickly she was making friends with the regular theatre nurses. One day, a few days after first meeting her, she spoke to him. She asked him to get something for her. She had rushed out of a theatre with the surgeon's demands for a *protractor* ringing in her ears. She saw him strolling past, a newspaper tucked under his arm, making for the rest room. She knew he was an orderly, or as one of the staff nurses had said, *a kind of glorified cleaner*.

'Can you go and get me a protractor?' she said, and he walked right past her, as if she had not uttered a word, as if she was not there at all. 'Excuse me, can you get me a protractor?' she called out, and regretted the hint of desperation in her voice. She saw him stop and turn to look at her, and then start to walk back. She was not to know that the newspaper under his arm contained an article analysing the previous winter's disastrous tour of Australia by the West

Indian cricket team. He had glanced at it before he left home, and memories of those screaming, demented Aussies tormenting and taunting the poor lads in maroon caps had flooded back. He had had to force himself to start off for work at all, let alone be civil to some heartless, mindless Colonel's daughter who was demanding a *protractor* from him like he was the club punkah-wallah.

'What do you mean, protractor? What protractor? We don't keep protractors,' he said. 'Do you mean retractor?'

'Yes,' she said, relieved that *it* existed.

He showed her where the retractors were and went off while she was still trying to force a *Thank you* past her lips. He sat in the rest room and read the grisly details of the Australian tour, a tragedy that he found to be almost more than flesh and blood could bear. In any case, the open-mouthed emergency look irritated him. He would not have thought, in the first few minutes after meeting S/N Mason outside the eye theatre, that there was anything she could do to irritate him. *But these things happen*, he consoled himself. *Life is like that. And sad though it was to see such a gift of nature turning corrosive and rejecting his feeble homage, it would not make him sour. He would still go on enjoying her beautiful face and her body of lavish grace*.

It was his last day at work before a month of night-duty, and the custom was to allow the condemned wretch some degree of freedom during these last hours. Daud lounged in the rest room for as long as he could, accepting, with what he thought was a heroic stoicism, the commiserations of those who knew his fate. There were some advantages to a month of night-duty. The money was better and there was more time off, but Daud hated being forced to sleep during the day and eat sandwiches in the middle of the night. The nights were long and boring. Nothing happened except occasionally some unfortunate who had fallen down a mine shaft or plunged his head into a hungry piece of machinery was brought in to be poked about and messed around by the doctors until he died. There was always, of course, the possibility of an emergency Caesarean when the hospital would at last come into its own. Doctors would bark down the telephones, midwives would strut into the theatre and shift the furniture so that their view of the baby's entry into the world would not be impeded. The anaesthetist would check and double-check his drugs and gases and the nurses would remember again the sense of vocation that had sent them into the profession. Daud would know that the patient would be heavier than most other patients, and that lifting her on to the table would be more difficult. There would also be a lot more blood about as the surgeon slashed his way into the uterus. The baby, though, was always nice when it came out. He had seen the most hardened cynics in theatres turn suddenly human at the sight of that snuffling slug, and break into smiles and applause.

He would have refused night-duty if it had been an option, as it was for the nurses. The orderlies had no choice. At the end of the month he always felt a little crazy and his stomach was in a mess. It was as if he had been hidden away and the world had passed him by. He returned to it with a sense of having missed, something, of having wasted time. All the books he would have promised himself to read during the empty hours he would not have read. All the letters he had intended to write would still be buzzing in his head. *Dear Theatre Superintendent*, he began. *I greet you, Ineffable Solomon. An orderly is an orderly, and little can be done about that. I write simply to register a protest concerning your cruel rule that I should have to do a month of night-duty. I am of a sensitive disposition, and*

I find the solitariness of those long nights turns me into a hysterical paranoid. I cannot promise not to run amok in the plaster store.

He checked to see who would be on duty on his first night: Sister Wintour and Staff Nurse Chattan. Both were night-duty veterans and could be relied upon to disappear for several hours sometime during the night. Any possibility of conversation, which the long empty hours invited, was unthinkable with those two professionals. The Staff Nurse usually made a little effort to hold up a conversation, less out of interest, Daud thought, than out of a misplaced notion of what politeness required. The Sister, he knew, would have no such silly concern. She would talk for half an hour about her latest dinner party and then retire to the doctors' rest room for a long snooze.

When he turned up for work the following Monday, it was in the expectation of a quiet and cosy night, boring and uneventful, like spending an afternoon with relatives at home. The sense of being incarcerated in a futuristic tomb did not usually strike him until the third or fourth night. He discovered as soon as he arrived at work that his expectations were to be disappointed. Staff Nurse Chattan, alias the Dodo because she came from Mauritius, the last and only home of that now extinct creature, had suffered a serious attack of venereal phlebitis, requiring that she spend a day and a night helping at the wedding of her younger sister which was being held at the family manse in Tooting SW17. Her relief for the night was a student nurse.

'Morgan or Moore or something. She's been in theatres for forty-eight hours and they've forced her to do nights. It's disgraceful. Just because they're too bloody lazy to do ...'

'Mason,' Daud said. 'And she's been here two weeks. Her father's a Colonel in the Coldstream Guards.'

'Really,' said the Sister, wary and watchful, but suddenly raising the register. 'This is not one of your little fibs, is it?'

They found S/N Mason in the rest room, looking as if she expected someone to give her something to do. 'Catherine Mason, isn't it?' the Sister asked. 'I'm Sister Angela Wintour and this is Daud, our orderly. Although I gather you've already met … Now there's quite a lot to do, so we'll have coffee first of all. Daud tells me that your father is a Colonel in the Coldstreams. You must have seen a lot of travelling … although less, of course, since the pull-out east of Suez. We were in the other army, doing mission work in Eastern Nigeria. My son was born there.'

Plucky devil, Daud thought.

'I was talking to Bernard Findlay the other day … Do you know him? Oh, I must get you to meet him. Next time he comes to dinner … He's wonderfully expert on the Army. He was Chaplain in something now, the Gurkhas or one of the Frontier Corps. Native troops but I can't remember the regiment. He was saying that there is this remarkable connection between mission work and the Army. It appears that most missionaries came from military families, including himself, and certainly my husband. Isn't that a remarkable connection?'

Daud watched the results of his handiwork with complacent glee. Catherine Mason was too polite to tell the Sister that she was mad, and Wintour was too thoroughly in her stride to notice the look of bewilderment on the young woman's face. After a while, even the Sister's suspicions were raised and several knowing looks were directed at Daud. She consoled herself with a ritual account of her last dinner party: terrine of veal *farcé*, devilled *poisson* accompanied by countless salads, and *flambeaux* pastries washed down with an ancient Sauternes. The Sister liked to make a bit of a show of her dinners, and had tantalised Daud several times with vague invitations to *come and eat with us some time*, all of which had come to nothing. He was always happy to offer suggestions whenever she chose to consult him, though. The curried mussels were his idea, as was the papaya and mozzarella flan for a troublesome vegetarian guest. It was soon clear that the dinner had exhausted Sister Wintour. She found herself so tired that she was forced to retire to the doctors' rest room for a while.

'Coffee?' suggested Daud as he got up to put the kettle on.

'When did my father join the Army?' Catherine asked, smiling to show that she could take a joke. 'He was a conscientious objector when he was called up for National Service, you know. I don't think he would take kindly to being described as a Colonel in the Coldstream Guards.'

'What's wrong with the Coldstream Guards? Is your father a communist?' he asked.

He saw her face waver between a frown and a sneer – was he a shit or a dunce? 'Well, he's not in the Guards, anyway,' she said, ignoring his question. 'The Sister said your name was … Daud? Is that right? Where do you come from?'

'Do you take sugar?' he asked.

'No,' she said, and burst out with a sudden, loud chuckle. 'Why did you say that? About my father being a Colonel? I know you were only teasing the Sister, but what made you think of the military?'

'It was the way you said protractor,' he said. 'It sounded like a Colonel's daughter.'

'Really? Did it sound posh?' she asked, laughing with surprise.

'Very posh! As if you were addressing the club punkah-wallah,' he added since he guessed that she liked this image of herself.

‘Punkah-wallah sounds colonial,’ she said, sensing that he was laughing at her.

‘Only the best colonial could’ve said protractor like that.’

‘That was so stupid! Rushing out like that without listening properly,’ she went on, changing the drift of the conversation, and making a face. She spoke in a different voice, one that insisted on not being laughed at. ‘It could have been important. Instead I just ran out and cried for help … which I almost didn’t receive.’

He stopped pouring water into the mugs of coffee and looked at her from under lowered eyebrows. ‘I can’t take criticism,’ he said.

‘All right then,’ she said after a moment, smiling. ‘Notice how politely I’m asking the question, which means you have to give a helpful answer. What am I supposed to do here? Can you show me?’

‘Drink your coffee. It’s only your second cup and you’ll have plenty more yet.’

‘Is this all that happens?’ she asked.

‘Yes,’ he said, grinning at her. ‘Unless somebody falls sick. You can go to sleep, of course. Everybody does.’ He told himself to calm down, not to strain so much with the jolly conversation. That was the least likely way of persuading her to like him, and he knew now that he wanted her to think him smart and pleasant. It was nothing so deliberate as a campaign to win her. She looked too secure and self-confident to be the kind of English woman who would respond with anything but fastidious alarm if he showed interest in her, he thought. He liked the way she looked at ease, and the light in her face when Sister Wintour was making a monkey of herself. He liked the stillness in her blue eyes as she listened to him talk, and admired her unflurried replies. He suspected that the assurance was partly a hoax, a manner; but he was still made envious. It was as if she spoke without calculation, although he knew this could not be so.

She gave him a little nod as he handed her the coffee. 'Anyway, I thought night-duty in theatres meant coping with terrible emergencies. Accidents and minor catastrophes and things like that. I didn't expect things to be this relaxed.'

'Sometimes it gets very dramatic,' he said. 'Most of the time it's quiet … sorting out the shelves, changing the gas cylinders, packing instruments, generally re-stocking for the day. How long are you on for?'

'Only one night,' she said, folding her legs under her and curling up a little in the chair. 'Then it's back to days.'

'You don't like it in theatres?' he asked.

She made a mildly disgusted face, and they shared a smile.

Daud's prediction turned out to be correct, and nothing dramatic happened. The Sister appeared now and then to replenish her cup, or to complain about some chore that the day staff had not performed, but otherwise left them to lounge the night away drinking coffee and talking. She talked about her parents and about her year at the hospital. He told her about his home, going on and on, he thought afterwards.

'What made you decide to be a nurse?' he asked her. She looked at him for a moment longer than she needed to. He saw the blue of her eyes turn darker, and she looked in some pain. 'You don't have to bother answering that,' he said. 'Don't worry about it.'

'No, no,' she protested. 'It's just complicated.'

'Well, tell me another time,' he said.

'I'll tell you now. Don't make such a fuss. Why should you think I wouldn't want to answer? I didn't expect you to ask, that's all. Nobody has since I've been here. I *wanted* to be a nurse, I think. For the same reasons that everybody else does … My mother tells me that even as a child my favourite game was playing nurses. When I was thinking of it as a career … vocation,' she corrected herself with a smile, 'I told myself that I was not going to be romantic about it. I was not going to expect to have to care for a handsome pilot or a quiet, intense young poet. But I think that's exactly what I have been expecting – you know, the kind of thing you read about in teenage novels, romantic intrigue in the hushed light of a ward at night. You see, you're laughing.'

'You hate nursing, I can tell,' he said.

'Of course I don't hate nursing,' she objected, laughing. 'It's a bit boring, the work is hard and dirty, the hours are too long and the money's terrible. Why should I hate nursing, for God's sake? But I think my father was disappointed.'

'The Colonel,' he said. 'Let me guess. He wanted you to be … er … a physicist.'

'He's not a Colonel. He's a solicitor. And he wanted me to study music, not physics,' she said. He winced from the rebuke in her voice. Perhaps the Colonel joke had had its run, he agreed. Or perhaps she had resented it from the very first, and now felt the time had come to lay it to rest. 'He'd encouraged me for years. He used to say I had talent in music but I could never believe him. I couldn't take it seriously. Nobody else I knew was bothered. I think I was afraid of being exposed, of turning out to be just another mediocrity. My brother thought I was. Richard … he's the star of our family. Shall I tell you about him?'

'Yes, do,' he said. He watched her as she talked, and wondered if he should feel his pulse to see if he was falling in love. *Not your type*, he admonished himself, remembering other rebuffs.

'Richard's a solicitor too,' she said. 'He runs a Legal Aid clinic in east London. He's always busy ... involved in a crucial test case or something like that, you know. Really enjoys his work, and works very hard at it. I lived with them for a while, him and his girlfriend Chris, before I came down here. He used to treat my musical accomplishments as something of a joke, turning up the volume on his radio when I was practising, that kind of thing. Or complaining that he couldn't get his work done with all the noise. My mother used to make me stop, because Richard's work was important. Then when things had quietened down, and I was sitting in a corner sulking, he used to sneak away from his work to come and gloat.'

He sounds charming, Daud thought, hearing the sense of inadequacy in her voice.

'We didn't really get on then,' she said, and from the way she smiled he guessed that this was an understatement. 'But things are much better now.'

'Does he approve of you being a nurse?' he asked, wondering if he should have kept quiet. She wondered too, looking at him before being seduced by an intimacy prompted by the lateness of the hour.

'I don't know,' she said. 'I don't think he approves of *me*. No, that sounds pathetic. I don't think I want to talk about Richard after all.'

'Time for another coffee and a change of subject then,' he said. 'Unless you plan to go to supper, in which case you have twenty minutes before the dining room shuts.'

'Oh God, you must be joking. It's nearly two o'clock. I can't eat that stuff at this time of night.'

'Exactly! Another coffee coming up, then,' he said, rising.

'No thanks,' she said. 'I think I'll go and check what the Sister is up to. I don't want her to think that I've abandoned her. I'll probably find out later that she has to write a report on me. Maybe later on.'

He felt worse than he knew he should, as if he had made a fool of himself in front of her. He realised with her departure that he had been feeling elated by the openness with which they had been talking, and had been misled into asking that prying question. He knew what would happen now. She would avoid him because she had shown too much of herself. She would shun him for the intrusion into her life. At such moments, he thought, they resented him more for being a foreigner, as if he had touched their inner selves with unclean and leprous hands. He hated most of all the unspoken rebuke that he had been trying to gain some kind of advantage.

She came back sooner than he expected, and he was almost too angry to worry about the reasons. He saw the regret in her eyes, and the way her lips pressed together as if to check the torrent that would burst from her mouth. He was distant to her at first. *What a carry on, just because he asked a question.* It was obvious that she was embarrassed by his hostility, but she went on talking, and he responded, if only to prevent a complete disaster. They were more watchful now, without the freedom of earlier in the night. The Sister took her away towards morning, to help with the packing for the day's cases. Daud went into the instruments room once, but he was in the way, and did not like the amused glint in the Sister's eyes. Catherine was not around when he was ready to go off duty. The Sister had let her off early.

He knew she would not be on duty the following night, but he went to work looking forward to seeing her. The Dodo might have collapsed after her exertions on her sister's behalf. Tooting might have been cut off by a transport strike, or be in the middle of a reign of terror by the A-team, making movement difficult and travel impossible. But the Dodo was there, skinny and cheerful as always, her gold teeth flashing with pleasure at the sight of Daud.

'Did you enjoy your holiday in Mauritius?' he asked her.

'Stupid boy, I only gone to Tooting, to my girlie sister's wedding,' she said, giggling with indestructible silliness. 'Look what I brought you. I knew you were on, so I saved you some *halwa* and *ladhoo*.'

'You been in Tootingji,' he said, imitating her voice. 'Is it safe with all the *hubshi* there? They always be thinking of only one thing when they see a woman, you know.'

'Ignorant boy, we all black in this country,' she said, and laughed with enough force to convince anyone that she was lying.

3

The buds on the chestnut trees in the hospital drive were now fully open in early summer. He walked down the avenue and turned his back on the portico tower above the main entrance of the hospital. The grass verges along the drive were wet with morning dew. Daud glanced once over his shoulder because the prospect of the huge trees always pleased him. He crossed into St Jerome Street, a quiet road with neat little houses on either side. The order and the neatness appealed to him, as a condition he would only ever be able to admire, he thought, but never achieve. He had once seen a man down this street picking up pieces of dried dog-shit with a pair of tongs, sniffing them and putting them in a dustpan. When he realised that Daud was staring at him, he glared back an angry challenge. Daud had envied him the passion that he had brought to such a task.

The street turned sharply, and he glanced behind him again before crossing the road. He was a tall man, but slim and light like a distance runner. The clothes he wore did not fit him very well, nor were they clean. The large yellow jumper had shrunk at the back and was pulled out of shape at the elbows. He tugged the back of it down whenever he remembered. His green trousers carried the tide-marks of months of dirt. With his close-cropped hair and untidy stubble, he gave an impression of hard-headedness, a fact of which he was unaware.

It shamed him that his clothes were always so dirty. He had, after all, been brought up by a mother whose regard for hygiene bordered on the religious. There were times when he wallowed in delicious remorse, seeing his squalor as an eloquent manifestation of his decline. At the beginning of every week he promised himself that he would wash all his clothes, mend the hems of his trousers and stitch the buttons back on his shirts. On occasions he soaked his clothes in a bucket of soapy water for a few days and then rinsed them. Sometimes the few days extended to a lot of days, and he daily avoided the stinking bucket and its gradually thickening contents. He always had to concede defeat in the end, and plunge his hands into the glue, and try to rub the stink off. *Your uncle gave his life to defend the empire from the yellow peril*, he lectured himself on these occasions, *and you wallow in the stink of rotting clothes. Was his sacrifice, and that of his comrades in the King's African Rifles, for nothing?*

In the mornings after night-duty, despite the long, sleepless hours, he always felt that he was the one who was fresh, while the people he met looked tired and full of sleep. He watched out for the smart secretaries because he admired their bodies and the way they decorated and clothed them. He recognised some of them from previous encounters, and was always down-hearted if he failed to catch sight of his current obsession. He passed conventionally attired young men, accountants and solicitors' assistants, he guessed. Sharp young men with homes to go back to. He envied them their clean jobs, their prosperous futures, and their smart dark jackets.

The traffic was thick and swift on the road by the common, the drivers gazing ahead of them with grim concentration. Daud waved to a gloomy-looking man with a square face, who was sitting in a brown Maxi, becalmed in the queue of traffic. The man looked behind him to see whom Daud might have been waving to. Daud waved again, and added a powerful smile. The man shut his eyes, and opened them again, looking ahead. *Dear Sir*, Daud complained. *You don't know me, that is obvious and no fault of yours. It may therefore come as a surprise to you to hear from me in this way. You look like a fine, generous man to me – a little gloomy perhaps, but kind, most likely. I'm not being facetious. Without another glance I can tell that you will not allow your mother to be taken to an old people's home when she gets too feeble for the stairs. I would guess that you are either a bowler or a wicket-keeper for your local team. Am I wrong? A noble sport! So how can a man like you, civilised to a fault and warmed by the love of your family, drive past me on this fine morning without a wave, without even asking me who I am, or where I come from or what I am doing here? Don't you care?*

He saw a girl approaching on the other side of the road. She was slim and tall, with a long, pale face. She walked slowly over the bridge, blank-faced and indifferent. She stopped across the road, looking away from him. He was struck by the confidence with which she could seem so cold. There was a hint of arrogance about her wretchedness. He studied her furtively. Her eyes were very dark but with a kind of liquid light in them, as if she was about to burst into tears. She had a small mouth, gathered into the shape of a diamond by the stray lipstick that was smeared and spilling over her upper lip. Her face had an abruptness about it, as if its maker had rushed to complete the lower part. She was wearing a very tight pair of jeans, rolled a little up the calves. Her jacket, faded and grubby, reached down to her thighs and gave her a top-heavy appearance.

As if she had known his presence all along, she looked straight at him. He looked hastily in the other direction, keeping his eyes away from her as he crossed the road. *Dear Pale Face*, he grumbled. *What was that look for? Did you think I was studying you with desire throbbing through my veins? Is that why you looked so amused? Black Boy Lusts After White Flesh: This morning a girl was accosted by a red-eyed black boy on the Kingsmead Bridge. He stormed towards her through raging traffic, oblivious to the cars, goaded by a mad lust. 'Who am I? What am I doing here?' he screamed, tormented by a clash of cultures. The girl has asked for her name to be withheld, but the alienated creature's name is Daud. You have been warned.*

On the path across the playing fields, he saw an old man. The man smiled behind his spectacles and said good morning. Daud was always respectful to such men, reminding himself that they had probably killed human beings during the wars, perhaps with bare hands. He replied to the greeting and stepped briskly aside, suppressing a military salute. *Dear Corporal, I've written several letters this morning already. Some mornings are like that. Only I don't want you to think that you fooled me for one minute. It's a clever disguise, but not clever enough. I recognised your face from the Tana River campaign, where I saw you chasing the Mullah's men out of Bajun country. I hope you haven't forgotten the lessons you learnt then.*

On his first night off he went to the pub where he had arranged to meet Karta. Karta was late, as he usually was, and Daud waited with customary unease as the pub filled up with the Friday night crowd.

'Chin up,' Karta said when he arrived, leaning forward and making to chuck Daud under the chin. Daud looked up and smiled with relief. Karta took a step back and opened his arms wide, inviting Daud to admire his costume and appearance.

'Stunning,' Daud said, smiling at his friend's indestructible vanity. 'You look like a young Harry Belafonte.' Karta swivelled on one leg, showing Daud a back view and glancing over his shoulder to watch his reaction. He swivelled again and turned to face Daud, a happy smile on his handsome face. He was tall and a little heavy, although his head was small for the size of his shoulders. His belly was beginning to bulge, but he carried this off with casual grace, thrusting out his buttocks and chest whenever he remembered. His voice was deep and rounded, so that even when he was being harsh and strident, it still kept its form. He laughed with a soft, throaty growl. As he did so, he became conscious of it, and cleared his throat before laughing again, trying too hard to make his laughter heard. 'Eat your heart out, bro,' he said, thrusting his hips out as he played out his pantomime. Some people close to them in the crowded pub applauded, and Karta acknowledged them with a curt nod.

'You're wasting yourself,' Daud said, leaning back and feeling that a burden had been lifted off his shoulders. 'You should be modelling for a mail-order catalogue. Nearly a third of their customers are now black, and they're always looking to fulfil their three per cent.'

'Don't be insulting,' Karta said, then pointed a dramatic forefinger at Daud's empty glass. 'Broke again! You should leave that job. I'll buy you a drink now in case that English Ape turns up.'

'African hospitality,' Daud said solemnly when Karta returned with the drinks.

'I'll drink to that,' Karta said just as solemnly. 'What three per cent?'

'Wogs in the population. You may not have noticed it, but mail-order firms, in a selfless act of community responsibility, have chosen to make the pictures in their catalogues reflect this. Three per cent of the population is black, so three per cent of their models should be black. That's the democratic tradition for you.'

'To the mail-order firms,' said Karta raising his glass again.

'How is the exploration into the effects of Christianity on African societies going?' asked Daud, nodding to encourage Karta to bare the fruits of his research. 'Have you got to the abolition of human sacrifice yet? Have you exposed all the lies that Europeans told about savage practices in African religions?'

Karta shook his head, grinning at the provocation. 'I can't get past the parading of the maidens,' he said. 'Anyway, let me tell you about my new outfit.' He stood up and took his denim jacket off so that Daud could admire his black trousers and green silky shirt. While he talked about where he had bought the clothes and how much they had cost him, Daud noticed that several people were watching them. Karta seemed oblivious to them, and needed none of Daud's feeble encouragement to complete his performance. When he sat down again, he was grinning with self-congratulation. He took a long draught of his beer, and then turned to the nearest of his audience. 'What are you staring at?' he asked.

Faces turned quickly away while Karta glared with puffed-up indignation. Daud watched his friend with amusement, remembering how he had been when he first came the previous year, full of jokes and cunning, and unsparing in the mockery of his own absurd expectations of England. A year ago he would have played his audience along, teased them and persuaded them to make fools of themselves. 'Look at them,' he said. 'What a craven bunch of conquerors! The sun never sets on their cowardice and hypocrisy. They don't even have the nerve to look you in the eye and tell you *I hate you, black man*. This shit-hole of a place!'

'You really want them to do that?' Daud asked. 'Spit in your eye and tell you how much they hate you? And put chains round your ankles and whip you morning and evening?'

'And force me to sing "Rule Britannia" before breakfast, as they used to at school, I might add,' Karta said and glared around the pub, blaming everyone there for the indignity he had suffered.

'Exactly,' Daud said. 'And call you to lunch with the Angelus and send you to sleep without supper. I'd rather take the craven bunch of coconuts myself.'

'Conquerors,' Karta corrected, then sighed. 'I am so fed up of this place, this arm-pit of the world. I'm pining for the motherland and some sun on my back.'

'Yes,' Daud sighed too. 'The steamy afternoon aromas of the mangrove swamp, and the grease and wood-smoke of the overflowing Freetown streets. I bet you pine for all of it! The ineluctable musk of the city bar! The stench of rotting garbage in the roads.'

'Oh, you're making me homesick, you bastard. Stop!' Karta cried, laying a hand on Daud's arm.

He had met Karta at a party for foreign students, given by the Society of Friends. Daud was very surprised to receive the invitation, not only because he was no longer a student, and the invitation referred to his studies, but because he was alarmed that they had discovered his presence in this country of millions. Did they have access to Immigration files? Or would he come under Customs? Would they force him to kneel before the cross and then steal his immortal soul? Would they trick him to eat pig meat and then sell him into white slavery?

He had his own image of what the Quakers were like: intense, slightly intolerant eccentrics who wore long beards and burnt witches. He saw them as the English version of the Afrikaner: obscenely pious, resourceful and self-righteous. He went to the party because he found the image irresistible. He told himself that it was a mistake, that he would be forced to drink orange squash and listen to an ex-settler talking about *good works*. Nobody that he knew had ever mentioned these gatherings, so he was not surprised to find only eight foreign students when he got there, being entertained by four normal-looking natives in their forties. The party was in the hall of the meeting house. One corner of the huge room was occupied by a trestle table on which were scattered a selection of viands and colourful beverages: biscuits and squashes. Another corner was noisily occupied by a Dansette record player. The dozen people who were there were marooned round the old, ribbed radiator, doing their best.

Of the eight foreigners, four he guessed to be West Indian nurses. All four were wearing bright, chiffony dresses – pinks and blues with satin petticoats. Powder covered their black necks, and their mouths glistened the colour of moist blood. He knew that if he spoke to them they would ignore him and walk away, taking him to be after only one thing. Two of the other students were Malaysian, he guessed. One wore a red cummerbund. They were smiling at the tall English woman who was talking about the difficulties of educating an apathetic public in the benefits of multi-cultural and multi-racial exchanges. *There is so much we can learn from each other. I myself do not believe in the divinity of Jesus Christ, and I have found it so immensely rewarding to discuss this with Muslims, who, of course, do not see Jesus as divine either*. He wondered if that was his ex-settler. One of the students was a European of some kind, dark-skinned with bright-red hair – Bulgarian or Greek or Armenian – with a firm touch of the tar-brush. The remaining student was Karta, only recently arrived from Sierra Leone, and not yet confident enough to express his full horror at the ugliness and complacency of his laughable hosts. He was dressed in all-black.

Daud's arrival was greeted with howls of joy by the two English couples, who rushed over to ask his name, check it off a list clipped on to a board and ask him what he thought of England. The four West Indian nurses ignored him when he asked them if any of them danced. He had only asked them to prove himself right. The two Malaysians smiled and smiled, and asked him if there were many Muslims in his country. The Bulgarian watched him warily, admiring his English. Karta made a fist with his left hand, and Daud nodded and smiled at him.

The party ended abruptly at nine. The four West Indian nurses said they were on early duty the following morning. Daud had noted Karta's bewildered failure to obtain even a greeting from them. By then the small group of revellers had sampled the refreshment and almost made the complete round of their range of conversation – and were back with the benefits of multi-racial and multi-cultural exchanges. There was a moment of panic when one of the hosts asked Daud if he was happy at the institution where he was studying. He replied that he was not a student and saw a momentary hardening in his host's eyes. Gate-crasher! By an unspoken agreement, everybody ignored his reply. Karta called him *brother man*, and they decided to go for a drink, to celebrate the reunion of exiles from the black homeland.

Karta had complained bitterly. They were so dirty. The food was so horrible, it either gave him the shits or indigestion. Everything tasted like pulped cabbage. Was the water safe? The television was all dancing girls and racist jokes. Everything was so squalid, so mean. And yet everyone was so mighty, so pleased with their Englishness. How long had he, Daud, been in this arsehole of a place? Was he at the university? That was where he, Karta, was. He was doing a Masters. Thank God he was only going to be here for a year. What did Daud say he was studying? *Man, this is one racist arsehole of a place. Haba! How could they force someone of your intelligence to work as a cleaner in a hospital?*

Daud had invited him round for a meal. Thinking back to his own early days, he made Karta a pepper stew. Karta ate with relish, closing his eyes and humming with ecstasy as the pepper burnt his palate. Marie, the pretty, dark-haired German girl who was Daud's latest *conquest* on the *au-pair* circuit – this was in the dark days when he still thought of such things as conquests – was sitting at the table but not eating. Karta kept glancing at her and she frankly returned his interest. Karta enthused: excellent food, *wonderful* company, almost as good as being at home. Daud was flattered despite himself, and told Karta to come round whenever he felt like it. Karta had looked at his black brother and then glanced round triumphantly at Marie, whose own eyes were beginning to water. *That's African hospitality*, he said. Marie was so moved by Karta's performance that she went to see him in the hall of residence the next day. When Daud discovered how he had been jilted, he pretended that it did not matter to him. He admitted to himself that he had treated her very casually and deserved the casual way she discarded him. She was only the first of many for Karta.

Karta had told stories endlessly. He told stories of his pompous school, Prince Henry the Navigator, he called it, which tried to maintain British standards in the heat and shanties of Freetown. He told stories of his father, a solicitor's clerk, whose love of the English extended beyond his cruelly self-mocking name. He had been christened Edward Samuel Benson-Hylen. The Edward was after the King of England. The Samuel was after Smiles, the self-help evangelist. Benson-Hylen was the name they had brought with them from the West Indies, from where they had been repatriated by a philanthropic master whose name they then adopted. Edward Samuel Benson-Hylen named his son less ambitiously. He called him Carter, after the senior partner of the law firm he worked for. Karta called his father *the black monkey*, when he was not calling him *Daddy* with perfect devotion. 'Daddy likes being described as an English gentleman. The biggest compliment you can pay that African monkey is to tell him that he sounds like Mr Carter, of the firm Carter, Sinclair and Hogg, Solicitors. I always wondered what that white man was doing in Freetown – hiding from Interpol probably. At least I can thank de Almighty that Daddy didn't choose to call me Hogg.'

Mr Benson-Hylen collected pictures of British royalty in the same way that other people collected posters of the black athletes giving the black power salute in the 1968 Olympics, or of Bruce Lee destroying another slit-eyed fooey with the sole of his foot. His constant adversary was Karta's English literature teacher, a man called Hitler Jones. *I swear to God, bro. That was his name. Hitler Kitchener Jones*. Mr Jones had been christened by the same priest who had warned his flock against reading *The Heart of the Matter* because it was immoral. Mr Jones thought of himself as young and radical, and rejected *The Heart of the Matter* for quite different reasons – because it revealed a colonial indifference to Africa and its people, and saw both as simply an exotic and dangerous background to its banal tale of middle-aged discontent and lust.

'It was Hitler who introduced us to Soyinka and Ngugi. Radicals like myself, he used to say. And introduced us to Naipaul. He's sick in the head that Naipaul, he told us. But Daddy wanted us to read Dickens and Shakespeare, or at least Sheridan, so he went to see the Headmaster to complain. He reported him for the books he made us read and because he taught us about the Yoruba pantheon. Daddy used to get so angry. God of Thunder indeed! he always said. He said to the Headmaster: How can you allow your school to teach that heathen, mumbo-jumbo voodoo to modern African boys?'

Karta had felt so ashamed of his father that he decided to change his name to Karta Benso. To his friends and to the world at large – he did not dare mention his change of identity to Daddy – he was no longer Carter Benson-Hylen, but Karta Benso, the New African, disciple of Hitler Kitchener Jones, scourge of the imperialists and their comprador lackeys, excoriator of the racist literature of Graham Greene and Joseph Conrad.

There was a time when Karta told such stories against himself. Daud had admired and enjoyed his benign anarchy then, but Karta had changed during his few months in England. He had become intolerant and irritable, full of mockery and a bitter, angry cynicism. He brooded now over small insults where he would have laughed and manufactured worse ones in reply. They sat in the pub,

Daud looking at his empty glass while Karta fulminated against *these arseholes*.

'And when are you going to be able to afford to buy me a drink? It's time you got yourself a decent job,' he said, allowing his irritation to reach Daud. 'Every time I see you, you're broke.'

Daud gave Karta a long, patient smile. 'African hospitality done finish?' he asked.

'Done gone!' Karta said, turning his pockets out. 'We now have to wait on the generosity of that English Ape, that Boy Monster ... if his daddy lets him out of the house.'

'No problem, *oga*,' Daud said, pulling out a bundle of notes. 'Night-duty is double money. I was just testing your African hospitality. Let's have your glass, I go show um real hospitality now.'

Karta sucked his teeth. 'I don't know why I bother with foreigners like you, but at least we're saved from begging the white man again. But I mean it about the job,' he continued when Daud returned. 'You should leave that damned place. Apart from anything else, it's bad for your health.'

'Lloyd is here,' Daud said, relieved to be able to change the subject.

Karta picked up his glass and emptied it. 'Let the Englishman pay for the pleasure of my company.'

4

'I'm in love,' Lloyd announced after he had paid the price of admission. Karta looked frankly disbelieving. He thought Lloyd was ugly, and often took the trouble to say so. That was how they were together: Karta who cared everything for his appearance and Lloyd who believed he could do nothing about his. Daud was convinced that they would come to blows sooner or later. Not that he cared that much, he protested. At every opportunity, Karta sought to lash Lloyd with his tongue while the latter used his full array of abuse to defend himself. Daud knew it would be up to him to ask the questions that would draw the story out. Otherwise they would sink into bickering and sulks, and turn the evening into an interminable squabble. Karta had already turned away with elaborate disgust, sipping the drink that Lloyd had bought him. For that was another curious thing, Daud thought, putting on his pince-nez to examine the specimen, the way that Lloyd tried again and again to buy his way into Karta's affections. As if a pint of beer could do anything but nourish the loathing that Karta felt for him.

'Who's the lucky girl?' Daud asked. Karta spluttered into his beer, and Lloyd smiled to acknowledge the sarcasm and to concede what he thought an undeniable fact. He *was* ugly, big and formless. That was how he described himself once. *Like a maggot*, Karta had told him with relish. His face was small and pointed, and was topped by a large, inverted bowl of black hair, falling in a fringe round his face. The smooth black dome was like a compound eye, glaring sightlessly around it and, viewed from the appropriate angle, carrying the same undiscriminating menace. The rest of his face was like the confusion of an insect's jaws, all the features delicate and indistinct, immemorable like the sunken chin of a cockroach.

'You wouldn't know her,' Lloyd said, dropping his eyes as if to hide the hurt that Daud's words caused him. 'She's much too grand for a yob like you. I mentioned you to her. I said I've got this friend who's the most civilised person in England.'

'A paragon!' Karta said.

'And he's a wog,' Lloyd continued, cheering up and raising his voice when he got to the word. 'She wouldn't believe me. She said she'd never met a civilised wog before. And she should know! Her granny lives in Chatham and half her street's been taken over. The pungent aromas of curry powder …'

'All right, cut that out,' said Karta, jaws working with anger as he glared at Lloyd.

'I wasn't talking about you, love,' Lloyd gasped, pretending innocence. 'I wouldn't dream of calling you civilised. Anyway, she was very impressed. I suggested that perhaps she'd like to meet you and … and …' He struggled to complete his sentence, hindered by bursts of laughter. Karta made a disgusted face and turned away again, shaking his head.

'But she said no,' Lloyd continued. 'She said she didn't fancy the idea of meeting … a smelly wog!' He finished triumphantly and burst into squeals of laughter, pointing first at Daud and then at Karta.

Daud saw the glass quivering in Karta's hand, its contents about to be dashed in Lloyd's face. He waited for Karta to raise his head, and when he did, he caught his eye. Daud knew that Lloyd was rarely embarrassed by public commotions and enjoyed them with the same delight that children found in romps and squabbles. He took to them with zest, like a shaggy dog its evening rumpus across the common. Karta's gesture would only involve him in further indignities.

'You're being more offensive than you realise,' Karta said, biting his words off to dramatise his anger.

Lloyd glanced at Daud. 'Oh, come on, you know I don't mean anything,' he said, looking suddenly stricken and demanding Daud's concern and care. 'It was only a joke. I'm not a racist! You know I don't—'

'Yes, all right,' Daud interrupted. He hated the way Lloyd made these slithery guerrilla raids on his sympathy, civilised wog and such like, and paid for his insults with exaggerated concern.

'But you know I don't mean anything,' Lloyd protested.

'Just shut up, you fat Englishman,' Karta said, his teeth still clenched.

'I don't understand why you have to go on like this,' Lloyd said. 'You call me these names, I don't get offended. What makes you think you have a right to abuse me for my race when you find the slightest remark about yours offensive?' His voice had risen to a quarrelsome whine, and they had arrived, Daud thought, at their usual impasse. 'Why do you bother getting upset? Why don't you just ignore me? I say the same things to Daud. He knows I don't mean anything. Why do you have to be so over-sensitive? Are you something special?'

Daud watched Karta sigh, and struggled to suppress a smile. 'I've got a chip on my shoulder,' Karta said. 'You carry on and tell your civilised wog friend here about how he smells and has a big penis and things like that. I think I'll go mug an old lady or something. I don't think I can listen to this arsehole any more.' Daud nodded and said nothing. All along he had refused to join in their fights, and ignored the opportunities they offered him to declare himself on one side or the other. Lloyd never talked this way when he was alone with Daud. He did it for Karta's benefit, and Karta knew that but could not resist the provocation. He found Lloyd's very presence a provocation, and had the matter been up to him, he would have despatched the monstrous slug long before.

'Why do you have to take it like this?' Lloyd asked, looking first at one and then the other. 'I'm not a racist! I was going to say why don't we go for an Indian. I'll pay. Come on, I'll treat you all.'

'I'll see you some time during the week, bro,' Karta said, ignoring Lloyd. He could not quite keep the hurt out of his voice, that Daud should choose to stay on in the pub and drink with Lloyd. 'You'll be in?'

'Glued to the telly watching the Test Match,' Daud said, happy to be reminded of the pleasures in store for him during his week off.

'It's going to be a draw,' Lloyd said, nudging Daud to claim his attention. 'Rain stopped play, or the bloody batsman fell asleep before wicket.'

'I don't know how you can watch that stupid game,' Karta said, rising to leave. He gave Lloyd a last baleful glance and then blew Daud a kiss. Lloyd made an obscene gesture as soon as Karta's back was turned.

'How about an Indian?' he suggested. 'I don't feel like staying on here.'

'You carry on, then,' Daud said. 'I'll hang on here.'

'There's no rush,' Lloyd said. 'We can go a bit later.'

Daud was sure he did not want the homage that Lloyd insisted on paying him. He refused the endless kindnesses that Lloyd was always extending to him. Lloyd took this to be an example of Daud's modesty and simply became more cunning with his generosity and more free with his advice. *You've got to look after yourself. You let people walk over you too much. Nobody gets anywhere if they can't be ruthless. That's just an invitation for people to crush you. I know you don't like to hear this, but that's because you're generous and you don't want to think that people are that way. But they are! You even walk in the streets with your head lowered.* Daud had been struck by that last description, and had examined it thoroughly, catching himself unawares in his wanderings and trying to surprise himself in his humble nigger slouch. But in the end he decided that that was the way Lloyd liked to think of him, as the retiring foreigner whom he would help come out of himself. Without question, Daud discovered, he walked with his back ramrod-straight and his head held high.

Lloyd would invite himself to dinner and bring a shopping bag full of food with him, which he would then insist on leaving behind. He visited Daud frequently and never came empty-handed. The gifts were more helpful than Daud liked to admit, but he would happily have done without them to escape him. He did not even want Lloyd's company, but he did not know how to chase him away. He could not bring himself to perform the necessary cruelties that would convince him. There were many times when he thought that his fastidiousness came from a reluctance to have Lloyd think ill of him, that he really quite enjoyed the elevated opinion that Lloyd gave him of himself. He hated most of all the pretence of sympathy and interest that Lloyd forced him into. What made it worse for Daud was that he suspected that Lloyd really was the little racist he played to Karta. Daud had been uncertain at first, afraid of misunderstanding him. Perhaps it was nothing more than boisterousness, a boorishness that Lloyd indulged in to disguise his isolation, he had thought.

'Well, how are things?' Lloyd asked, breaking the silence and nudging Daud's leg under the table.

'Fine,' he said.

'How's work?' Lloyd asked again.

'The night-duty wasn't too bad in the end, and now a few days off. It could've been worse.'

'That's good,' Lloyd said, leaning forward. 'I'm really bored actually.' Daud had recognised the movement. It meant that Lloyd was about to lay a burden on him, was about to *talk*. He would be forced to listen and, worse still, would have to say something in the end. He guessed that he was the only one who did listen.

'That shop depresses me! It's destroying me!' Lloyd said, gritting his teeth comically, making a joke of his desperation. His father owned a footwear business, and insisted that his son learn all aspects of its workings. He had spent six months in the factory as a costing clerk, and was now enduring a six-month stint in the shop. His father had allowed him to open a bank account at the end of the first six months, and had promised him a loan for a car at the end of the second. 'I'm sorry about all that ...' he continued after a long silence. 'You know I don't mean anything, don't you? It's him, that bloody Karta. He makes me act like that. He treats me like a fool, as if I'm something ridiculous. So I react that way.'

'Shall we go for this meal?' Daud said, but it was too late to stop him.

'I'm not a racist, you know that. But that bastard really makes it difficult,' Lloyd said when they were on their way. 'He's hardly down from the trees and he acts like he knows it all. Sorry, but I just can't stand that kind of behaviour. From the very first day I met him! Do you remember?'

Daud nodded. He remembered that Karta had turned up with Rosa, a Dutch girl with hair the colour of dark honey, and that Lloyd had been unable to keep his eyes off her. She had said afterwards that he had made her feel *sticky*. Her English was rudimentary but Daud had no difficulty understanding what she meant by this.

'He was talking to you most of the time,' Lloyd said. 'He didn't even speak to me. He ignored me as if I was dirt under his feet. He had this Dutch floozy he had picked up somewhere, and you could see him touching her up as he was talking. God, he was disgusting. I'll tell you something else that really pissed me off. The way he looked at me whenever I said anything, as if I was talking rubbish. It was the contempt. He's a fine one to complain about prejudice if that's how he treats people. He had that horrible sneer as he looked at me. I really can't stand people like that.'

Daud smiled to himself. He knew that Lloyd had been frightened of Karta. He had jumped, a small start, every time Karta spoke to him without warning. Later on he found out that Lloyd had never spoken to anybody black before meeting Daud. At that time they were on the same evening course, Lloyd trying to find a way of escaping his father's shoe shop, while he was trying to find a way of escaping the hospital. Daud had enjoyed the course, goading and provoking the tutor into hilarious displays. Lloyd had attached himself to him, and Daud had been relieved that he was not to be shunned by everyone. Then he had seen how Lloyd was rejected by the others, how they laughed at his accent and his boisterous ways. Whenever he said anything in class the other students stopped paying attention, and the teacher sighed gently while she heard him out.

He had been generous from the start, bringing him a chocolate bar or offering to buy him a portion of chips after class. Without any embarrassment he told Daud how surprised he was by his first black. *Sorry, I didn't catch your name. Where did you say you come from?* Daud told him that he was named after the slayer of the Philistine Goliath, and the father of Solomon via poor Bathsheba. *That doesn't mean anything to me. I'm an atheist*, Lloyd told him, pleased with his wit. Of course he had never believed the cruel exaggerations about black penises, he assured Daud, but he had expected his black to be always on a short fuse, on the point of eruption. Like the hysteria of the song-and-dance coon with his rolling eyes and blubbery lips. That was how he had thought of them, he confessed. Excitable and a little dumb, and not really interested in very much. He could not imagine one of them writing a symphony, for example, or being a philosopher. Daud egged him on, wanting to know the worst, taking comfort that this was all they thought of him and no worse. He smiled his superior smile and left the man to his ignorance, judging him beyond the reach of irony or sarcasm.

Karta would have nothing to do with such scruples, and licked his lips with anticipation when Daud told him the story. 'I'll make that racist cunt eat shit!' he said. 'How can you sit and listen to somebody saying all that and not stick a fist up his arse?' When Karta finally cornered Lloyd, he preached at him like a demented evangelist. His tongue rolled over centuries while he claimed everything within sight. He claimed the civilisation of the Pharaohs, before the envious and greedy Greeks under Alexander conquered

Egypt and transformed that African country into an exotic brothel, complete with its brothel queen, Cleopatra. He claimed Leo Africanus as well as the first Augustine. *Yes, Saint Augustine, you ignorant man. What did you think he was? A Viking?* He ranted about Pushkin and then gleefully destroyed Lloyd's scepticism by recounting in precise detail the history of the Pushkin family, and the astonishing rise of Grandpa Pushkin from slave boy at the Court of Peter the Great to a General in the Russian Army. He claimed Alexandre Dumas, all three of them.

'Fifty million black people, fifty million Africans were kidnapped from their homes,' he raged at Lloyd. 'Although the exact million is still being argued over by rigorous academics who don't want to get the odd million wrong. God knows how many others were slaughtered because they were too old or too young or too thin or too fat. Can you grasp that, you arrogant imbecile? Can you even begin to understand what you left behind you? You took only the best and the healthiest. You didn't want any weakling to cut your cane and pick your cotton, and produce your bastards. Can you imagine the havoc your little business left behind? Why should you? It was you who discovered us anyway, wasn't it? We didn't exist before you Christian bastards with your religion of life after death came and discovered us. You brought God to us. You saved us from eternal damnation. You brought light into our heathen darkness and led us from our barbarous natures. I know what I'm talking about. My father is a lay preacher. You forbade us human sacrifice, taught us the true meaning of compassion, taught us restraint in government, and opened our eyes to our pitifully primitive condition. You taught us how ugly we were, how we smell and how we are lazy and stupid. You even changed our names for us. You made monkeys out of us!

And now you laugh as our Casely-Hayfords and Jean-Louis and Benson-Hylens strut and preen for your approval. It's not us who are depraved, it's you! You and your fathers and grandfathers and your allotted and self-besotted kith and kin and clan. One of these days, my ugly Englishman, we're going to rise and chop every one of you, and rape your daughters and boil your vicars and slaughter you in your beds. As you've always wanted us to!'

And Lloyd swallowed and trembled and, Daud was sure, an inner foundation shook. 'What a load of codswallop!' he said. 'What a load of rubbish! What has all that to do with me?' Every Friday, without further invitation, he turned up at the pub, loathing Karta even as he feared him. Karta abused him endlessly but Lloyd always returned. He fought back with a tenacity that Daud found hard to understand. What for? Why did he not just go away?

He was sure they would come to blows sooner or later, and suspected that both men were looking forward to that day. He had tried to persuade Karta to leave Lloyd alone. *What are you trying to do? Educate him? Punish him? Let him alone*. Karta had shivered with a loathing that Daud had found shocking. *I'll kill that bastard one day*, he said. Daud tried to discourage Lloyd from coming to the pub but did not know how to say the words that would drive him away. With each day he understood that Lloyd had nowhere else to go, and came to him with the unerring sense of someone who had already suffered many rejections. It was all Daud could do to keep refusing invitations to tea with Lloyd's parents.

5

When Daud returned to day-duty, he found that Catherine Mason had left theatres and had been sent to another ward. He conceded a sense of disappointment, but in his mind he shrugged her departure off. She would not have wished to do more than talk to him now and then anyway. Some days later he met her in one of the hospital corridors. She was amid a large and noisy groups of students, whose striped uniforms looked to him at that moment aggressive and hostile, like the intimidating abdomens of fierce hornets. In his embarrassment he smiled distantly at her. He may even have seemed cold to her, he admitted, although he was only thinking to pre-empt a rebuff. He had imagined he would run into her, and had planned a smooth, sophisticated smile, accompanied by a nonchalant piece of wit, but he had been too surprised to think of all that when he met her. Her smile was even more limp than his, and they passed each other without exchanging a word. As the days went by, he became angry with himself when he remembered the freedom with which he had spoken to her on that night. It was no wonder that she ignored him. It would not do for her friends to think she was showing interest in a *coloured* ancillary. Next time he met her, he vowed, he would invite her to plant a smacker on his right royal black arse.

He ran into her again in the dark and decrepit pre-fab hall where non-nursing staff took their lunch-time cup of tea. The hall was cavernous, large enough to be the venue of the hospital amateur dramatics productions. Daud had seen an ambitious performance of *Peer Gynt* there once, and had applauded for so long at the end of the play, to make up for the tardiness of the rest of the sparse audience, as he saw it, that the producer refused to speak to him for several weeks, assuming that he was mocking them.

Daud liked the hall for its hugeness, and the gloom of its distant corners. At one end was a tiny cubby-hole, across which ran a counter. Two tired-looking old ladies lounged behind it, stirring now and then to pour tea for the occasional ancillary that appeared. Half a dozen tables were generously scattered over an area the size of two tennis courts. It was not surprising then that he saw Catherine as soon as he entered. She was leaning forward over a book and took no notice as he slid into the chair opposite her. He saw a frown pass across her lowered brow. He was sure she had already seen him in the time it had taken the old ladies to pour him a cup of tea. After a second or two, although it seemed longer, he asked her what she was reading. She looked up sharply and stared dumbly at him as if she had no idea who he was. He smiled to encourage her recollection. She returned a polite, non-committal smile and pushed the book towards him, grudging and unfriendly. It turned out to be a book he knew, and he said something. She made a knowing face and he assumed that his conversation was too obvious as well as unwanted. He admired this stiffness, he told himself, and much preferred the resentment to a hypocritical show of friendship. He persisted, and although she was reluctant at first, sighing with impatience as she listened to him, gradually she joined in and began to talk.

In the end her eyes sparkled with pleasure again, and gave him new courage.

'I really enjoyed that night,' he said at last, when the time to return to the infernal regions was fast approaching. 'When we were on night-duty together.'

'Yes,' she said, smiling, her smooth skin filling up and turning dark. 'It was good. I talked too much, though, didn't I? Like a kid! And all that coffee didn't do my stomach any good either.'

'It must have been a lot better going back on days, then,' he said.

'No, it wasn't,' she said, grinning. 'It was too busy.'

She rushed off back to work, glancing at the watch pinned to her bodice. He thought it would be easy after that, and he passed happy hours contemplating and planning his best approaches. In the midst of his euphoria, he had many moments of sinking despair. These occurred after he had seen her. He saw her several times but she was always with other people and he could not bring himself to detach her from the group. Or they were hurrying in different directions. Or it was the wrong time of the week when the coffers were empty. *For God's sake*, he ranted at himself. *Why can't you just ask her? It's humbling to sit here, nursing little fears and worries about inviting a woman out, when others with the power to change the world are brooding in some bat-infested cave, waiting their moment with steadfast will.*

The more he saw her, the more his desire and his loneliness seemed like self-mortification, like something he did to himself. Eventually he saw her in the dining room one lunch-time, and he was determined that this was the day. She was ahead of him in the line, and he hid himself carefully between heads and bodies of the nurses in the queue.

From there he could watch her without being seen. He pretended that he was stalking her, and that if she saw him she would dart into the safety of another group, as if all the time she had been hiding from his intense courtship.

The line moved slowly towards the counter. Another line worked its way back. Steam rose from the trays of food and from over-heated bodies, mixing into a fug that was thick with the smell of stewed meat. She had her back to him, and he saw how the snugly fitting bodice followed the contours of her shoulders and hips. A strand of hair had strayed on her brow and she pushed it away absent-mindedly before bringing her arms together again across her chest.

The women behind the counter were all dressed in white, starched and stiff and wretched in the heat. He wondered again why it was that so many of the people who did menial jobs in hospitals had that wasted, worn-out look. The older women looked unkempt and prematurely grey. The younger men had moustaches and a victimised appearance. The older men were always lounging against linen bags, scowling at passers-by, having developed the conviction through long practice that their duties consisted of resisting all efforts to make them do anything. *Do I look like that*, he wondered? The nurses did not, but they were different.

He saw Catherine pick up her tray and turn to squeeze past the queue that was waiting behind her. Her eyes went straight to his face. It was difficult to miss him as he was the only man in the whole line. She paused beside him, smiling with what was unmistakably pleasure and surprise. He grinned back, unable to think of anything suave to say. She glanced beyond the line and then nodded, and he hoped that meant that she would keep a place for him. He had no time to dwell on this happy prospect as ahead of him loomed the domestic supervisor. In her dark-blue uniform and lace-fringed cap, she looked the very picture of Victorian respectability. People spoke of her as a kindly lady but he was not fooled. He could see her strutting and parading in the Crimean concentration camps, holding Florence Nightingale's lamp and barking words of cheer to the starving and the wounded. She was ample and wide, the epitome of the mindless maternal shape, he thought, except for the diminutive heart.

'Hello,' she said, smiling. 'From St Nicholas, are you?'

St Nicholas was a nearby psychiatric hospital from where male student nurses came for general hospital practice. It was a loony bin. Daud knew, from the general rumour, that syphilis was rife there and reincarnated Nietzsches two-a-penny, and that abuse and self-abuse were the normal conditions of existence. The supervisor insisted, on every occasion she met him, on asking Daud if he came from St Nicholas, and in any case always spoke to him with that patient and accommodating tone of voice that suggested that perhaps he could be doing something other than working there. The first time, she had insisted on calling theatres to check his story, licking each syllable of his name before spitting it out. He had worried that she would call St Nicholas to see if there was a loony on the loose. Or that he would be refused a meal, and would be sent to eat in the lower dining room with the porters and the floor cleaners, *and God knows what was in their stew*. He called her *The Lark of Bloemfontein*, because he was sure she must have been there too during the Boer War, lecturing the starving women and children in the concentration camps on the wisdom of defeat and British rule.

'Can I have a few more potatoes, please?' he asked the grey-haired old lady bent over the vegetables, offering her the greasiest smile he could manage. In the background he heard the domestic supervisor tutting with distaste. The woman frowned and took a firmer grip of her spoon. He wondered how old she was. Did she look like the kind of person who could have given birth to sons that now roamed the globe killing and torturing people in World Wars? Had she herself manned the ramparts of some obscure battle to hold the line against howling dervishes and smelly wogs? Spoon held firmly in one hand, she covered the potatoes with the other, as if she expected him to lunge for them.

He saw Catherine sitting at a table by the window. She did not look to be in a state to help him repel the blood-sucking ghouls of the old Empire. She seemed tired and dejected. *Catherine dear, have no fear*, he whispered. She looked up and smiled, and he felt his spirits rise. What could be denied a man like him, a man who dared so much? He had eaten hog meat when he was hungry, sinning against all the observances of his people. He had swallowed alcohol in defiance of his God. He had crawled on hands and knees in search of a living. He had taken on the Gorgons and the Cyclops of the empire and put them to flight. Would he now dare proposition one of that empire's fairest maids?

'Delightful,' he said, pointing to the gristly stew on his plate.

'It's every bit as bad as it looks,' she said unhappily.

Sweat shone on her face, and her eyes seemed watering with exhaustion. His stomach grumbled insistently, coiling into painful knots and then flying open with a dramatic growl. He forced a forkful of watery potatoes into his mouth to keep it quiet. He sorted out pieces of meat and swooped them up towards his mouth in an act of blind courage, with his eyes shut. It was almost too much, and peristalsis briefly rebelled. *Don't get so worked up*, he patted his stomach sympathetically.

'I can't eat any more of this,' she said suddenly, looking at him angrily, as if it was something to do with him. 'It's disgusting. How can they expect us to eat this?'

'I couldn't agree with you more! That's what I was trying to say,' he replied, ignoring the howls of betrayal from his stomach. 'What about the fruit salad? I don't suppose that's any good, is it?'

'It's too sweet. It's awful,' she said.

'It's always too sweet.' He cast a mildly regretful look at it. 'To be honest with you, I don't think I can eat it either. How about a cup of coffee? We can get some downstairs.'

'I don't drink coffee in the middle of the day,' she said.

'Tea?' he offered feebly, beginning to feel that he had picked the wrong day for his assault on the summit.

'It stinks in here,' she said. She stood up abruptly, picked up her tray, and waited for him to rise. He ignored the furious rumbling of his bowels and rose to follow her. The corridors were dark and silent. They passed a window which overlooked the back lawns of the hospital, stretching away to the white hedges that formed the boundary with the county cricket ground. He thought of calling her back to see the view but she seemed too tense. What was she so angry about? He assumed it must be work. She walked a little ahead of him, looking miserable. Her hair was streaked with white as light from the window flashed on her. The purple lines of her uniform striped across her shoulders, hugging her flesh. As he drew level, he stole a last look at her from the back, finding himself contemptible for this act of disrespect.

'Do you really want a coffee?' she asked as they descended the stairs.

They walked down the avenue of chestnuts instead, sitting at last on one of the benches outside the nurses' home. He saw that her tiredness had turned into something harder, irritation perhaps. He tried to think of something to say, but their silence had cast a grip on his mind. He watched her as she turned away from him. When she turned back, his eyes roved over her face with a hurried intensity, as if he was gorging himself with a last, full look before she left him. She laughed. 'What's the matter?' she asked.

'You seem tired,' he said.

She coloured a little. 'It's nothing. The ward is getting me down. I'm sorry, I don't mean to be rude.'

Dear Catherine, he began. *Here I sit, making a meal out of asking you to dinner. Do you not pity my fumbling clumsiness? You have to realise that asking you out has no cultural relevance to me whatsoever. I don't really know how to do it. I don't have an instinct for it. I think you understand me. To have cultural integrity, I would have to send my aunt to speak, discreetly, to your aunt, who would then speak to your mother, who would speak to my mother, who would speak to my father, who would speak to me and then approach your father, who would approach your mother, who would then, if all had gone well so far, approach you. Then vice versa.*

'Have dinner with me tonight,' he said.

In the silence he heard the breath wheeze out of him. The light was gentle, the sun having disappeared behind a cloud. A sudden burst of bird song reached him across the glade. The sedge swayed along the margins of the lake. The sound of water rippling over rocks was hushed by the fragrant bushes that surrounded the pavilion: lavender and jasmine and sweet oleander. In the distance, he heard the sound of bells pealing the hours, joyous and lifting. She smiled at him, her lips flushed and parted, the vein in her neck fluttering with excitement. She lowered her eyes from his dark, implacable gaze and stared unseeingly at her fingers, knotted into each other in fear.

He struggled to prevent a grin of triumph from breaking across his face. He had swept her off her feet, that much was clear. He had breached and laid low all her defences. He could already see the acclaim his conquest would bring. His landlord would grin with the smug joy of the earnest liberal, and wait his moment before bringing in piano keyboards again. *Do you see what you have given the world, W.E.B. Du Bois?* Lloyd would probably bring him a whole bag of shopping and wait his chance to tell her his *smelly wogs* joke, to show her what a buddy he was. Karta would see it as a victory for black humanism. *You are the slime and plasma of the green spring of the world*, he would exult. But that will be nothing, he thought, compared to what the crowds will do. They will make offerings of magnificent opulence in recognition of his heroic stature, head and shoulders above Prometheus and Sir Gary Sobers. They will come to show their gratitude for all the lives he had been instrumental in saving, for all the rivers of blood he had staunched, for all the myths and taboos he would have made redundant by his ineluctable will. The men, draped in glittering splendour, *none of your ostrich feathers and solar topees here, if you please*, will precede the women, carrying sticks of jasmine and shards of sandalwood in glowing embers. In the rear, among the perpetual motion of gently vibrating naked flesh will come the eunuchs and the virgins. On their heads they will carry straw trays laden with fruits, cooked meats, cakes, jellies, and wriggling, steaming, dark-red *halwa*. Flanked by the chanters and the praise-singers, robed in cloth of copper and amber, he will stand silent, impassive, detached, erect. As they pass in homage before him, he will decree that all cripples, and other general eyesores, should be held, collected at one place and tossed into pyres lit with Kismayu *ghi*. Then all will be invited to a feast of tender goat meat, dripping with juices and saffron-soaked spices. They shall wash their mouths with juices of pineapples, and dig their teeth deep into the soft flesh of blood-red pawpaws, and sate themselves with the jellies and the *halwa*.

But she said no. 'I can't go out tonight,' she said. 'I'm sorry. I'm expecting a phone call. Perhaps ...'

'Don't worry,' he said quickly. 'It was just a thought.'

Dear Catherine, It was a mistake to ask you, an even bigger mistake to panic when you said no. I panic at the slightest excuse, I'm ashamed to say. My cowardice, which is immense, is due to the sort of upbringing I had. My mother listened to too many of those hygiene programmes on the radio. I grew up in the dark days of imperialism, when Public Health officials took their duties seriously. What else could they do in the God-forsaken places they chose to install themselves in as civilising czars? One of these duties was the broadcasting of horrifying and, no doubt, accurate accounts of the depredations the human body was prone to in a tropical climate. My mother listened to all these broadcasts, and took them all very seriously. So, if there are any retired officials listening, out in the fastness of Cumbria, or snug in some Cotswold cottage, thank you. You can stop luxuriating in the lower infant mortality rate, the virtual extinction of malaria, the control of epidemics of intestinal diseases, and consider the harm you have done to the molly-coddled survivors.

My mother boiled our water, dosed us with castor oil and quinine, and washed our arses twice a day with soap and water. We were not allowed to buy cooked food, wash in the river or sleep in the open. We were not allowed to ride a donkey in case we became infested with fleas. She was worried about TB, bilharzia and VD, and she did her best to protect us. An unusually smelly fart earned you a double dose of castor oil, and on bad days, an examination of the orifice. A mildly festering wound aroused fears of gangrene and amputation. An itchy penis provoked lengthy and detailed scrutiny of the abused member. A careless cough precipitated a merciless interrogation about the state of health of the chests of one's friends and associates. The result of all this, dear Catherine, although I'm sure you've already guessed, is that I'm afraid of everything. And you said no when all seemed well. Why did you do that? Where will I find the strength to ask you again?

During the afternoon, which he spent entirely in the disposal corridor, he contacted most of his usual correspondents. He paced up and down, reviling himself for being so laughably clumsy, and abusing her for being a sulky foreigner. Whenever things looked as if they were getting out of hand, he dashed off a calming letter. *Dear Sir Gary, May you live for ever.* The thought of Sir Gary never failed to soothe him. *Dear Herr Nietzsche,* he ranted when irritation overcame him. *This obsession with the will seems to me just a short-cut to beastliness. Endless monsters have tormented us since fuck knows when, all screwed up with their wills. Why bother making a formal declaration out of it? If you had asked Idi Amin what it was that he thought he was doing, he would have explained himself in your terms. Assuming he was capable of something so inexpressive of the will! There's no need to scoff. Take Macbeth if Idi Amin does not suit you.*

Dear Catherine, he began again. *I wanted to tell you about my mother's obsession with hygiene. I wanted to tell you about my separation from my people, and about the guilt I feel that they seem to have abandoned me. I wanted to tell you this.*

6

He lived alone out of choice, he insisted. He relished his solitary existence, and did not usually invite people to visit him at all, or only very occasionally, and never out of necessity. He was self-sufficient, sophisticated and utterly without fear, the very model of independence and grit. So she needn't think that just because she had refused his invitation to dinner that this mattered in any way at all to him. It might have ruined his weekend and filled him with thoughts of his unworthiness but that was no stranger to him. Was that clear?

He knew that she lived near the hospital, in one of those large Edwardian houses whose owners had moved on to other things. The houses were now flats and bedsits, let out to nurses and students to provide a tidy income for the owners, until the next wave of gentrification hit the district and they could be sold for a fortune. On the Sunday evening he went strolling in that general direction, retracing his morning route to work. It was a warm, dry evening, and the streets had a dishevelled, impromptu appearance, as if caught out by the fine weather.

He did not intend to call on her. He would prowl in her garden or hide in the conifer hedge and wait for her troubled face to appear at the window. Then he would set up a howl of distress in the quicksilver twilight, and watch her start with knowledge of her guilt. *Catherine, Catherine.* He would leave before she could speak, scuttle into the laurel bushes before she could redeem herself with a few words of kindness. He might even strangle her puppy, and leave it dangling off a branch at the end of her handkerchief. He turned back before he reached her street. *What did you take me for?* he scoffed. *A character out of a book? Some hysterical, alienated foreigner or something?*

The neighbours on both sides of his house had their televisions on, blaring through the thin walls as if they were in the next room. He tried his own set, with the sound turned down, to check what they were watching and decided to retreat upstairs. He did not grudge the extra rent he paid to live this way, partly because he did not always pay it. Karta had suggested moving in, but Daud had refused. He kept the extra room as a place to go to for a change of scenery, he told him. Once or twice Lloyd had muttered about needing somewhere to go for a day or two, to escape his parents, but Daud had played dumb, as he had to discreet attempts by some of the foreign student friends of Karta to hire his room for a little private screwing.

He had once shared a house with another student, a Nigerian called Ray. They had been friends before they found the house, talking for hours about politics and music, arguing about football and cutting a caper in the streets when high spirits overcame them. They had ended up not speaking to each other, and Daud knew that the fault was as much his as it was Ray's. He could not bear the way he lost control of his own life. He had to consult Ray about what they ate, had to worry about what Ray was doing before he could play a record, go out or even go to bed. Sometimes, in the middle of the night, he would hear him pacing around in his room, talking to himself.

And Ray never flushed the toilet. Daud would go to the toilet in the morning and find great logs of shit in the pan. When he could bear it no longer, he asked Ray if he would mind using the flush. Ray had not said another word to him for the two months that remained of his academic year. He did not even talk to himself any more. There was an uncanny silence in the house that was only ever broken by the sound of *things*: footsteps on the stairs, a door banging, the clank of crockery being stacked on the drainer. Ray flushed the toilet, but when the time came to leave, he returned to London without saying goodbye, and Daud had never heard from him again. On the few occasions he went to London, he worried about running into Ray and dreaded the embarrassment of having to pass him without a word.

It was after Ray's departure that he had inherited 9 Bishop Street and since then had ruled over it in unquestioned supremacy, living a life of self-denial and squalor, of quiet desperation and inner frenzy, as was his right and choice. He reflected that it was after moments of rejection such as he had suffered at the hands of Catherine that his mind became a moral battle-ground, a victim of competing desires and a prey to the conflicts in his soul. Should he allow himself to become demoralised or should he grit his teeth, clench his fists and demonstrate the black man's dignity in adversity? Should he run amok or retreat into an incredible sulk, singing spirituals like Sidney Poitier in *The Defiant Ones*? Should he give up his job? Grow locks? Should he become an existentialist and achieve his apotheosis at the moment of his destruction? Why couldn't she have dinner with him? He hoped she understood the responsibility of her actions.

He had his late duty on a Monday, at his own request. The shift started at one in the afternoon and finished at nine in the evening. This gave him a longer weekend, and nothing ever happened on Monday evening, so he was not missing anything by being at work. Nothing ever happened during the weekend either, but that was not the point. Mr Solomon, the Superintendent of Theatres, was sitting at his desk complacently regarding the work rota when Daud arrived. Solomon was cleaning his fingernails with a pen-knife, now and then putting his fingers in his mouth to suck a stubborn bit of muck out.

'You're in the back this afternoon, my lad,' said Mr Solomon in his abrupt voice and twitched his mouth in a parody of a smile.

Daud always took care with Mr Solomon, who was unwaveringly hard with him. It filled him with awe that he had never seen Mr Solomon sweat, or go red in the face. He kept himself steady whatever the provocation. He never changed, and so far as Daud was concerned, he never even tried to pretend that the world was inhabited by anything but monkeys. Daud left Solomon's office without expressing his fulsome admiration for such a desperate philosophy. *Dear Ineffable Solomon, It's a relief to find you the same when all about you are losing their marbles and refusing invitations to dinner. Only do you always have to put me in the wash-up? Can't you be a paternalistic racist and put me somewhere less messy? Can't I be your token ethnic minority equal opportunities showpiece?*

He saw on the list that Dickie Bird, the orthopaedic registrar, was wielding the knife. Mr Richard Bird quite liked being called Dickie Bird, especially by the menials like orderlies and porters. He was an unpleasant man who enjoyed making faces about *our coloured brethren*, by which he meant the Pakistani who was his staggeringly inept assistant. *Dear Mr Dickie Bird, This is one of your coloured brethren speaking. I get tired of these innuendoes you are so fond of. Does it occur to you that the great-grandaddy of you all, old Hippocrates himself, could trace his ancestry to a bean merchant from Harar? So there.*

He was pleased to see also that the instruments Sister for the afternoon was Sister Lucy Williams, a soft-spoken, polite lady whom he always thought of as a reincarnation of Jane Austen. Her hair was thin and dark, and parted in the middle. He had once overheard her having an argument with Florence Nightingale. He had been cowering behind the steriliser for warmth, during the depths of winter when the thin glazing of the disposal corridor was no protection against the weather. She had been filling the machine with instruments, and became irritated with something that kept going wrong. Suddenly she lashed into the memory of her holiness, the Great Florence, unaware of his astonished presence. *This is your fault, Miss Nightingale. If it wasn't for you I wouldn't be here.* He knew nothing of her personal life, for she was one of those people who rarely figured in conversations over coffee. He hoped she enjoyed what there was of it. Perhaps, though, she spent endless, lonely hours at home, drinking herself to death and wishing that a Russian cavalry officer would leap her garden fence and have dinner with her. Perhaps she was not arguing with Flo at all but *writing* to her.

Dear Catherine, The ennui is getting to me out here. It can kill you sometimes as it stretches endlessly ahead of you. I pace up and down these long empty back corridors, counting until the numbers are just a jumble in my brain. Sometimes I hide in the disused radium store, so I can talk to the skull and cross-bones warning on the door. Admit it, you were pleased that I asked you, weren't you? But you were right to refuse, I think. You probably found the idea quite strange. I understand why you refused more than you do yourself. I know that you will dutifully protest at this. You see, I know you better than you realise, although not as well as I would like to. And without saying so, you will feel impatience at my absurd sensitivity. Good Lord, you'll think, don't they ever give it a rest? Can't these buggers sing any other tune? Can't we just be people living in the same place, sharing and learning from each other? Can't we just make the decisions that seem right to us without having race or something thrown at us? Well, no, you can't. I know it's a dreary business, especially when you give so much of your time and selfless concern and your generous care. This is not to mention your quiet and unsung rejection of cheap racism, and your approval of such measures as Bengali folk-dancing on TV and your often declared crush on Sidney Poitier. I kinda dig him myself, honeychile. After all this, do I dare connect your rejection of me with my socio-cultural and sub-cutaneous deprivation? How can I explain to you that we are an unfortunate people who don't know about gratitude? We know about resentment, about frenzy. We are quick to take offence, primed to blow. So next time I invite you to have dinner with me, your best course will be to say yes, and look pleased about it. Otherwise I will make up my mind to be annihilated. You have heard about how we do it, haven't you? How, when the time requires, we can glaze our eyes and go off in search of the leaf-mould dungeons of our benighted grandfathers? How we can let the precious gift of life depart from us as if it were a trinket in order to show somebody how upset we are? You have heard, I'm sure, of the spiritual intensity of our sulks. I've thought a lot about you since I last saw you, and I feel that it is in your interest to be associated with me.

Dear My Daddy, This is long overdue, I know that. The only good thing about what I'm doing is that I can see the avenue of chestnuts from here. The trees are full of leaf at the moment. It would have pleased you to see them. The work is dirty and my position is humble. I bet you never thought I would be doing this kind of thing when you handed over your life's savings to me. Regards to everybody.

When Daud first came to work in theatres, Solomon had put the word out that he had been in some kind of college or seminary. For reasons that Daud never understood, Solomon announced him as formerly studying to be a priest. There were many such occasions when he suspected that the old desperado was making fun of him but he was always won over again by his utterly unflappable cynicism. Sister Wintour, who had been a missionary in Biafra, was one of the few people who remarked on his studies. Everybody else ignored the interesting possibility that Solomon had presented to them. To have a refugee from a seminary in your midst, reduced to the humble calling of wiping pus off an operating table, and not to pursue him with impertinent questions and wild prognostications! Nothing more was required to convince him that he was dealing with a bunch of dumpling-eating Moloch-fodder. Was this what the Ineffable was trying to show him? Was this his way of telling him that imagination died in these catacombs? *O Wisdom Incarnate!*

Sister Wintour had already heard of him when Daud was sent for a short, introductory spell of night-duty. She had a reception ready for him. She was the Mother Superior taking confession, gathering the prodigal son to the bosom of Mother Church. Staff Nurse Chattan was to be the bemused heathen who might inadvertently be struck by the Light while witnessing this touching scene of spiritual reunion. The Sister spoke to Daud as if they had a great deal in common: God, the desire to serve, Africa. She told him she could guess the doubts and terrors that would have driven him out of the seminary. She could understand how after witnessing the incredible degradation to which man had been reduced in Africa, he should begin to doubt the wisdom of the controlling Hand. But God works in His own ways, and places the burden of understanding on us more often than we realise. Do not spurn this opportunity of advancing Christ's message on earth, she begged. *I'm a Muslim*, he announced, entirely to her disbelief. The Staff Nurse giggled and the good missionary was routed. 'Islam has done nothing but harm in Africa,' the Sister counter-attacked. 'As if things were not hard enough for the black man already!' It turned out also that the soul of the black man was being destroyed by smoking and drinking. His whole culture was under threat from eating bread and tinned mackerel. *Tinned mackerel?* Instead of yam and stockfish, she explained.

About Biafra she said only that it became very difficult once the war started. Both their house boy and their cook had gone off to join the Army. 'To do a bit of looting, most likely,' she offered. 'Honestly, as if anyone could imagine Boniface and Barnabas with guns! It meant the mission had to find us another boy to serve at table. It wasn't easy at that time to find anybody who was properly trained. And we had to find another cook. Oh, the meals this new cookboy turned out! The most ridiculous things! Boiled beef and carrots, liver and onions! Good Heavens, where was the pepper soup and the pounded yam? We ate African food. It was so annoying.' The Staff Nurse, wiser in the ways of the world than appearances suggested, spoke to him quietly after the Sister had gone for her snooze. He told her that he had to leave his studies because he ran out of money. She nodded sympathetically. 'I'm a Muslim too,' she told him, giving him her skinny smile. 'Take no notice of the missionary madam. Islām is good.'

That was also the night when he witnessed his first emergency Caesarean. The panic was prodigious. The telephones were ringing, the Sister was running, and the Staff Nurse was hysterical. When the midwife arrived, she was out of breath, her glasses were all steamed up and she had no time to change into theatre clothes but stormed in wearing her ward uniform. The patient, a Nigerian woman called Mrs Abubakar, followed close behind her, attended by an Egyptian surgeon. The woman was obviously in agony, and when the blankets were removed, her bedding was covered in blood. *Where's Mr Waring?* the Sister yelled. The midwife hushed her and the young Egyptian surgeon looked even more frightened. He slashed the belly open and yanked the baby out, but it was too late. Mrs Abubakar lost her baby and very nearly her own life. The surgeon did not know how to stop her bleeding. He was complaining as he worked. Waring, the consultant, had told him to see to the patient because she was one of his people, he said. By the time Waring arrived, furious at not having been called earlier, he found his frightened assistant in tears. The midwife had just been in to announce the baby's death. Waring completed the operation in a silence that was broken only by the soft, suppressed sobs of the young doctor.

Waring did not even look at his assistant after the operation. He thanked the Sister with his pretence of Old World politeness, and then gave Daud a long, curious look. 'Aha! I see we have a new bod here,' he cried, advancing towards Daud and cleaning his pince-nez. 'Where is it you come from, son? India or Pakistan? The Dark Continent! Having a lot of trouble out there, you chaps, aren't you?' He left the theatre closely followed by the Egyptian, whose career was certainly in ruins, and on whose head was the blood of the young Abubakar, one of his people.

Daud wondered if it was time for a tea break. With Solomon on duty, that was always a hazardous manoeuvre. He loved nothing better than to flush out orderlies and assorted ancillaries from the rest room. He took his overshoes off and strolled into the theatre corridor in search of adventure. He glanced into the reception area, wondering as he did so whether there was any chance that Catherine might be sitting there, waiting to hand over a patient. He found a pretty student standing by a patient's trolley, holding his hand and speaking softly to him. Leaning against the opposite wall, and watching her with an unnervingly blank stare, was the tall, dark-haired porter with the Zapata moustache. His name was Michael but everybody called him Mick because he was a porter. He was well-known as a gourmandiser of pretty young students, and Daud imagined that he achieved his nefarious purposes by first hypnotising his victims with his blank stare and then eating them.

The nurse looked up gratefully at Daud, and so she should with Mick taking up station beside her like that, but he beat a quick retreat before she tried to hand the patient over to him. He saw Dickie Bird coming out of one of the theatres and strolled back to the wash-up, knowing a dirty trolley would soon be on its way out.

The list cases finished at five. By then Daud was close to tears with boredom. He knew that if he made his presence known, he would end up cleaning the theatres while everybody went off duty. *Dear Colonel Alexander, Let me congratulate you, first of all, on your appointment to chair the enquiry into the noxious smells that have troubled the estate by the abbatoir. In these days of hardship, I can only envy you your good fortune. I am sure you will make a first-rate job of it. They did not name you after the conqueror for nothing.*

The Most Sterile Majesty, the Enlightened Solomon, he chanted. *Once again I pick up thoughts and groans to commune with your wise nature. You know the esteem in which I hold you, and I beg that you will not dismiss my little plea because it seems a touch disrespectful. Why do I always work in the disposal corridor when you are at the helm? Can't you see what it's doing to me? Can't you see how the boredom is getting to me? It is time, it seems to me, that the duties of a theatre orderly were clearly defined. My contract states that I will carry out general theatre duties, assist in the anaesthetic room, clean and maintain instruments and equipment, and shave patients in the pubes if nobody else wants to do it. May I respectfully submit that the way you are treating me is tantamount to slave labour? You will concede, Wisdom Incarnate, that this is nothing short of barbaric exploitation. Is this what I sacrificed my education for? What do you take me for? A monkey? I look forward to hearing from you.*

When he next heard from Solomon, it was to be told to clean the theatre, a duty he performed with resignation. He contented himself with writing obscene letters to his erstwhile hero. Solomon offered him a lift home as they left together at nine. In the car, he told him of his experiences as a tank sergeant during the war. Daud could hardly believe his good fortune. This was yet another piece of evidence, unlooked for but most welcome, to confirm his general theory of a gifted killer race that roamed the globe, slaughtering wherever it went. It had to be admitted that they had slaughtered with impressive efficiency and a degree of moral economy. It did not surprise him that Solomon saw nothing to be ashamed of, for example, in spending his youth sitting in a metal can dismembering people. It was not as if he took pleasure in it, or did it too successfully, or ran amok and carved up the vanquished as well. He did what nature had created him to do. Daud shivered slightly as he discerned the beginnings of a staggering revelation. *It was not that war made people ruthless and cruel. It was ruthless and cruel people that made war*. Was it possible that the race needed to feel and hear the gurglings of its dying victims in order to be at its most creative and alive? Like vampires? Was that why the nation was going to the dogs, getting so badly hammered in cricket and generally turning into a bunch of effete wankers? He offered Solomon a drink, hoping to delay him long enough to pop the question at him, but Solomon smiled his thanks and refused. 'My children are at home alone,' he said. 'Another time perhaps.'

'How old are your children?' Daud asked. It was a random question but one never knew what it might yield.

'Nine and thirteen,' Solomon said, grinning in the dark but none the less changing gear in preparation for leaving. 'I don't like to leave them alone any longer than I have to. They're quite used to it but …'

Daud waited, unable to save Solomon from the misery of having to complete what he had started to say, and unwilling to stop him in case he should misunderstand.

'Their mother died about seven years ago,' Solomon said.

'I'm sorry,' Daud replied, shamed by his own frivolity.

7

He queued up with the other ancillary staff outside the accounts office. When it pleased her to do so, the wages clerk opened the door and admitted them. Her name was Mrs Coop, and it was obvious from the tone of her address that she felt nothing but contempt for the people she served. She turned the smallest query from one of them into an excuse for a merciless, wheezing interrogation. Cigarettes had ruined her chest. Daud took his wage packet without looking at it. Mrs Coop rapped on the counter behind which she stood and summoned Daud back with a hooked index finger. He grinned at her and turned to continue on his way.

'You!' she called, and the cramped accounts office fell silent. Every week somebody fell victim to Mrs Coop's particular disdain and this week it was to be him. He checked over what had just happened to see if he had done anything wrong. He was reluctant to upset the old bag. She found breathing so difficult that usually he watched her with fascinated horror as she took deep, whistling breaths before gasping out a phrase or two. Often he found himself so absorbed in this primeval struggle for life that her laboriously crafted words failed to register. 'Can't you read?' gasped Mrs Coop, her finger tapping the sign on the counter. It asked all staff to check their wages before leaving the office.

Her white hair was hennaed and tortoiseshell spectacles swung on a cord round her neck. Daud looked at her wasted old face, then dutifully checked his wages. 'It's never wrong, Mrs Coop,' he said, thinking to flatter the old woman and add a few days to her life.

'Well, next time make sure you check it. I don't want you running back in here in the middle of the week complaining that your wages aren't right,' she called out, struggling with each word individually, as if it had required a particular effort to bring it out into the world. The last syllable reached him after he had gone through the door, and was standing outside the office, on the brink of going out of earshot.

'Stupid cow!' said a woman's voice in the queue. 'She'll kill herself with them horrible fags.'

'I wish she'd just get on with it,' growled a beefy, balding man in blue overalls, grinning to acknowledge the deliberate ambiguity of his exhortation. Daud looked at him with interest. Could this man have led charges across strange and blood-stained terrains, cut railway tracks into mountain-sides and brought order to warring peoples? The man caught Daud's glance and gave him the imperial smile. 'I wouldn't let her talk to me like that if I were you,' he said, grinning and looking at faces in the queue to signal that this was a send-up. 'I bet if you were back in the jungle, you'd have just chucked her in a pot, wouldn't you?'

'What?' he asked, momentarily taken aback by this brazen assault.

'Ha ha, I was only pulling your leg, mate,' the grinning man said, pretending to hush down the titters of the rest of the queue.

'Pulling my leg?' Daud said. 'You ignorant fat man! You wouldn't know my leg from your arsehole, you penis sucker.'

'Now you just wait a minute,' the man shouted, trying to raise his voice above the gleeful hoots of the women in the line.

'Shit-eater,' Daud called out, even though he felt that honour was already satisfied.

'Come back here and say that,' the man yelled.

Daud waved two fingers at him and beat a tactical retreat. He was pleased with himself as he strolled to lunch, and neither the meal nor the thought of the man could diminish the euphoria of the handsome pay-packet in his pocket. He saw Catherine ahead of him on the great, curving stairway, descending towards the main hospital entrance. 'Hello,' he said, hurrying to her and touching her on the shoulder. She looked round, and her face changed with a slow smile.

'Where've you been? I haven't seen you for ages,' she said.

'What do you mean, ages? Thirteen days ... or something like that,' he said, not wanting to be too exact.

'Really? Is that all?'

'You look ... good,' he said. 'You look lovely,' he added, laughing at his own caution. He saw a *Thank you* beginning to form on her lips, but she only mouthed the words. 'You look somewhat pissed off, though. Come to think of it, you seemed a bit pissed off the last time I saw you. This nursing isn't such fun, is it?'

'You're determined to make me dislike nursing. I don't feel pissed off,' she said, in a voice that was cheerfully hinting that it did not wish to discuss the subject. 'Where are you off to now?'

'Peer Gynt Hall,' he said, and went on to show off by explaining the name. She took him instead to the common room in the nurses' home, saying she found the gloom of the hall depressing sometimes. He felt like an intruder as he followed her in, and stood close by her as she poured from the huge pot. The room was crowded with students, most of them in uniform. He saw Roger Churchill, a Barbadian student nurse from the psychiatric hospital. He was sitting sprawled out in front of the television, watching the immolation of the England cricket team. This was the second day of the Third Test, and England were having serious problems with Michael Holding's bowling. Roger Churchill waved to Daud and then shouted out the score. They were nodding acquaintances but in this crowded room it had been necessary to show that they knew each other. Heads turned to look at Roger while he became absorbed again in the cricket. His middle name was Winston and in the one long conversation they had had together, he had made Daud green with envy by telling him that in Bridgetown he had often ridden on the same bus as Seymour Nurse. Later, Roger Winston Churchill was to be expelled from the psychiatric hospital after being discovered in a store cupboard with a teenaged female patient, soothing her shattered psyche in the time-honoured manner. But there was no hint of this as he lay sprawled in front of the television, shouting out the cricket score. The pause in the buzz of conversation was only momentary, and the murmur picked up again almost immediately, flowing round the oblivious Roger with effortless accommodation.

They sat under a chestnut tree in the garden that led off from the common room but was enclosed from the road by a hedge, and talked comfortably and easily together. She told him of the awfulness of the ward she was working in. He asked her if she would like to get away from the hospital regime and go out somewhere. A meal or the cinema?

She said yes. *Just like that!* He said he would wait for her at the bus station, near the clock.

He hurried home after work, washed the clothes he was wearing, and then ironed them dry, rushing like a maniac, watching the steam rising off his trousers, fearful that the appliance would explode. With his clean clothes draped over chairs to air, he stood in the living room for some moments, gathering strength for the next task. Shouting obscenities and prayers as if he were once again at the Defence of Kut, fighting off the mad charges of the Imperial armies with his bare knuckles, he made a dash for the shower. He shouted down the disgust that he felt as his naked toes touched the slimy shower floor and scrubbed the smell of theatres from his body. When he had finished, he mopped the floor, sluicing the last obstinate bubbles on to the toilet area. The floor-boards were soft and spongy with rot, and swallowed the water gratefully. Karta called it Daud's *slum*. A fair description, Daud thought, as he watched woodlice crawling along the margins of the floor.

He felt clean and dressed up as he waited at the bus station, and felt that everybody who walked past him knew what he was standing there for. He thought of walking towards her flat, but he was afraid of missing her. He passed the time by practising his opening words. *You're beautiful*, he would say.

He had taken girls out before, and felt he ought to say something like that to them, something winning and flattering. Even when it was true, he had never been able to say it, had always fumbled and fudged and made a joke out of what he really wanted to say. These women had been foreigners like himself, most of them in England to learn English. They spoke to each other in a kind of minimal language, bending rules to suit their own grammars. It was easy to avoid having to say things to them. He had gone out with homesick German *au pairs* who had surprised him with their frankness, which he found little short of brutal. They told him openly that they just wanted to sleep with him, did not want any complications. There was a young Syrian midwife who clung to him in a way that was flattering at first but quickly became frightening. He had mistreated her shamefully to persuade her to leave him. He preferred not to remember how he had behaved with her. There had been an exceptionally kind and intelligent Swiss woman who was an assistant at the local grammar school, who tried to talk to him and communicate the beginning of the affection that was growing in her. He deflected her by pretending that her English was worse than it really was, and that he could not grasp the subtleties she intended. In due course they all went away and sometimes wrote him affectionate and adoring letters. The letters arose, he assumed, out of the desire to glamorise their sojourn in England with a fiction of the dark lover abandoned in the wastes of Albion.

Sometimes he wrote back, and invented without compunction. The Swiss assistant had brought out the best in him. For her he conjured picnics he had been invited to, boat rides on the river with two Polish students who were on a walking tour of the world, his arrest and incarceration by a bigoted, fascist and sadistic police. He even invented a family with whom he often went to eat, and who invited him to join them on High Days and Holy Days. This had gone down so well that she had returned the following summer with Suchard chocolates, two bottles of wine and a basketful of marshmallows for which he had a weakness. She stayed with him for two days, breaking her journey in the hope of meeting these wonderful people he had come to know. Unfortunately none of them was around. And they could not go to bed together because there was something wrong with him. *Wrong?* A meaningful glance at his astonished loins that had known nothing about this part of the plan. It had come to him all of a sudden that he did not want to sleep with this woman, could not be bothered with the labour of it, did not want to demean both of them with an act of spurious intimacy. So she had continued on her journey to New York or somewhere like that, baking him an enormous cake before she left. He never heard from her again, and never told her that she was beautiful, although he often felt he ought to.

When Catherine arrived, she was hurrying. She saw Daud, smiled and slowed down. She looked slimmer and more glamorous out of her uniform. Her hair was pulled away from her face but a few strands had escaped and grazed her temples like a halo in the setting sun. Her skirt swished round her calves as she hurried to him. 'You look beautiful,' he said, astonishing himself with his boldness.

She grinned and shook her head, surprised by his abruptness. 'Thank you,' she said. 'That's kind of you.'

This is easy, he thought. He had to be careful, of course, that he did not ruin a good thing by making it cloying. Or allow himself to seem too overwhelmed that she was actually out with him. 'You're a bit late,' he said.

'I'm sorry. Everybody was going out tonight so I just had to wait my turn for the bathroom. They're going to a big do in Dover at the Yacht Club ... a barbecue and dance, for the county cricket team.'

'The Yacht Club! Do you go there?'

'I've been there once,' she said. 'Just for a drink.' There had been the briefest of pauses and Daud waited for her to say more, but she glanced away, dropping the subject.

He was disappointed that she moved in those circles, was part of that jolly world besotted with fantasies of glamour and fun. The doctors at work talked about such moneyed pleasures, and described their friends who were farmers or racing drivers or journalists, reported their witticisms and their drinking habits. Some of the nurses were allowed into this world too, and after paying the price of admission, became victims of their own fantasy of capturing a rich farmer or a deeply tanned airline pilot for a husband. But if she was part of that, he admonished himself, what was she doing with him? He acknowledged his own feelings of inadequacy, for if she knew that kind of excitement then she would find him dull.

'You look very tired,' she said.

'It's been a hard day,' he said. 'I spent the whole day patrolling the back corridor, washing instruments and putting dirty towels in linen bags.'

She was a little ahead of him, and she glanced over her shoulder. The sun was in her eyes and she squinted a little. When he said no more, she stepped off the pavement to have a good look at him, walking beside him. She looked him up and down once, and then she smiled.

'How do you think I look?' he asked, assuming that she was laughing at his clothes. He turned round slowly with his arms stretched out by his side, but he was too self-conscious to do a Karta twirl. 'I took out my shark-skin, my leopard-skin, my sequins, my leathers, but I just could not make up my mind. So in the end I wore these rags.'

'You look all right,' she said, smiling. She came back up on the pavement and took his arm.

They stopped under St George's Tower while he showed her the inscription that said that Alderman Spencer had laid the foundation stone for that edifice. Behind this, under the arches of the tower, was another inscription, very much smaller, which said that Kit Marlowe's family home had stood thereabouts.

'At least for the tourists' sake they should have made that Marlowe one bigger,' Catherine said, tightening her hold on him. 'And given a little more information about him.'

'They should've emblazoned it across the clock face, with a slot machine at the bottom. *For only 50p you can hear the first 100 lines of* Tamburlaine,' he declaimed, conscious of the slightest alteration of the pressure of her arm. '*Read by David Gower, local boy made good*. But the burghers are more honest than that. Kit Marlowe was a scandal who shamed his parents with his whoring and his boozing, and founded nothing but a couple of plays. You can get that kind of information from the tourist centre. Here they are concerned to celebrate their own more solid achievements.'

'What a philistine,' she said, dragging him away from the tower.

'You're a fine one to talk! An *habitué* of the Yacht Club.'

She coloured a little behind her smile and he could not restrain a pang of envy. *Who is it? Who is the bourgeois shrimp who's been chatting up ma chick?* It was still very early in the evening, and very quiet even though it was Friday. He suggested they went for a drink first, but she said she was too hungry. They stopped in front of the theatre while they debated where they should go. He entertained her in the meantime by inventing histories for the actors whose photographs they were standing in front of. She moved away from him in the end, saying she could not think with all that chatter and clatter going on in her ear. She came back, demanding a Chinese meal. As they walked away from the theatre, she took his arm again, holding tightly to it and leaning on him.

'What exactly are you doing in that place?' she asked, softening her voice to show her sympathy. 'A clever man like you?'

Her arm seemed a great burden to him. By small, irritable movements he conveyed this to her and she withdrew it, looking at him with surprise. He folded the arm across his chest as if to keep it out of reach, as if to control himself from using it otherwise. 'Perhaps you'd like to suggest that I become a nurse,' he said, glaring at her.

'I'm sorry,' she said, laughing out of embarrassment. 'I don't understand. What do you mean, a nurse? What have I said wrong?'

He ignored her, caught now in the dynamic of his hurt. That was what people who decided to treat him kindly said: *Why don't you try for a nursing course? I'm sure they'll accept you.* He resented that he was vulnerable to them, that he did not have a mother and father at the end of a telephone to tell him to hang on, to learn to labour and to wait. He detested the meaningless pity of people who knew nothing about him but could still hector him. *Make something of yourself. You are not doing yourself justice. We all know that you are capable of a great deal more than this.* He was doing his best to keep his head above water, keep despair at bay by mocking the afflicted, spurn the culture clash with surprise forays into forbidden territories. Why could he not be left alone to the quiet contemplation of his failures? Why could he not be left to wallow in self-pity?

'What is it? What have I said?' she asked, challenging him to explain himself. She stared angrily at him, stopping on the pavement and turning to face him. 'I actually meant to be flattering, not critical. What annoyed you?' She saw the look of anger in his face turn to pain. He shook his head and sighed, and gave her a shame-faced smile. She resisted a temptation to reach out and touch him and comfort him. *There there.*

'I'm sorry, I get hysterical about some things,' he said, surprised by the challenge and wanting now to win her back to his side.

'But I still don't understand,' she said. 'Why did you get so angry?'

'I suppose your words imply a criticism ... even if you don't mean to be critical. That I'm resigned to that dirty place. Not doing anything for myself. That I'm here simply because I haven't had the good sense to do something better with myself.'

'I didn't mean that,' she protested. 'I didn't mean anything like that. I was just prying, trying to find out how you felt about it. If you had ambitions ... Or how you found yourself where you are.'

He made himself keep silent, feeling that he had come near enough to embarrassing disclosures, had come close to chasing her away with his sensitivities. 'Please forgive my peculiar behaviour,' he said, bowing slightly with a pretence of cavalier charm.

She made a solemn face, then laid her hand on his arm the way she imagined a strong, sophisticated woman of the world might a few minutes before dinner.

8

The waiter hovered over the spare ribs and asked if *it* was all right. Catherine looked up from her eager munching and smiled brightly at the boyish-looking man. 'It's delicious,' she told the waiter. She invited Daud to contribute and he added several nods and an appreciative mmmhm. The waiter straightened with an eager smile. Smile is good for business, but it was, anyway, no less than he had expected to hear.

'Isn't he sweet?' she said after he had gone. 'The way he comes and says *All right?*'

'Don't patronise him,' he said. 'If he didn't want your money so much he'd probably chuck a handful of rat poison in your food.'

'Charming. Am I patronising him?'

'All that *sweet* business … because he is a small man or gives you that bizarre smile.'

'Are you like this all the time?' she asked. 'Anyway, stop being so unpleasant and tell me about your true ambitions.'

'To leave that place,' he said, leaning back from his gnawed bones.

'Is that all? And go where?'

'To the university … this autumn perhaps,' he said.

'Really? That's good.' She paused in her chewing and dropped the bone on her plate. 'Tell me more.'

'Can I tell you about the cricket score first? At Old Trafford this morning England were all out for 71 …'

'No,' she said sharply. 'I hate cricket. Tell me about going to the university.'

She sighed after a moment and then smiled an apology. *It's the Yacht Club again*, he thought. He told her about the evening classes and the examinations he had recently taken. If the results turned out to be reasonable, he would start at the beginning of the new term. He had kept quiet about it in case things went wrong. Oh, she was pleased! Evening classes! She had tried to attend evening classes while she was living in London, and she just could not do it. Mind you, it was a secretarial course, deadly dull. What was he going to study? History! *And* literature! He laughed with the pleasure of explaining how he had arrived at the choices, while she became absorbed in the pleasure of living somebody else's life. He paused while the waiter brought them the rest of their meal.

'Beanshoots in everything,' she said.

'The authentic traditional Chinese flavour. And this padded cell that we sit in, with the muted lights and the hideous canopy of silver-spangled stars, is probably a mythological representation of the contempt they hold us in. We're probably sitting in the middle of a painting called "Cultural Chaos" by Lin Ah.'

'You're too sensitive,' she said. 'Smile at the sweet little man. Can't you see he's beaming at you? Anyway, so you're going to get away from that horrible job. But what about money? Will you get a grant? You have! It sounds as if it's all worked out. I envy you, I think. Oh … what about sending money home … to your parents? How will you manage that on a grant?'

He remembered that on that night they were on duty together she had asked him why he had left the college where he was a student and he had lied. He lied to everybody about that. Usually he said that he had to go out to work, earn some money, because his father had been taken ill with meningitis or something like that, and his family needed him to send money back to support them. Very few people ever asked any further questions, and if they did, he volunteered hints that there were other unnameable diseases in the family. This was usually enough to force the hardiest into retreat, in case they got embroiled in an endless family saga.

'What will you do about that?' she asked, carelessly pressing him into a corner.

He shovelled a forkful of beanshoots into his mouth, undecided about how much to concede. He tried to resist the temptation to unburden himself. He told himself, as he always did, that he would feel no relief but only shame and remorse. She was waiting for more, holding her fork in the air as if she knew she would soon tire of the waiting and would have to prod him into speech.

'I don't know yet,' he mumbled.

'But you used to send money to them, didn't you? That was why you stopped being a student before, wasn't it?'

It was a lonely winter. The days were grey and dark … never seen such days. The damp, the chill in the evenings, and nowhere near home. The long evenings muffled to the noise of human laughter. The nights were frightening as men and women grew in size, adding inches in girth and adopting lowering looks at chance encounters. The cold froze the sweat in the anus, running out of fear and anxiety. The wind blasted the cracks open. Gloomy, long winter evenings of painful regret. Gloomy, long winter evenings when the thoughts of friends and home were like torture.

'No,' he said lightly, all at once indifferent to what she might think. 'I never sent money anywhere. I lied to you.'

She looked sad, and he wondered if she had guessed all along.

'Does that break some code of honour?' he asked, watching her with a look of fierce, angry attention.

'I guess so,' she said, watching him back with wary surprise but with the beginnings of anxiety in her eyes. His look of fury confused her, and she was afraid that she had missed something, had misunderstood. 'I think I tell too many lies too,' she said, feeling foolish but trying to think of something encouraging to say.

'I'm sorry.' He was too absorbed in himself to notice the help she was trying to offer. *What was he saying sorry to her for? Why was he apologising to her?* 'I wounded them so much … beyond remedy. I disappointed them so completely. And I could not bring myself to be abjectly contrite and penitent enough in my letters to console them.'

'Your parents?' she asked.

Something abject would have appeased them, he thought. Or at least would have allowed them to feel that there was something he still needed from them. Instead he could feel only the injustice of their rejection of him, and could respond only with hurt silence. They took his silence to mean that he did not care, that he was not worried about their approval any more. Now so much had happened that he had no idea where he would begin to explain to them the sheer misery of all the things that had happened.

When she spoke again, repeating her question, he raised his eyes to her and she saw that they were liquid with a pain he was trying to subdue. He looked away quickly, not from embarrassment, but as if he would leave. 'Tell me,' she said, feeling she should touch him, stop him from going. 'I'd like to know.'

She was nothing to him. He thought that with a mental swagger. She would understand nothing of this. Why did she ask about things she could not possibly understand? Forcing him to talk about events he would rather forget. He did not even talk to others like himself about this … others who had also come to conquer the world and ended up as car park attendants and accounts clerks. But still she waited, expectant and serious, waiting for him to bare his soul. She wanted to help him, he could see that. Save him from himself. She wanted him to prove to her that he was not just wallowing, that he had cause and reason to wander around the countryside looking tragic and interesting.

'My father didn't need my money,' he said. 'I stopped being a student because I failed all my exams.'

Yes, he thought, *all* my exams. The shame was not in the failure of intelligence, because he knew it was not that, but that those two years had shaken the sense of himself as hardy and resourceful. He had ended up a shambles of bitterness and despair, weeping with loneliness in his grubby, boarding-house room, his books and notes open before him, demanding to be studied. But his mind could not study anything, overwhelmed as it was by a relentless internal sobbing. 'Why?' she asked, frowning and direct. 'Why did you fail?'

'What?' he said. His voice sounded distant and thick, disturbed by an idle question in the midst of tricky ruminations. It was intended to discourage conversation, to imply that he had not really heard the question, and did not really want it repeated.

'Why did you fail?' she asked, direct and insistent, but now soft-spoken and kind. He sat more upright in the chair, the palms of both hands pressed downwards on the table. She said nothing while she waited for him to speak, wishing she could, and thinking only that this was not what she had expected.

Holton, the head of department, had gleefully sent a copy of his report home. Daud had deliberately given the wrong postal address in his enrolment papers, not because he feared that reports might be sent to his father – he had not expected to fail then – but out of a duplicity that had become part of their lives. It was a habit of fear that the years after the revolution had taught them all. But he could not, it had never occurred to him to, give the wrong name for his father. He had picked a post box number at random, anything. It had never occurred to him that whoever the letter reached would simply put his jacket on and take it round to his father's house. Why should he not give the wrong address? There was nothing to hide, but it would give the postal censors a conundrum and a small headache.

At the end of his second year, when it was clear the way things would turn out, the head of department asked Daud where he should send the report. Should he send it to Daud's home address, all those thousands of miles away, where it would arrive like a lethal curse that would sweep the memory of Daud from proud parents and show that the assurances of well-being that he had plied them with were nothing but lies? Or should he send it to Daud's boarding-house address, where he could shred it and throw it in the bin and write instead some more lies to his parents? Daud told him to send it to his parents, daring him to indulge his petty, official revenge. The head of department took him at his word and sent the report to his father. He wrote to Daud too, enclosing a copy of a report that detailed his various failures with complacent satisfaction.

Daud had hoped that the report would not arrive, would get chewed up by the revolutionary censors or would sit and rot in a mail-bag at the airport. It took his father more than three months to write, and then only a dozen terse lines, congratulating him and wishing him all the luck for the future. *Your mother has not mentioned your name. She has sworn not to until God has shown mercy and shown you the way out of your waywardness*. Could they not bring themselves to say one word of kindness? Could they not have enquired if he was in some kind of trouble, if he had enough to live on? Could they not have said to him: *This is bad luck, but don't be too disappointed. Keep trying*. Did they have to make him feel as if he had strangled their first-born? What wayward ways? He had missed them so much. Them and Bossy, and his people and his land. He had driven himself to the very edges of despair … cold and hungry and filled with hate.

'By the end I had no money left anyway,' he said, grinning at her, 'so it wouldn't have made any difference. I hadn't paid any rent for months. I was lucky … the landlord had had lots of overseas students at one time or another. It was a boarding-house, you see, for students. I used to tell him that I was expecting a draft from my father and he would say: *Of course! Pay me when you have the money*. He was into racial harmony and all that. He's still my landlord and I still owe him money.'

'Is that what happened?' she asked, her face flat and unresponsive, as if she suspected him of trying to escape a necessary but unpleasant fate. He smiled as he watched her put her fork down and cross her forearms on the table. *Now this is for your own good, my lad. Just spill it out and you'll feel much better afterwards*. 'But that's not why you failed,' she said.

'My stomach was always rumbling with hunger. I used to feel puny next to these hale and beefy young Englishmen who were always shouting or getting excited about the smallest things. They were always eating: sweets, crisps, chocolate bars. Sometimes I used to stay away from class because my stomach made too much noise.'

'What!' she cried, incredulity in her dilated eyes.

'I felt so silly.'

'But that's stupid!'

'They laughed at me when my stomach rumbled, so I stayed away. They were always laughing at me. It sounds ... pathetic, doesn't it? You hear stories of these great people who battled against hunger and cold to complete a brilliant piece of learning. Now I always wonder: Didn't their stomachs rumble?'

'You're joking!' she said, but she could see from the patient way that he waited to continue that he was not.

'I used to stand outside the college canteen during the lunch period, hoping that somebody I knew would walk by and ask me what I was doing there. Hoping that one of them would say *Come in, I'll pay for you*, or *You can have a share of mine*. And they did, they used to. It couldn't go on of course. I used to see this hunted look my class-mates would give me at lunch-time. They were stupid shits on the whole, always making jokes about coons and wogs and smelly niggers. Really to be despised by them was more than I deserved. I went for long walks in the town. Sometimes I stole something from a shop, chocolate or a bag of sweets. I wrote to my father asking him for money. I knew he'd given me all that he had when I first came, but what was I supposed to do? He wrote back saying there was no more ... unless I wanted to go back and drink his blood.'

'Why didn't you get help?' she asked, her voice squealing with irritation and annoyance. *Nobody could be that gormless. God, aren't you savouring this a bit? Perhaps seasoning it as well*, he could hear her say.

'I didn't know where to get help. I tried to speak to my tutor at the college. I went to see him ... but as soon as he thought he had the drift of what I was saying he stopped me and told me to go and see somebody at the British Council or the Students' Union. I went to the doctor,' he said, clowning as he said this, as if he had found something at last that would make her pleased with him. She nodded, meaning to show her approval, joining in the joke.

'What happened?' she asked, smiling.

'He told me to go home and eat more, and drink more milk,' he said dejectedly.

'All right, all right.' She was suddenly unable to contain her impatience, not wanting him to continue. 'There's nothing you can do about it now. Why are you telling me?'

He poured himself another glass of wine and then held the bottle inclined a little towards her. She nodded and he filled up her glass. She said *Thank you* quietly. He should have known better, he told himself. Should've kept his mouth shut.

'So you think these are just excuses?' he asked, pushing his plate away and picking up the glass of wine. He was tired of beanshoots anyway, he told himself.

'No,' she said. 'I don't know.'

'Or you think perhaps I'm enjoying myself too much and you don't want to encourage me,' he said. From the way she dropped her eyes he guessed that he was not far off the mark. She looked up again quickly and shrugged.

'It's just unexpected,' she said. 'It wasn't what I thought ... I don't know what to say. Why didn't you go to Social Security?'

‘I didn’t know about it,’ he said, smiling. ‘I really was pathetic, wasn’t I?’

‘No, you just make me feel guilty I think, like you expected me to apologise, take the blame. Anyway, I’m surprised you didn’t know about Social Security. I thought that was what you foreigners came to Britain for.’

‘It was easier to tell the lies, wasn’t it? Terrible tragedy! My father … such a charming man, a philosopher and a gentleman … forced to retire, I’m sorry to say. In the prime of his intellectual powers … a bad attack of elephantiasis of the testicles. It’s a common disease out there in the trops. Also, he isn’t quite himself, you know, in the head. There’s a history of … er … his sister had to be hospitalised. To add to all this, he never really recovered from an attack of typhoid when he was a baby. So I had to give up my studies and go to work. Who would object to that? Nobody bothered to ask how you could send money home on the wages of a theatre orderly. These people, they need much less than us. Look at the way they live sixteen to a room and survive on rice and peas. They’ve all got stacks hidden under their beds. Wasn’t it easier to tell the lies?’

‘No,’ she said. ‘I don’t know what hurt it’s been causing you but it would’ve been better to talk about it to somebody. Then you’d have seen that there was nothing to be ashamed of.’

‘Aah, thank you,’ he said. ‘I wish I’d known. I can just see myself, unburdening to some anonymous victim cornered at a party, who’d have gone home amazed at her own virtue for having spent the whole evening listening to a lonely young man’s confession.’

The waiter walked slowly past, attracted to their table by the noise of their raised voices in the silent restaurant. He saw that they were still hesitating over authentic traditional Chinese flavour and could not blame them. It was disgusting muck and he himself would not eat it if the manager paid him to. Smile good for business, so he scraped past them with a happy grin. The more he saw people enjoying authentic Chinese flavour, the happier he became. It was almost cruel to make money this way. It was like robbing a child. *The girl was pretty, but the man … ugh! How can she touch …* He smiled to himself as he wandered round the empty restaurant.

'You could say something encouraging,' he suggested. 'Instead of all this hostility.'

'Like what?' she asked, pretending to be chastened and eager to please.

'You could say: "You didn't give up, though, did you? It shows a lot of strength to do things that way."'

She did as he asked, and they smiled and drank their wine quietly under the canopy of silver stars. The waiter walked past again and this time hesitated, but Daud immediately picked up his fork and started eating, not wanting him to come yet and bustle around them. She laughingly joined in. The waiter smiled too. Smile good for business.

'Can I tell you about the Test Match score now?' he asked. 'England were all out for 71 in their first innings. 71! You'll never guess who did all the damage!'

'I don't want to hear about the Test Match, please,' she pleaded through gritted teeth.

'That's a very selfish thing to say, so for your own good I'll ignore it. There they were, poor old England, with the chance of behaving honourably for a change. They were given a reasonable start by Mike Selvey who took four whole wickets on his own. Ha ha ha, grovel grovel grovel, Tony Greig was saying. Then Michael Holding started on that long run-up of his that the commentators love to make fun of. Crack! Smash! Ooops! 71 all out.'

'Thank you,' she said. 'Now can you stop?'

He looked at her for a long moment, then sucked his teeth with powerful disdain. 'Explain this incredible prejudice that you have against the great game. On second thoughts, don't bother. Tell me something interesting instead. How long do you have to wait before you are awarded your cap, earn your wings, finish your training or whatever you call it?'

'No,' she said, glaring at him.

'All right then, tell me about your brothers or sisters, or maiden aunts or your local vicar. Or how you lost your virginity,' he persisted, thinking this was the wrong way to go about winning hearts and minds in the jungles of Kent. It was the thought of the Yacht Club *beau* that was irritating him. No doubt he was always going on about cricket, without really appreciating the finer points of the game the way Daud did. And because of some pampered, plump Englishman, he was not to be allowed to gloat and crow over England's disastrous display.

When the bill came, his consternation was real. The waiter smiled and smiled while Daud peeled off note after note from his small wad, wondering if anything would be left after he had finished, or if he would have to put up with Karta's nagging about the job. He did not want to explain to Karta that another job like the one he was doing would be no improvement. If that was how things were, then he might as well stay where he was. He suspected there was something illogical in his explanation and so was reticent with it. She watched him pay the bill and pursed her lips with incredulity.

'Those were very expensive beanshoots,' she said.

'There's no problem,' he said, adding another note as a tip. Catherine gave it her serious consideration and then wrenched her eyes away. Daud took the note back with a smile.

They walked around the quiet streets afterwards. She asked him again about his first years in England, made him talk about the events he had described at dinner. He was not so tense now, and told her different stories of the clever things he had got up to, or how awkward he had felt in his home-cut clothes, how difficult it had been to understand what people were saying to him. They caught glimpses of the cathedral in their wanderings, its formal, lit-up splendour crossing the lowering, medieval alleys down which they strolled. He tried to persuade her into the County Hotel for a drink. The barman there was a Venezuelan he knew, a man called Ricardo who claimed that his father was the Chief Justice of Venezuela and directly descended from Francisco Pizarro, the butcher of the Incas. Ricardo was patently a self-invention, another stranger passing himself off as an exotic-in-exile, and more grist to the Englishman's self-esteem. He wanted to take Catherine in there to show off to her. *I know some very weird people*. But she refused, with an instinct that he had not yet grasped. She was put off by the hotel's appearance of burgher stuffiness, the kind of place where the Rotary Club would hold its dinners, she said.

They met other couples strolling in the long summer evening. He took her down a dark street which suddenly opened out into a small clearing. They were on the edges of Westgate Park. The houses were run-down here, and some of them looked dark and empty. There were skips full of rubbish on the road. The area made him feel vaguely anxious, and he laughed off his nervousness by making fun of the names people had given their houses. They went down another dark street. He heard her sigh wearily.

'Are you all right?' he asked, although he guessed that what she was trying to tell him was that she was getting bored. They walked down a gloomy, leafy lane which smelt of mould and damp, and passed a dark, shadowy lump in the evening murk. 'That's the oldest church in the city,' he told her. She agreed very readily when he suggested that they go for a drink. She would even have agreed to the County Hotel and Ricardo to escape the gloomy streets.

He took her to the Black Dog. He explained to her that this was a kind of pilgrimage. 'When I first came,' he said, 'the biggest surprise was the constant mockery ... Racial taunting seemed so much part of English life that I began to take names like the Black Dog as an intended insult. Even now, when I go into a place called the Black Dog or something like that, I have to nerve myself to it.'

'Let's go somewhere else,' she said.

'No. I've been in there before. I was just explaining. Because we were talking about those days ...' The pub was surprisingly plush and quiet, an atmosphere that seemed to mock his pretensions. He felt he did not have a right to be there. They stayed until closing time. Could they meet again tomorrow, he asked, walking her slowly home? She was working the next day but she was free on Sunday. That suited him better, although he did not say so. It would give him time to wash the sheets on the bed.

When they reached her flat, he stood awkwardly in front of her for a moment and then leant forward to kiss her lightly on the lips. He kissed her again, but made no further effort to detain her. On his way home he thought of all those years. He had kept that to himself for too long, and he was glad that he had spoken to her about some of it. It felt like he imagined confession would feel. He wished he could treat it all casually, but he knew he would never be able to do that. It was nothing very much really. He had been too young and feeble to grit his teeth and keep his head down. He had allowed himself to be overcome, had spent his evenings huddled over a tiny gas fire, wondering for how long he could keep going.

He reached home with a sense of relief. He had given the racist monkeys the slip for another night. He did not linger. In his bedroom he began a letter to his father which he knew he would never finish, or if he did, would never send. What could he say to him? And he had to go to work the next day.

9

Lloyd arrived with his bag of shopping late on Saturday afternoon. Daud was watching the final session of play in the Third Test. He had gloated over every run and grinned at Tony Greig whenever his baffled face appeared on the screen. *Grovel, you Boer!* Lloyd's arrival was unwelcome on several counts. Clive Lloyd had just declared the West Indies' second innings closed at 411, a lead of 551. Daud wanted to give his whole attention to the impending destruction of the flower of England, and not have it distracted by one of its idiot sons. Also, Lloyd's presence meant that he could no longer make faces at the screen and give free vent to his derision of the England Captain. He did not want to look childish and vindictive. He did not want a heathen to lecture him on fair play and how to be a good sport.

'They're useless, aren't they?' Lloyd said, putting his shopping bag down and inviting himself to a chair. The bag meant that he would be staying for the evening. 'They're getting thrashed.'

'Don't write them off yet,' Daud said, reluctant to have the matter dismissed in this blasé style and wanting the agony prolonged, and properly analysed and relished. Couldn't Lloyd at least show some patriotism? Stand up for his brothers? And allow Daud the pleasure of telling him what a bad leader Tony Greig was?

Daud wondered what the bag contained. He was ashamed of himself and vowed to resent afterwards the bucketful of trinkets, or the plump joint of something juicy, with which Lloyd was buying him. It was no more than tokenism, condescension and bad conscience, and Daud would be as humiliated and angry as decency required later on. For the time being it was necessary to be thick-skinned. His romantic excesses with the beanshoots had left him with the prospect of bangers and mash for the rest of the week. And although the butcher round the corner prepared fine sausages, it was not a prospect Daud relished. Sausages gave him indigestion. It was such things that convinced him that he was not intended to live rough, or to turn ascetic. Spinach gave him diarrhoea, cheese blocked him up for sure. Yoghurt made him nauseous. Breakfast cereals made his stomach bleed and biscuits made him sneeze. This was not the result of a congenitally weak gut, but the insistence of a stubborn one. It thrived best on subtly spiced curries and rich casseroles served with mounds of rice. Or fat, bulging meat pies, on their own or with a bit of salad. Or fried red mullet, prepared to a recipe that was a family secret, and served with flat bread and green chillies.

Daud cheered, unable to control his joy as he watched Holding running in to bowl to Brian Close. Out of the corner of his eye, he saw Lloyd watching him with a smile. When he glanced at him, Lloyd bent down to unload the shopping and lay it out on the table. He did this one item at a time, putting it down and then glancing at Daud with a smile, waiting for him to look and respond. He was like a child, asking and inviting approbation for some good deed. *Good boy, now just leave the stuff there and piss off.* Daud saw a chicken and some cans of beer, along with a pile of vegetables and fruit.

He hated his vulnerability to such largesse. He had tried to persuade himself to laugh at Lloyd, to see him as egotistical and ignorant. He took these offerings to be Lloyd's way of pre-empting rejection. *Look what I've brought you. Does it please you?* A gift as well as a means of pacifying his own fears about scrounging off other people. He did not want to believe that Lloyd could be bringing the food out of the selfless kindness between friends. He could not believe that Lloyd was naive enough to think him that kind of a friend. *Live off the Englishman, my bro*, Karta advised him. *They stole all this money from us anyway. Suck his blood! Make him pay for his wicked history*.

'I thought I could persuade you to turn out one of those interesting chicken casseroles of yours,' Lloyd said, cringing with exaggerated anxiety. 'I hope you don't mind. It's a bit of a liberty, I know. But you make them so magnificently ...'

'It's a diabolical liberty,' Daud said, unable to resist such an opening.

Lloyd grinned with relief, assuming that Daud did not really mind. 'It's sheer desperation,' Lloyd said, laughing now. 'It makes me reckless. And you'd understand why if you took up the invitation I'm always extending to you. Come and try one of my mother's dinners. Dad is really keen to meet you as well. He says you must be the only intellectual left in England.' Daud understood, from the way that Lloyd chuckled as he said this, that the *intellectual* was not to be taken as either true or as a compliment. What it was meant to say, he assumed, was that he must be one of these Babus. A *monkey see monkey do* type of swot, affected and clownish like a Benson-Hylen strutting his Englishness across the world stage.

'Well played,' Lloyd applauded ironically as Edrich ducked under another bouncer.

He came round two, maybe three, evenings a week and Daud was tired of it. Daud sometimes heard him walking up and down on the pavement outside the house at night. He knew it was Lloyd because the first time it had happened it had terrified him. He assumed it was a racist freak that he had dodged at one time or another who had recognised him and followed him home, and had now come to post a Molotov cocktail or a carrier bag full of shit through his letter box. He had peeped out carefully from an upstairs window, debating the range of weapons available to him, only to discover Lloyd strutting up and down on the pavement outside his front door. He had ignored him then, and ignored his other late night visits. Lloyd never knocked on these occasions, waiting to be discovered there. *Fancy seeing you here! Come in, have a nip of brandy before you continue on your inspired stroll round the deserted streets of the town. Tell me, since you're stopping for a few minutes, what are you working on? An ode or a canto this time? Or is it an entirely new form that you have invented?* He sometimes brought a bundle of papers that he left casually on the table, as he would a pound of apples or a bottle of milk, saying nothing until Daud asked him. It would turn out that they were poems or a story. There was nothing else to be done then but to ask if he could read them. Lloyd protested that he carried them around because they comforted him. He did not intend to impose ...

Once he left three pages of a story on the table, and Daud left them alone. He did not ask anything about them and casually moved them aside when the food was ready. Lloyd *forgot* the papers when he left, and Daud heard him tramping the pavement the following night. When he turned up on the third evening, his eyes went directly to the table and to his pages, spotted with splashes of grease now and filmed with a fine dust. That was at a time when Daud was trying to chase Lloyd away with cruelty. He failed in the end, unable to sustain the necessary callousness.

Lloyd liked to read the poems aloud, speaking them gently and never looking up while he read. He had seen Pablo Neruda do that on television and had admired his dignity and modesty. Lloyd's attempt at the pose was a much cruder affair, the cringing poet making an offering of his labours and his craft while all the time suspecting that he was much better than his listeners were likely to give him credit for. Daud found the poems dull and rarely said anything to Lloyd's requests for a comment. That was not the end of his misery, though, for Lloyd would launch himself on an interminable monologue about the shifts of style and imagery, the pun here and the primordial there, archetypals jostling with mnemonics enough to do justice to his education at the renowned public school in the town.

Daud watched as Brian Close and John Edrich played the West Indian fast bowlers. It was as if they were the last two Englishmen on the walls of Khartoum or the beaches of Dunkirk, refusing even to duck or evade the ball. They were demonstrating their moral superiority over their torturers. *Britons nevernevernever shall be slaves*. Holding, Roberts and Daniel, the West Indian bowlers, seemed incensed by this display and bowled even fiercer bouncers. They were determined to make the England batsmen *grovel*, to make them eat the words of their Captain. The harder they tried, the prouder stood the England batsmen, and the more triumphant became the voices of the commentators. Daud was sorry to see the boys goaded into a frenzy in this way. Even Lloyd was sitting with his mouth open, and Daud could sense him stirring with patriotic passion. *Oh, I say, look at these brutes running amok. Surely! Surely!*

He went into the kitchen to clear the decks for the meal, and to escape the outburst that he could see Lloyd puffing himself up for. The kitchen was a narrow ante-room to his rotting shower, cold and damp in all weather but becoming uninhabitable once the cooking was under way. A back door led into a garden which was littered with broken paving-stones. He kept the door open when it was warm, to *air* the cubicle and rid it of the smell of damp bricks.

'This is savagery!' Lloyd called out from the other room. 'It's nothing to do with sport now. Those bowlers are looking to kill. Christ, this Daniel looks mad. If I was one of those batsmen I'd walk down the track and wrap my bat round his neck.' Daud exchanged a chortling grin with a saucepan. He felt sure that Daniel would have no difficulty in dealing with such a challenge. BRING ME HE BLOOD!

'You'd burst into tears before you even got to the wicket,' Daud went into the living room to tell him. 'You don't even know what those two men are facing out there … but I'll tell you. They're suffering for the sins of a cruel leader, who could not resist blustering when the West Indian boys were being humiliated by those demented Aussies. Now he's waiting up there in the dressing room while the brave infantry are getting slaughtered. This match is over now. All that's left is to humiliate England, and that's what those two old men out there are resisting. Even in defeat they want to conduct themselves with honour. It's that big-mouth that those bowlers want. You wait, they'll make him suffer before this series is over.' As he spoke Daud saw Close turn his back on a ball that thudded into his shoulder with the crump of distant, heavy artillery. The camera zoomed on his face, which showed hardly a wince. The old pro's loving it, he thought. He knows he's won this one. He's made them look foolish. Even if they get him out now, he's looked them in the eye and said *You've done your worst and I'm still here. You ran amok, lost your rag and ranted and raved all over the park but I'm still here, bruised but still grinning at you.*

Karta arrived during the last few minutes of play and made a face when he saw that the cricket was still on. He clasped Daud's hand and pulled him forward into a half-embrace, but he did not even glance at Lloyd. He was wearing skin-tight red trousers and a grey shirt, carrying a zipper jacket in one hand. He put the other hand on his hip and took up a pose. Daud looked him up and down, as he was supposed to. 'Up to your usual standard,' he said as Karta turned this way and that to demonstrate his new clothes.

Karta laughed and reached past Lloyd without saying a word to him. He helped himself to a beer while Lloyd looked indignant. It was a moment or two before Karta realised what was happening at the cricket. 'Knock that old honky's block off,' he encouraged the glowering Roberts.

Lloyd was worried about the rate at which Karta was consuming the beer, and he glanced at Daud, looking for support. He picked up the cans to take them to the kitchen. Karta watched his retreating back with loathing. 'Kill the white man!' he shouted, and grinned as Lloyd's back winced. 'What's on the menu, bro? You know, it's one of the highlights of Saturday evening, coming round here for a meal. It's one of the few things I'll remember from this place.'

'Coming round here on the scrounge?' asked Daud. 'I don't think I'll forget it either.'

'African hospitality!' Karta admonished him. 'Where's your African brotherhood? Don't show yourself up in front of foreigners. Anyway, I know this came in the form of development aid from the Englishman.'

Play stopped with England on 21 without loss. Edrich and Close survived eighty minutes of scary cricket, and long before the commentators had finished the summing up of the day's play, Lloyd stood up to switch to another channel. Daud collected the meat and vegetables and went to the kitchen to start the meal. Karta followed him to get the last can of beer. As he pulled the ring off Lloyd suddenly stood up.

'Going somewhere?' Karta asked innocently, the first words he had addressed to him.

Lloyd made a face and seemed on the point of following this with an obscene gesture but his nerve failed him. 'I'm going to get some more beer,' he said, spitting the words angrily to hide the apprehension of the moment. 'You've had three of the four cans I bought, and you're not touching the next batch.'

Karta waited until the front door had slammed shut. 'I'm going to teach that man some manners,' he said. 'Why do you let him come? He's such a stupid, ignorant … turd! And he gets on my nerves. I don't know how you can stand him hanging around you.' His teeth were gritted with anger, and on his face was a grimace of revulsion. His body shivered with disgust. The first time Daud had seen Karta do that, he had smiled at the melodrama. He soon found out that Karta was not faking, and he was silenced by the intensity of his loathing. Karta clucked angrily, irritated with himself. He looked over his shoulder to catch Daud's eye. 'He's exploiting you, can't you see that?' he said, smilingly inviting Daud into the joke.

Daud moved away from the kitchen door and returned to the cooking. He heard Karta shout from the other room but made no effort to understand. A moment later he heard a sudden burst of applause and laughter as Karta switched to a comedy programme. He heard Karta's shout above the noises of mad glee. 'Something smells good, countryman.'

The neighbours had complained before about the noise. The walls separating the houses were paper-thin and hollow. Sometimes at night he heard what he thought were individual grains of crumbling plaster falling down in the gap. He heard mice walking up and down the walls and between the floor-boards, sometimes stopping to hold a squeaky conversation. When they came into the house, he chased them wildly between the decrepit sticks of furniture. He chased them more for the pleasure of the hunt than because they were unbearable. He had grown up in a house infested with mice and had long lost any fear of them. For some reason, they never appeared upstairs, but only in the living room or the kitchen. The mice he had known as a child were of a hardier and more adventurous stock. They had no difficulties getting about and climbed up and down stairs without any apparent fear.

The kitchen walls were beginning to stream with condensation. The aromas of cooking were comfortably held in abeyance by the smells of damp bricks and mouldy wood. Every dark corner harboured woodlice and earwigs. The open shelves were rough and splintered, and had shown no gratitude for the coat of paint he had put on them. His antique oven was rancid with grime. He never used the tall wall cupboard because an uncontrollable mould grew in there. He frightened himself that the mould would one day break out of the cupboard and take over the whole house while he was sleeping. What would Catherine make of him when she saw all this filth? Perhaps she would be so distracted with passion that she would not notice. Or perhaps, he guessed with a sinking sense that this one had the ring of truth, she would walk into his hovel, take a couple of sniffs and make her excuses. Phew!

On one side of him in the terrace lived an old couple. They never spoke to him. If they saw him coming, or caught sight of him in his rock-strewn garden, they went inside the house and shut the door. They seemed frightened of him. He guessed that they were deaf from the way that they shouted at each other, and the volume at which they watched television. He rarely heard the woman's voice, but the man sometimes became very angry.

On the other side lived a young couple. They had been interested in him when they first moved in. He was a student of architecture and she was an assistant in an art gallery in the town. They had invited him to their house, and he had looked with envy at all the clever things they had done with the small space. They had ripped a wall out here, and put in a new window there. Pictures and objects littered the rooms, and plants flourished under the kitchen window. They showed him photographs of their travels and overwhelmed him with their sophistication and wealth. One Sunday they took him out to a country pub in their blue sports car. Daud sat in the passenger seat while Susan perched behind them, her arm on his shoulder and her plump breasts leaning against him.

Within three weeks of meeting, he was spending several evenings a week with them. Susan came for him as soon as he arrived back from work. Tony told him about wines, and also explained the new plans the council had for pedestrianising the town centre. Some evenings they played records, and once Susan danced with him, clinging to him without shame in front of Tony. She insisted on reading his palm, rubbing it first with gentle pressure and then holding it in both hands while she pored over its mysteries. She told him he would realise his dreams in nine years. Tony smiled at this, as if he was sharing a joke that Daud could not understand.

In expansive mood he told Daud that he had spent a year in South Africa, working in an architect's office. He had relatives there and would gladly go back there to live, he said, but there was going to be trouble so why take the risk? When Daud did not challenge him, his narration became warmer and more detailed. He had been surprised by the amount of contact between black and white ... multi-racial parties, children playing together.

'Like piano keys,' Daud suggested.

'Absolutely,' he agreed.

'That's lovely, Tony, isn't it?' Susan asked, squirming on her bean bag and smiling at Daud.

The best-loved character in the architect's office, it turned out, was Amos the black messenger. He kept everybody in tucks with his antics. 'My nephew's wet-nurse was a black woman,' Tony declared. 'Christ, how far can you go to show that you don't have any racial prejudices? To let your own child be suckled by a black woman!'

Daud had asked for another helping of the moussaka, and sensed that his reply had disappointed them. They never invited him round again, suspecting him of secretly laughing at them. When he met them now they were barely polite. After a noisy gathering at his house, Tony would come round to see him, to complain about their disturbed sleep. *Susan is highly strung and gets very upset if she can't sleep. So please show some consideration.* Once he had come storming round when Karta was noisily demonstrating some new dance steps, and had angrily demanded of Daud that he *show some human decency*. Daud was a little past his best at the time and had told him to go and suck a black tit. Daud sometimes banged on the wall to irritate them or shouted abuse into an upstairs cupboard that he knew adjoined their bedroom. *Go home you Boer fascists.*

Lloyd came back with a large can of beer, and stood in the kitchen, drinking and talking to Daud, leaving Karta to the television. 'It really smells good,' he said, feeling pleased with his recent mission of mercy. He talked about William Blake, whose poems he memorised and loved to recite. Daud listened with only half an ear, but he knew that Lloyd spoke Blake's poems with feeling and love. He was concerned not to overcook the rice.

They were all more cheerful by the time they sat down to eat. Daud put a jar of chilli sauce on the table for Karta, who licked his lips noisily, exaggerating his anticipation. 'When are you going to grow up and stop eating chilli sauce with everything?' Daud asked him.

He was pleased with his efforts and ate the chicken stew with relish. Eating his own cooking had taken some getting used to. After he moved out of the boarding-house, when he stopped being a student, Ray did most of the cooking. When he did not feel like doing so, they bought some fish and chips. Whenever Daud suggested that he would cook, Ray hooted with laughter and begged him not to. After Ray stopped speaking to him, he ate tinned foods and sandwiches. He was too ashamed to start learning under Ray's hostile scrutiny. Sometimes he cooked sausages because there was nothing he could do to make *them* go wrong. When he became sole lord and master of 9 Bishop Street, he allowed himself more licence. His landlord called round one evening to check something and found him in the middle of his latest creation. *I'm experimenting*, Daud told him. The man had taken pity on him and the next day brought him a battered copy of a cookery book. That had initiated him into the mysteries of lamb chops and boiled cauliflower. None of it tasted like food but it was filling.

His new skills were too quickly put to the test. He had visitors. A Norwegian couple turned up one evening, asking if he knew where Tony and Susan were. They told him that they had got married that morning, had been travelling all day and now had nowhere to stay the night. The woman was visiting England for the first time. Daud offered them his bed and something to eat. They accepted both. He had bought a chicken earlier that afternoon, intending to cook his most ambitious meal yet: roast chicken, roast potatoes and runner beans, followed by apple crumble and custard. He set about his task self-importantly while the Norwegian couple retired upstairs to make the bed and then try to smash it to pieces, as he could clearly hear. It all ended in disaster. The book did not tell him that he had to thaw out the chicken before roasting it. It did not tell him how big the potatoes should be for roasting, and he had sliced them. When the Norwegian couple appeared after the hour and a half he had suggested to them, they looked sleek and content. His breath smelt of alcohol and she looked round his hovel with some suspicion. They said nothing as he served them bloody meat and soggy slices of potatoes. They pushed the food about for a while and then went back upstairs. He heard them laughing. He cleared the table and sat down to his apple crumble.

They left early the next morning but came back a week later to take him round to the house they had newly rented. He was surprised by its affluence, which was not unusual. He was surprised by everybody's affluence. They did not offer him the roast chicken dinner which he had assumed would be the humiliating high point of his outing. After the tour of the house they drove him back without even troubling him to refuse a coffee. He suspected that he was being put in his place in some way.

Should he tell Karta and Lloyd about Catherine? Not yet, he decided. He watched Karta wolfing down the stew and felt the contentment of the successful cook. 'Listen, bro,' Karta said, leaning back from the wreckage on his plate and fishing in his jacket pocket for a cigarette. 'There's a meeting of the Afro-Asian Society tomorrow. You should come. It's going to be an interesting one.'

'What exactly does the Afro-Asian Society do?' Lloyd asked, waving Karta's smoke away haughtily. 'Does it plan the revolution?'

'No!' Karta said, blowing a stream of smoke at Lloyd. 'We sit in dark corners and try to think of ways of cutting English throats. Usually we sacrifice a chicken or a goat, unless we can find an English virgin, which is rare these days. Then we perform secret rites and do crazy dances and have orgies.'

'Why can't you be civil for once?' Lloyd asked, flushing with anger. 'Don't you ever stop?'

'I bet your great-grandpappy didn't stop when some ridiculous old black chief asked him not to take away his people's land, eh?' shouted Karta. 'You don't like what I say, take your arse out of here! Fuck off!'

'Karta,' Daud warned.

'Tell him!' he said, pointing at Lloyd.

'You're too pathetic for words!' shouted Lloyd, turning away from the table.

Karta stood up angrily and switched the television on. Daud gathered the dishes and took them to the kitchen. He washed them immediately, before the cockroaches and mice appeared to feast on the leftovers. The effect of the beer had worn off by the time he returned to the living room. The three of them sat in a tense silence, watching television and waiting for the football to start.

He hated the way they bickered like that, Daud thought. Karta was staring stonily at the television, his face puffy and hot with injury. Lloyd was breathing noisily, huffing with indignation. He should get out more, get away from them. If he entered all the competitions that promised holidays in Bali or Rhodes or Hawaii, he would be bound to win one. Then he could escape them for a blissful fortnight of flesh-pots and decadence. In the meantime, he should go to the cinema or join an amateur dramatics group. He went with Karta to the Afro-Asian Society once, but the grandiose rhetoric left him numb with boredom and on the brink of tears. He should take a boat on the river, go for picnics in the countryside in the summer, go for a hike along the Pilgrims Way. Take Catherine with him, have fun!

What a horrible little room, he thought. The paint was grimy and cracked with age. The furniture, which Piano Keys had delivered in an orange station-wagon, was worse than junk. The table was scored and runnelled, as if it had once served as a chopping board. Daud had painted its legs yellow to brighten it up, but only succeeded in making it look more squalid than ever. A small, lumpy settee was wedged under the stairs, kept company by the scabby, brown armchair in which he was sitting. He was the only one who could sit in it since neither Lloyd nor Karta, nor anybody else who had seen it, could contemplate its touch. Daud thought of it as like touching a leper: good for his soul and it made the leper feel good.

Still, it could have been worse, he reassured himself. The story Karta told of his first few weeks in the hall of residence returned to disgust him. Karta had moved out in the end because he could not stand the smells in the toilets first thing in the morning. *It was like a ritual with these English students. They couldn't use the toilets in the afternoons or the evening, they had to do their crap in the morning. And all the doors had these springs. They shut behind you and sealed up the smell of turds in the corridors.* In the end Karta had not even been able to shake hands with anybody without thinking of their turds. When he went for a bath he took his own supply of scouring powder, and used his own bar of soap. He never went near the showers, afraid he might have to get close to one of the maggoty bodies with crumbs of turds still stuck to its hairy arse. *To think we allowed these molluscs, these shit-sniffing slugs to rule over us. That was the biggest shame, my bro.*

When the football came on they started to talk again. Every time a black player touched the ball, Karta cheered and stamped on the floor. Lloyd cringed but did not say anything. When a black player scored one of the goals, Karta rose and banged on the wall, inviting *the Boer* to take note. They switched channels after the football. Daud said he would go to bed soon but they could stay and watch TV if they wanted. They were just in time to catch the news, and a filmed report on the murder of Dora Bloch in the aftermath of the Entebbe rescue.

'They are savages!' Lloyd cried. 'Nothing more than savage murderers. Look at that pot-bellied monster! The very personification of evil! There is nothing you would not believe about that greasy bastard. He is a killer, nothing more or less, a merciless bastard!'

Daud watched with his chin in the palm of his hand, silent with shame, while Lloyd exacted his revenge against Karta.

10

They stopped by the river to watch the water streaming underneath them. The light had gone by then and they could see the water only as turbid shimmerings of reflected street-lights. 'During the day,' he told her, 'you can see the shingle on the river bed, and the spindly weeds bending under the force of the water. You can see the slime on the river banks, and the allotments on the other side sprouting brassicas.'

She nodded as if she had never heard of such things. They stood that way, leaning against the parapet of the bridge.

'Behind us,' he told her, 'you can just make out the shadows of the cogs and wheels of the old weir. Can you see them? The mill was on the bank behind the weir but it's all gone, washed away by those same waters that had turned its stones. Can you hear the water rushing through the sluices in the cogs?'

'Yes,' she said.

'Well, if you really strain you can hear a hum, a noise in the distance,' he said, smiling self-consciously under her stare. 'That's the new mill now, grinding day and night, its yards crawling with fork-lift trucks. I used to hear that hum on quiet nights, and then found out what it was quite by chance. At night it looks like a prison camp, a floodlit yard surrounded by high-wire.'

'I can't hear anything,' she confessed.

Two men came walking towards them, and Daud felt the dregs of an old fear. He turned back to the river to avoid their sneering faces but his body was tense and alert. He heard their conversation change, and then knew they had stopped behind them.

'Have you got a light, mate?'

Catherine glanced at them and turned back to the river. Daud saw that the men were watching him unwaveringly. Their bodies were hunched forward. Their enormous shoulders were so muscle-bound that with one tweak of an index finger they could send him flying into the cabbage patch across the water, he thought. Or sprain themselves to perdition, if he was willing to take the chance and make a fight of it. He could see that they were struggling not to laugh.

'No,' he said.

The man who had spoken reached into his pocket for a lighter. He lit his cigarette and puffed it twice, then curled his lips into a caricature of the Crown Prince of Pongoland.

'Give us a kiss, nigger,' he said. The two men laughed, turning their backs on him with complete assurance of their strength. They were both in their thirties, dressed in jeans and jumpers with the sleeves pulled up to reveal muscular forearms.

Catherine had whipped round, staring at the two men in astonishment. It was as if she was taking them in for the first time, their cruel laughter and their gross muscles. 'Let's go,' she said in a soft, frightened voice. The men heard her and shifted themselves a little to block the way.

'Where are we going then, love?'

She leant back with surprise, then Daud saw her frowning and beginning to get angry. *It's all right.*

They're Englishmen, he wanted to say. *They won't hit a man who wears glasses*. Her arm was trembling on his, and he could feel his own lower lip beginning to quiver out of control.

'Is it true what they say about them boys?' It was the same man doing all the talking, the more rugged-looking of the two. The other one's role seemed to be to laugh and support, and put the boot in when the time for that came. 'Cor!' he now said, sticking his elbow in his crotch and allowing his forearm to dangle between his legs.

'Oh, why don't you piss off?' Catherine said. 'You're pathetic!'

The two men were briefly shaken by the contempt with which she spoke to them but they began to grin. They will discover a new game soon, Daud thought, and will taunt *her*. None the less he relished the disdain with which she had sought to despatch the barbarians. He gently tugged at her arm and they walked away. He expected the men to follow and look to recover their supremacy by humiliating them some more, but they stood on the bridge, laughing and shouting abuse at them. A car drove slowly past, its occupants deep in conversation, unaware of the drama on the pavement.

'Stupid bastards!' she said.

He embraced her, flashing a strong grin at the starlit sky. He had seen Sidney Poitier do that in a film once. They stood in the middle of the pavement, tight in each other's arms. She laughed and drew away from him a little.

'Honestly, it's like a bad joke,' she said. 'Stupid shits!'

He kissed her. She leant heavily against him, her arms wrapped tightly around him. He smelt the perfume in her hair and nuzzled his face in its fragrance. She held on to him as they began to walk again.

'The fascist bastards,' she laughed. 'It's ridiculous, isn't it? I didn't know people actually said things like that. You'd have thought they'd be a bit more original at least.'

'I don't know what's funny,' he said, taking a deep draught of her fragrant hair, to fortify himself in case they suffered a brief rupture so soon after joining fates.

She leant back to look at him, smiled and pressed his arm. *Bear up, darling. Don't turn bitter and twisted. It's not worth it.* 'You're not going to get upset about those idiots, are you?' she asked.

'Where would they get the brains to be original? What do you think they are? Comedians making jokes? They do what they've always done, and what their fathers and grandfathers have always done. Why change a winning formula? The place is crawling with them. If you can step out of the line of their antics then they are ridiculous. But they demoralise me … The first time it happened I stood and stared, stunned. Who? Me? A man drove past and shouted, and stuck two fingers out of the window for good measure. Suck on that, you fucking wog. What's original about that? But when it happens to you it is shocking. And it goes on all the time. It's nothing much. People call you names or make faces at you. Kids shout at you like you're a naked lunatic. Clerks in offices get smart with you. When you get on a bus you feel the conductor marshalling the passengers against you, daring you to have the wrong change or name the wrong route. It's demoralising. I can do without originality on top of that, thank you very much. Let them come as predictable as they know how. It evens the odds a little.'

'I hadn't thought of it in that sort of detail,' she said after a moment, reluctant to concede. She was determined not to take the two men seriously. To her they were two yobs: they made stupid remarks to him as they might have done to her if she had walked past them. 'Perhaps you're being too sensitive, expecting too much,' she said.

He grinned at her. 'Perhaps I've got a chip on my shoulder. That's what it used to be a few years ago,' he said. 'Next time somebody tells me my mother is a monkey, or frowns because I've walked into a restaurant, I'll remind myself not to be too sensitive. I'll just blow them a kiss with my rubbery lips and carry on polishing my halo. Or if some high-spirited vagabonds chase me through half-deserted streets, looking to crush my infamous loins with well-aimed kicks, I'll appeal to their sense of honour as Englishmen. I won't think to curse their free-booting ancestors who rifled the treasure chests of the world for gewgaws, and then returned home like gleeful burglars, laughing at their victims. I won't expect too much or get upset over a bit of name-calling. Ho ho ho, not me!'

'I'm sorry,' she said. 'I hadn't thought ... That was feeble, what I said.'

'You just don't want me to make a fuss,' he replied. 'You want me to take this like a man, despise my tormentors and conduct myself with dignity. Be brave!'

She grinned at his sarcasm. 'I hadn't thought you would have to put up with that all the time. I don't think my parents would call you names, although they'd probably like to. I know they'd frown if you walked into their favourite restaurant. I don't know what that proves. That it wouldn't be amusing to be at the receiving end of it? I know they think it's silly of Richard to waste his talents on Bengali tenants who want to take their landlords to court. Especially since the landlord is often the Council, who own the courts as well. Did I tell you that's what he did? My brother?'

'Yes,' he said.

'Perhaps you should come home with me one weekend and we can ask my parents if they'd like to call you names. I can just see that,' she laughed. 'Especially if you give them that free-booting ancestors stuff. I expect my father will pour you a glass of his best whisky and then call you names behind your back.'

'It could be worse,' he said. He knew he had not made her understand the way the little acts of abuse and mockery became a relentless pressure. She wanted them to be more shocking before she could take them seriously, he guessed, not these silly gestures of resentment. Not all of them were as crude as the two men, he might have assured her. Some thought that a bland, dissembling smile hid their contempt from the victim. When the realisation came to him in those early years that he provoked such profound disdain, he had felt a bitterness that was now hard to credit. It had unnerved him, made him lose heart. But that was not how people were made, he thought, not to live on pain and bitterness. When he could, he hid his misery behind better things, covered the lesser with the pleasure that he took in small acts of recovery.

They bought fish and chips and ate them as they walked. He had never done that before, not strolled the streets eating out of newspaper, but he did not tell her. He wolfed the food down quickly to get it out of the way. His fingers were impregnated with grease, and he felt as if his skin was standing out in bubbles of oil. His breath had the smoky smell of hot, stale fat. He insisted that they stop at the Black Dog for a refresher.

They could not stay long because she was on early duty again the following day. They said long and lingering good nights at her front door. *Good night, good night! parting is such sweet sorrow* … He left her at the door and turned to hurry home. The men had frightened him more than he had admitted, and now as he walked home, the memory of the encounter made him rush. They could have tracked his every movement since the bruising they received at Catherine's hands. They could pop up from behind any dustbin, crawl out from any manhole. Or they might do something original for a change. He walked into the house with a bark of triumph. Ha! He had given the racist freaks a clean sight of his right royal again.

England duly disgraced themselves at Old Trafford, losing by 425 runs. Even this triumph over historical inertia did not make the rest of the week go any more quickly. He could think of little else but her. When Lloyd called, Daud could think of nothing to say to him, and Lloyd left after half an hour looking hurt. Karta turned up on Thursday to find out why Daud had not come to the pub. He spent the evening there, watching TV and helping himself to the soup that Daud had warmed up to convince Karta that he was too ill to go out.

He kept his eyes peeled for her at work but could not see her. They had arranged to meet on Saturday, because she said she had too much to do during the week, but he had hoped that they might run into each other at lunch-times. When he could not see her he began to wonder if she went out with anyone else. He thought of the person who had taken her to the Yacht Club, about whom she had been so discreet. He imagined a rich young farmer or a cocky surgeon with whom she would have a great deal more in common than with him. She had talked of other places too: a famous pub on the road to Margate, and a jazz club in the country that he had heard about. For all he knew there were others she had not even mentioned. And although she did not say so, he *knew* she would have gone there with the same man. He could picture them, he thought, sharing a joke and chatting, perfectly at ease with each other. With friends like that, what was she doing with him? Perhaps it meant nothing to her. He could not believe that was true. He guessed that she had not really thought the matter out, had simply followed an instinct, overcome by his great charm. He would be able to tell on Saturday, he thought.

What had she meant that she should have met him years ago? Was she in trouble? Perhaps the jazz club farmer was really something much sleazier, something truly sick and disgusting. Say a disappointed intellectual who relied on her for moral support and a platonic friendship. Perhaps that was why she went red when she mentioned the jazz club.

He thought of the way she had said *piss off* to those men with such irresistible contempt, of the way she felt as she leant against him, and the things she had said as they stood in the doorway. She had said she wished Saturday was not so far away. How sorry she was that the evening was so short! And how nice that she was free all next weekend.

He waited impatiently for her at the bus station on Saturday morning. She waved to him as soon as she saw him, embraced him and held him for a long moment. *I missed you all week*, he told her. She grinned and kissed him on the lips. They found a café and ordered coffee and cakes. She liked the coffee and he liked the cakes. They sat within sight of the cathedral gates, and saw hundreds of visitors pouring in and out in a constant stream. He imagined a time when the visitors would have dragged themselves from the corners of the land, to find succour at this shrine. How irritated those pilgrims would have been to see these curious unbelievers, wandering passionless through the holy places, clutching glossy picture-books of martyred saints.

'Tourists!' he said. 'They're so undignified, gawking like voyeurs.'

She was taken aback with surprise. 'That seems … harsh,' she said, uncertain if she should take him seriously. 'Isn't everybody a tourist the first time they visit a place? You must've been a tourist the first time you went into the cathedral.'

'I've never been inside the cathedral,' he said triumphantly.

'Never?' she asked, watching him with suspicion.

'Never!' he replied firmly.

'Why not?' she asked after a moment, intrigued.

He shrugged. 'I don't want to be like them,' he said. 'I'm on the side of the pilgrims in this.'

'But aren't you interested? Don't you find that great building challenging? Something you should go and wander in?' she asked, not satisfied with his explanation.

'I could discover it,' he said. 'As Columbus did the Maya shrines.' It came to him suddenly that he had wanted to visit the cathedral all along. Of course he had! He had scoffed at the idea because it was what tourists did. It was the kind of thing that drew attention to you, that forced you out of the woodwork and into the open. He told her this, and smiled at the look of smug vindication on her face.

'That's a silly excuse,' she said. 'You should've visited it instead of being scared … What do you mean forced you out of the woodwork?' she asked.

'If you look different in a place, you try and avoid making yourself conspicuous, don't you? You just go from one place to another, like everybody else, and don't dawdle in places that will make people turn and wonder what you're up to.'

'Like hanging around bridges in the evening, for example?' she suggested. 'Is that really why you haven't visited the cathedral?'

'Yes,' he said, listening to himself to see if this was true. 'Everybody gushes so much about the cathedral here as well. They're so enthusiastic about it. It's become a symbol, a kind of cultural testimonial. *Look at this thing we made, look at how clever we are*. I find it intimidating, I think. The cathedral, I mean. It makes me feel like a Pygmy, a hunter-gatherer grubbing about on the forest floor.'

'We should visit it then,' she said firmly, the way Nurse might insist on a necessary injection.

'Not today,' he said, alarmed by the resolute manner in which she spoke. Not after he had cleaned the house thoroughly, and washed and aired the bedsheets, and sprinkled the mattress with essence of sandalwood. All that remained was to do the shopping ... 'Soon,' he told her. 'We'll visit it soon.' He mentioned his grand plan for the summer, boat rides on the river, picnics in the countryside and a hike along the Pilgrims Way, perhaps ending at the cathedral. She became so enthusiastic that he was tempted to calm her down by suggesting an evening at the jazz club as well.

'I rang up my mother before I came out,' she said suddenly, and then turned to look for the waitress, trying to seem casual. 'Did you want some more coffee?'

'Is everything all right?' he asked. 'Is your mother—'

'Yes,' she interrupted him. 'Everything's fine. I don't know why I rang her.'

'Why not?' he asked.

She looked at him as if she suspected him of something. 'I suppose that's it,' she said, sighing. 'I do know why I rang her. To tell her about you. I thought this morning: What would she say if she knew? No, that's not true. What

I thought was ... What I've been thinking about all week is: Am I crazy, going to spend a weekend with this man I hardly know? A black man. And I found myself feeling relieved that she wasn't here, feeling relieved that I would not have to be faced with that complication. Part of me was ashamed of ... us. As if it was a kind of failure, coming to be with you. There's a part of me that said I should know better, should not indulge myself. Everybody will think there's something wrong with me, that I can't find anyone better. So I had to ring her and tell her, didn't I? I had to ring her and say: *I know you don't want to hear this but you're going to. Now what do you think about it?*'

'What did she think about it?' he asked gently.

'She was appalled!' she said, her voice still hinting at the shock she had felt. 'She was quiet at first and then told me to stop being so stupid. After a while she began to say the most grotesque things ... I had no idea she thought like that.'

He laughed bitterly. 'Why should it surprise you?' he asked. 'Nothing surprises me about the racist confusions of the European mind.'

'Not that!' she said, shaking her head urgently. 'I expected that. I expected her to feel revolted, to say something harsh at first. For all I know I might have said the same things myself in her place.' She wanted to explain, to be truthful. She waited to see if he would say anything, if he would take offence.

He waited, showing neither shock nor surprise. He wondered if she had considered that he might have asked himself what *he* was doing meeting someone like her. The thought made him smile. He knew the answer to that. But he also knew the pleasure he took in her was real, urgent ... not something he would leave at the mercy of the sanction that other people felt they could give him. He wanted her to feel like that too.

'I just said that I was going … to see this man I'd met recently. She told me to take care,' Catherine said, smiling. 'Then I told her that you were black. She asked me why I was going out with someone black, as if I was doing it deliberately, as if it was a principle. I said that I liked you. That you were like no one else I had ever met. She didn't say anything … and then exploded with all these things. She called me disgusting, told me I'd always been filthy. She'd never said anything like that before. And then afterwards I thought I must have missed something, I must've misunderstood. What could've possibly made her think that? I only went out with one boy all the time I was at home. Why did she say all that?'

He realised what it was that had wounded her – the opinion her mother had of her. Because she had answered her own question about him, he thought. She came to see him, and spoke to her mother about him, no less. Catherine turned round again to look for the waitress. The café was crowded with Saturday morning shoppers, whole families crammed into impossible nooks and crannies. Daud's frantic waving attracted their attention as well as that of the waitress. She hurried over to take another order of coffee. 'I mean I don't tell her anything about any men I see,' she said.

Who do you see? You disgusting, two-timing her. Who? It was the wrong place to be talking about these things, he thought.

'Does it surprise you that she was distressed?' he asked.

'No, of course not. Well, I suppose I hoped she would surprise me. But it was the things she accused me of.'

'Perhaps there's something …' he said hesitantly, conscious of the heads that were within earshot of them.

'Something bad at home. That's what I thought. She can't mean to say this. Something horrible's happened. That was my first thought.'

'Ring again and find out,' he said, squirming to end the conversation.

'She would've told me,' she said, her voice falling suddenly into self-pity. 'She seemed so pleased at first.'

'You should've told her I'm a Muslim,' he suggested. 'That would have reassured her.'

She smiled. 'I don't know why I said anything. I always thought she liked to pretend that I never did anything like that, she had saved me from all that. Maybe that's what is upsetting – after worrying about hiding these things from her, it turns out she thinks of me as some kind of a ...'

'Slut!' he pronounced with relish.

'I should've said that I was going to spend the weekend with this poverty-stricken black man who is a Muslim as well,' Catherine said, leaning back to allow the waitress to put a pot of coffee between them. He was filled with pleasure. *She did not care if the waitress heard*.

'Named after the slayer of the Philistine Goliath,' he said, gently tapping his chest with a fist.

'They would have been down here to prise me out of your clutches by the morning,' she said, laughing and reaching out to touch his hand at the same time. The waitress glanced at them and then retreated with a smile of complicity on her face. 'My father thinks we've become a society that no longer understands restraint, and that we'll watch ourselves turning degenerate without having the faintest idea what to do about it. He'll assume that I'm half-way down the slippery slope and come charging over to rescue me.'

'The Colonel! Really?'

'He's not a Colonel,' she said, laughing at the memory. 'But he really thinks that. He has furious arguments with my brother. Richard accuses him of being a proto-fascist, whatever that is. And my father says that anarchy is always preceded by misguided liberalism. And yesterday I heard another explanation. There's a new gynae house surgeon. He said he was from West Africa but he didn't say exactly where. Anyway, he came to the ward to examine two girls who were having abortions today. He told me, in front of the two girls, that they were an example of the breakdown of modern western society. He said that we had all become too individualistic, that we had no sense of community any more.'

'And then he asked you out?' he enquired.

She flushed with guilt and surprise. 'Yes, he did. But men are always like that. If you exchange a few friendly words with them they make a pass at you.'

'You should be so lucky!' he said, grinning while vats of sulphur and envy bubbled in him. *Would you like to come to the Yacht Club and catch a bit of community spirit with me?* She looked at him as if she was considering saying something but then shook her head. 'What did you say?'

'To him? I told him that I was seeing someone else. He was very apologetic when I told him you were African,' she said, beginning to collect her things and sort her bag for leaving. 'Where do you do your shopping?' she asked, folding her wrists across the handbag in her lap.

11

'This,' he said, pointing to a chipped and grimy door. The brown paint had cracked and peeled in places. He noticed for the first time that a large crevice was beginning to appear in the door frame.

'Is this where you live?' she asked, the disgust palpable in her voice. She touched the glass in the door as if expecting it to fall off. With a fastidious toe she pressed the spongy weather-guard, and to her alarm felt the rotting wood give way under what was no more than symbolic pressure. 'You live here?'

'Oh, only for the moment,' he said, but failed to persuade her to smile. Even as he watched her and felt guilty for his self-neglect, a part of him was doubled up with glee.

As he let her into the house, the smell of damp and rotting wood was almost overpowering. He wondered if she would gag and choke, but she held on bravely, her discomfiture evident only from a sudden and sharp intake of breath. Her face puckered sneeringly as she looked round his living room. He could see she was becoming hardened, for she released her breath carefully and took several gentle sniffs to test the air. He had cleaned the room earlier and in his eyes it looked quite pleasant. He put down the bag of shopping and invited her to sit. As if determined to demean herself fully in her descent into urban squalor, she sat in the dilapidated, scabby armchair. He stopped himself from moving forward to pull her out of the chair. *This is not necessary*, he wanted to say.

'It's a bit small,' she said with obvious distress. 'Can I open a window?'

'Sorry,' he said without the slightest sympathy. 'The window doesn't open.'

'What do you mean, doesn't open?' she asked, looking around her again.

He drew the curtains aside to show her where the nails had been hammered into the window frame. Clouds of dust billowed away from the curtains and hung suspended in the airless room. 'The window would fall down if you took the nails out,' he said.

She rose to her feet, and for a moment he thought she would leave. 'Show me the rest of the house, then,' she said.

'You'd imagined something more comfortable, no doubt.' He stood in front of her with his hands in his pockets. 'It's not as bad as you think, unless you're used to carpets and wallpaper and things like that. Come and see the rest of it if you want ...'

'It's awful,' she said when they were back downstairs. 'It's damp and dirty and stuffy. The furniture looks as if it's been salvaged from a dump. Finger-marks down the walls! The kitchen and the bathroom are just too squalid for words.'

He watched her fury with silent amazement, sitting at the table with his hands folded between his knees. He made to protest but was silenced by her hot, angry glare.

'How can you live like this?' she asked while his face quivered with sudden annoyance. 'You could at least *clean* the fucking place. That would be a start! Or have the window fixed so you could get rid of that putrid smell.'

He took her on another tour, this time pausing over the places that were the sources of the interesting smells: the damp bricks in the kitchen, the spongy bathroom and the rotting floor-boards everywhere. He conceded that the kitchen and bathroom in particular left something to be desired, but he vowed to attack their darkest corners with the most powerful chemicals known to man, to root out the filth and putrescence wherever it might lurk. Had she noticed the bedroom, though? Was it not large and adequate? Really quite a surprising room! When they went back to the living room, he noticed that she chose the other chair, glancing at the diseased one with a suppressed shudder. She looked at the walls with an appraising eye, and he wondered if she was planning his colour schemes for him.

She asked if she could get dinner, which disappointed him. He had wanted to cook for her, to show off. He went out to buy a bottle of wine while she unloaded the shopping. When he returned he found her cleaning the cooker. Strands of hair were plastered to her sweaty brow, and dirty splashes stained her blouse.

'What's in that cupboard?' she asked.

'A kind of mould,' he said with a tinge of fear. 'I can't stop it growing. Sometimes in the middle of the night I get this nightmare that it's come out of there. I don't know what it is but it's grotesque. I can't touch it ... like huge flaps of white meat, fluted and filigreed on the underside, growing in layers and multiplying all the time.'

'Yes, I saw,' she said, echoing the awe in his voice.

He opened the wine and fortified himself before he began to help her. He cleaned the sink while she battled with the cooker. She encouraged him with kisses and praise. He made trouble often, protesting and complaining about the futility of what they were doing, so that she would keep encouraging him. When she went back to the kitchen later to check on the food, she was disappointed that their efforts had not made the kitchen look much cleaner than before. He felt vindicated.

'How long have you been here now?' she asked. 'In England, I mean.' They had washed up the dishes and put them away, and Daud was beginning to think that the time had arrived to give lust its head, to invite it to open its innings. He watched her slide into the lumpy settee with the grace of a svelte sophisticate, and saw her wince with surprise.

'Five years,' he said. What a long time it had been. It seemed a time of such misery, even though he reminded himself of this or that event that had given him pleasure. He had stood by the mill, he remembered, and watched his soul rushing through the cogs and the wheels, and wondered what would come to save him. It was also there that he had kissed his Swiss girl goodbye and wrapped her round with his flimsy mac on the chilly September of her departure, promising to write to her every day. She had clung to him with gratifying abandon. While tears poured down her face she swore to love him for ever. A man in a leather jacket and with an Afro hairdo of serious proportions had walked past this dishevelled scene, glaring at him and raising a fist as both a salute and a rebuke.

'It doesn't seem so long,' she said. 'I would've thought you'd been here longer.'

It was also there that the car had stopped to disgorge him the morning after the booze-up in the historical grounds of a stately home. *How had he got there?* They had lit a fire in an old quarry and spent a reckless night smoking pot and singing folk songs which meant nothing to him.

'Do you miss your country?' she asked.

He sat beside her on the uncomfortable settee and caressed her face with both his hands. She drew nearer to him and then fell heavily into his arms, murmuring endearments and leaning on him. The warmth of her body and her breath made him growl softly with pleasure and excitement. She reached for his face with her hand and pulled his head down. She kissed him violently, roughly, muttering small sounds in his mouth. He held on to her, surprised by her passion.

'I missed you all week,' she said.

He whispered to her that he had put clean, fragrant sheets on the bed. She smiled and shut her eyes, then held her hand out to him, inviting him to lead her upstairs. They lay on the bed exchanging caresses. Before long he found himself in sole possession of two handsome and stupefyingly soft breasts. This calmed him, and he settled down to his new toys as if he would never tire of them. She had to nudge him in the end, demanding his attentions elsewhere. She grumbled when he forced himself to stop moving, but he had to wait for his shredded nerve-ends to lose the intensity of sensation. Anxiously she asked him if he had ... if he had. He answered her no and began again, but he knew that for his vainglory he would be unable to hang on. She held on to him while he shuddered and rocked. For a long time after, she would not let him move, her arms tightly wrapped across his back. In the end, laughing at him a little, she pushed him off.

'Sorry,' he said as he threw himself on his back.

'Later,' she said. She rolled over towards him and curled herself into his arms, stroking his damp flesh.

'I should've played a few defensive strokes first,' he said drowsily. 'Up and down the line instead of charging like that.'

He felt himself beginning to fall asleep but she started to talk. He dozed off for a second until she noticed and shook him awake. The drowsiness abated when he made himself sit up, turning to look at her and stroke her face, incredulous at her beauty. She showed him the mess they had made of the room and he grinned with satisfaction. The mess testified to their great passion, he suggested. She smiled pityingly. 'You'll have to do better than that,' she said and got up to switch off the light. When she returned, she lay on one elbow beside him, tormenting him with conversation while he pleaded with her to go to sleep. In the end, she too became tired and drew herself close to him. He asked her if she was all right, and she mumbled something which he did not really hear.

In the morning he woke suddenly, roused from deep stupor. The memory of Catherine came surging at him with the clarity of a vivid dream. In the grip of enchantment, he felt for her body beside him but no one was there. His hand, though, ran over the warm hollow where her body had lain, and he saw their clothes still scattered across the floor as they had left them. He smiled smugly and sank back to sleep. When he woke up again, he found her lying next to him, watching him. As his eyes focused on her, he expected her to smile or say something, but she lay watching him, the side of her face cradled in his right hand. He grunted contentedly and reached to shut her wild, wild eyes with kisses four.

'You were snoring,' she said, her voice breaking his customary morning silence with the unexpectedness of the hum of holiday mornings. It reminded him of waking up on days of Idd and hearing the distant sound of his parents talking and clanging pots and pans as they prepared the pleasures of the day.

'I was putting it on,' he replied, his voice thick with sleep. 'Don't tell me I actually fooled you.'

She grinned at him. He rolled towards her and she gently gathered him in and wrapped herself round him. He felt himself drifting off to sleep again and did not resist. It seemed only a little while before she shook him awake. He went for her like a bull at first, but she calmed him down with long, lingering kisses. She made him lie back and think to please her. They made love slowly, pursuing preferences and laughing at failures. He felt as if he had known her for a long time.

'I miss the people I used to know. You asked me yesterday if I missed home,' he said. 'I relive scenes that I remember in detail, but I can't test them against other people's memories. If I misunderstood anything, if I read something wrongly, I can't ask for reassurance. And I find that I only remember certain kinds of things.'

'What kinds of things?' she asked.

'Things that make me feel guilty. I remember saying goodbye to my parents, how my father held my hand as if he did not want to let me go. How my mother said nothing but watched me as if incredulous at my departure. I remember those things. I don't even know whether she was incredulous, but as time passes these things become true, because I think that's how she would've felt.'

He was quiet for a while, feeling his way, waiting to see if he should say more.

'I think I understand,' she said, leaning on one elbow over him. 'I'd never thought about never being able to go over anything important. Perhaps small encounters escape because they come back too faintly ... Do you know what I mean? But I do understand about giving people thoughts that they don't even have. I mean ... I think I've let my father down, and I imagine him thinking of me as a disappointment.'

'Because you're not studying music?' he asked, wanting to persuade her that he was talking about something different.

'Yes,' she said, frowning, dissatisfied with his summary. 'But in other ways too. Just that it doesn't look as if I'm going to be the kind of person he would think of as successful … and I wish I could've been. But I really am not like that. I imagine him thinking that I'm just not ambitious enough. That I'm … frivolous. Perhaps he doesn't even think that. Do you see what I mean?'

'Yes,' he said.

'I always felt nervous of him,' she continued. 'Always afraid that he would misunderstand me. You could tell with somebody like him … you could feel the things he wanted for you. He didn't push or anything like that, but you could see his disappointment when you failed him.'

'Like with the music,' he suggested.

She smiled. 'Yes. But in other ways too.'

'Do you feel that you've failed … yourself?' he asked. 'You said you didn't want to be what they wanted of you.'

'I don't know,' she said, lying down and turning away from him a little. 'I don't know if those are just excuses. I didn't want to be a nurse, I knew it as soon as I arrived here. I knew before, but I could not think of anything when they asked me what else I would do. I used to say that there were things I wanted to do, I just didn't know what they were yet. He was disappointed, I know that. But I didn't want to study music. It was such labour … and for so little.'

She turned over to look at him, to see how he was taking what she was saying. 'I'm sorry,' she said. 'I'm sounding pathetic. If I had anything in me I would've told them all to get stuffed, wouldn't I?'

'No, I think you're brave and interesting,' he said. 'Not a bit pathetic.'

She smiled her gratitude and stroked his face. 'But I was such a mouse, such a drip! I think I just desperately wanted to get away from home in the end.'

'Why did you want to get away?' he asked, watching as tears began to trickle down the sides of her face.

'It was stupid,' she said, turning away again. 'I thought they disapproved of me, all of them. There was my father wanting me to be clever and sensitive, and my mother resisting him and hanging on to me as some image of herself. And Richard was always mocking, mocking. And Hugh ... I blame myself really.'

'Who's Hugh?' he asked so peremptorily that she turned to him sharply, a frown on her face. 'Who's Hugh?' he asked with an oily, grovelling tone, and earned himself a caress that was something between forgiveness and gratitude.

'He was the first boy I went out with, and almost the last,' she said. Then collecting herself, she laughed. 'How did I get to be talking about him? Why aren't you stopping me?'

'Because I want to know who Hugh is,' he said. 'And I already dislike him. His very name turns to bile and corrodes my ears.'

'Oh, no no, he wasn't important,' she said, waving his jealous passion aside with an intensity that contradicted her words.

'Why were you so desperate to get away from him then?'

'He encouraged me,' she said. 'Tried to help me. He told me I could still play music in my spare time, and nursing was a good profession because I could have children and return to it later. He wanted me to do my training in Leeds where he would be going to university. He thought we would marry and live together for the rest of our lives. I refused to go with him. I went to London and then came down here.'

'Why didn't you want to go to Leeds?'

'We started sleeping together that summer,' she said, as if she had not heard his question. 'It was the first time for me. Usually he was gentle, almost timid, but in his love-making he was angry with me. He wanted me to go with him, but I refused. So he punished me, humiliated me for having lost my awe of him. Oh, I used to worship him!'

'You're lying,' he said. 'You've never worshipped anyone. You're too contrary, too full of grumbles.'

'That's nice,' she said, smiling at him and looking pleased. 'I used to feel proud that he'd chosen me.' She watched as he rose out of bed and wrapped a *kikoi* round his middle. 'Where are you going?' she asked.

'I don't really want to talk about this man any more,' he said, walking towards the door. 'And … it's time I got up. Those were the St Alphege church bells announcing midday, and I never lie in bed in the afternoon. He sounds great.'

'He was all right,' she said, sitting up and watching him.

'You should've gone to Leeds,' he said, with his hand on the door.

She nodded. 'Set up house and skivvy for him and provide him with all the comforts of home. I felt I was pushed into something permanent, that everybody was beginning to treat us that way. I wanted a place of my own first. I always had that ambition. There, one ambition at least, to have a flat of my own where I lived alone, and where I could come and go as I pleased. Not for ever … just for as long as I wanted to.'

'It sounds more fun than it really is,' he said, pulling the door open. 'You end up wishing for someone to burst into your room and ask interfering questions. To take your mind from recognising the misery of the memories that come back to you. You end up missing people that you never realised you even remembered.'

She sat watching him for a long while. 'You were talking about your parents before,' she said. 'And I never let you finish.'

'Shame on you!' he said, before running downstairs to chance his life in the shower. He had felt misunderstood at first, when she started talking about her people. He had never spoken about his parents to anybody, had been too guilty and pained to be able to talk about them, and was hurt that his effort to do so was unceremoniously pushed aside. He understood the inadequacy she spoke of, had sensed it from the beginning, and was now glad that she had offered him a glimpse of its meaning.

'Tell me,' she said when he came back. 'I'm sorry I went on like that. You were saying that the only things you remembered were those that made you feel bad. Tell me about your parents. I showed you mine, so you have to show me yours.'

'I'll tell you later,' he said. 'You'd better get up now or the powerful juju of the St Alphege bells will blister your bum with sores. There's a legend about them. If you hear the bells in bed in the afternoon you get bedsores.'

'Tell me,' she said after they had eaten a huge breakfast of sausages and eggs. 'Otherwise I'll feel you're just punishing me for talking too much earlier.'

He shook his head, not knowing what to say, not sure that he should begin at all. 'I don't think I'll ever see them again,' he said, beginning at the end, then sitting silently while guilt and failure overwhelmed him. She started to speak but he stopped her. He shook his head, apologetically demanding her silence. She started to rise, to go to him, but he shook his head again, peremptory with warning. She sat back in her chair and watched him in the grip of his misery. After a few moments he sighed and then puffed heavily, clowning the passing of the pain. It was then that there was a loud knock on the door, and its melodrama made both of them smile.

'Karta,' he said as he went to open the door.

Karta was made shy by Catherine's beauty. Daud had told him nothing about her, and he stared at her with a look of dumbfoundment. She smiled and shook hands with perfect ease, unaware of the effect she was having. Daud thought he understood how Karta felt. The women they knew looked damaged, like themselves. Always straining too hard and seeming to be dissembling, to be uncomfortable with themselves, out of their depth. That was what it meant to be a stranger in a place. Catherine shook hands without thought, completely confident of her social graces whatever doubts troubled her smiling face.

'How are you?' Karta asked, speaking with a serious voice. Daud watched with barely suppressed impatience as Karta tiptoed to the cupboard to fetch himself a glass. When he returned from the kitchen with his drink of water, he had obviously pulled himself out of his surprise. He talked about a film he had seen the previous evening at the university. 'Do you like films?' he asked Catherine.

'Yes, I do,' she said. 'Although I don't know the film you're talking about.'

'This bushman despises them,' Karta said, pointing at Daud. 'He thinks that people who like films are just incapable of reading books. That's the trouble with people like him. They read a little bit and discover their own ignorance, and then they think that everybody's in the same state. So they insist that we all take the same medicine. That's the trouble with you, bro.'

Daud was a little surprised at first by this assault but he did not defend himself against its injustice. He assumed Karta did not really mean him any harm but was just puffing himself up. He listened without protest or smile while Karta brought in his Masters and his trips to London and beyond. Most of what he said was addressed to Catherine, but he could not avoid a surreptitious glance at Daud now and then.

'Well, I'd better be going,' Karta said after a short while, putting his glass down on the floor. 'I only came round to say hello. I'll see you another time, my bro. I'll see you too, I hope.' This last was meant for Catherine, and was accompanied by a long look that made Daud feel a twinge of fear.

I'll kill you, you fucking baboon, Daud thought. He saw her smile at him and heard her say how nice it had been to meet him. He got up quickly and started to see Karta out. Standing outside the front door, Karta leant towards Daud and whispered *Good luck*. Daud restrained himself from smashing the door in his face.

Later in the evening they went out for a drink. As they walked round the spiked iron chains that surrounded the war memorial, he remembered a girl he had seen standing there once in drenching rain. She was selling poppies on Remembrance Day, in the shadow of the cathedral. Her raincoat was belted tightly round her waist, and with her free hand she beckoned him. She told him that she could give him a good time for a price. While he reeled backwards at the blasphemy, she undid the top button of her coat and leant a little towards him. He asked if what she was doing wasn't illegal, and she said she had a permit, grinning at his gullibility. He told her it was against his religion, and she said it was against hers too but she needed the money. He said he had no money. She asked him how much he had. She was slim and dark, as he remembered her, and at first glance he had thought her attractive. Her face looked ugly when she smiled, and the rain had reduced her hair to a trailing mess. He told her he had VD and made his escape. He told Catherine about her but she doubted that such things could happen here.

In the pub they found seats in a bay window that curved almost completely around them, giving them the feeling that they were sitting in a glass case, and that all comers could see them as they sat talking. A group of students, elaborately ragged and dirty, were arguing a point in the middle of the floor. One of them walked away in a huff to play the fruit machines by the toilet doors. She wondered if he would be like them when he was a student again, but the idea was so ridiculous that she chuckled. Elbows on the table, chin cupped in two hands, he too was watching the students, wondering at their swagger. At a nearby table, an idling young trendy shouted to the old man facing him that he was from Holland. *I'm Dutch, sir*. Elephant hide thonged his neck to set off his white vest.

'I used to share a room with a girl from Malaysia,' Catherine said suddenly. 'The way we've been silently sitting here reminded me. And this afternoon … She used to talk a lot. You couldn't stop her once she started. Something about her way of talking was wrong, though. It wasn't her accent or her English, just that despite her smiles and her bright voice she was on the point of cracking. She was utterly miserable. She used to get letters from home, every other day, and she used to read them out to me. Word for word! She used to explain what the meaning of this was and what the meaning of that. In Malaysia we have this, in Malaysia we have that. All the people in the letters had to be explained, whose uncle he was and what he looked like. Then the photos would come out, and then the tears. She cried every night. I felt sorry for her, at first. She was having so much trouble in her ward. She was so small and looked so fragile, and she was in a ward with one of those huge Sisters who terrified her.'

'A dumpling eater,' Daud suggested, making light of what he suspected she was going to tell him.

'I disliked her in the end,' Catherine said in an ashamed voice. 'I used to complain about her to the other students, saying that she was exploiting me.'

His heart ached for the Malaysian girl. He said nothing while he wondered if he went on at people like that.

'I was very cruel to her,' she said, dejection on her face. 'I requested a transfer ... because I could not bear to listen to her. I was thinking about this morning, when you wanted to tell me about how things come back to you. And I would not stop talking. That's how the Malaysian girl used to be with me.'

'Nothing like it,' he said, laughing with relief. 'I won't request a transfer.' He had imagined that she was going to say something about him, accuse him of burdening her with his misery, of being a morbid bore. Instead he found himself being asked to be magnanimous, reassuring her that she was unselfish to a fault. He took her hand off the table and kissed it. He thought of the way Karta had behaved and wanted to put in a good word for him. He did not want her to think Karta spiritless, and he disliked the way he had been with him, rushing Karta off as he had. In the end he did not say anything, thinking he would wait for her to see him as he could really be. Karta did not need any help from him.

The Dutchman at the next table was talking about cricket. The old man listened with a look of contentment. His hearing aid was turned down as usual, but he liked company and this seemed a good lad. Anyway, there was no point turning it up. He was speaking some foreign lingo, no doubt. The Dutchman repeated the word *cricket* several times and in the end got up to demonstrate an ordinary-looking off-drive. *We have been playing cricket in Holland since 1903*, he shouted as if he suspected the old man of doubting his word.

Catherine and Daud sat in silence, she leaning back in her lounge chair, he sitting upright on his padded stool. Behind him, the white-vested Dutchman was filling the air with his goodbyes, discouraged by the old man's unresponsiveness. The students were talking quietly, having settled their differences, laughing now and then with arrogant confidence. The old man at the next table, now deserted by the Dutchman, turned his attention to them. Daud had seen him countless times in the pub. He walked up to their table and stood uncertain for a moment or two, smiling at them his facile grin of the empire. Daud glanced at the old man's hands to see if they still dripped blood from the wogs he had slain across the globe. The old man said hello.

'Where you from then? Hong Kong, eh?' he asked cheerfully, sitting down. He glowed at them both, fractionally longer at Catherine. 'I spent a long time in Hong Kong. Travelled all over the world, matter of fact. Cape Town, Durban, Alex, West Indies, you name it. I've fought in Burma and Abyssinia for King and Country ...'

Daud gulped as he watched the old man's hands quivering with the atavistic thrill of remembered slaughters.

He glanced at Catherine, but she only had a distant, polite smile on her face, humouring the old man. *This man has killed human beings*, he wanted to scream at her. *Look at him! Look at those hands innocently quivering round the beer glass! Those same hands were wrapped round the throats of Allah knows how many innocent wogs across the globe!*

'I've nothing against you darkies,' the old man said, turning to Daud and making his mouth fall open with terror. 'I always say, you want to see 'em in their own country. Cheerful as you like, always eager to please. It's only when they come 'ere that they turn nasty, 'cause of a few rotten apples that give 'em a bad name. Oh, I got nothing against you lot. But it's cold here, innit? Whatchu think of the weather? Whatchu think of the winter, eh?'

They walked home by the cathedral gate, down the lane lined with shops. In between trying to persuade her to take the terrifying old man more seriously, he pointed out the inn where Charles Dickens had stayed. She tried to imitate the way the old man talked, holding her quivering hands out in front of her. Daud attempted to hush her, glancing round to see if the old man was following them. *I tell you that man's a killer. You heard him yourself.*

Approaching on the narrow pavement was a group of youths with wide shoulders, short hair and flashing grins. Daud groaned and covered his eyes for a moment. They were passing a paper parcel full of chips between them, and Daud remembered now why he had disliked eating chips in the street. He felt Catherine's hand tighten on his arm.

'I don't like Pakis,' said the beefy leader.

'Get out of our fuckin country, nigger.'

'How much didcha pay for her, you fuckin wanker?'

'You Tarzan me Jane.'

They parted in the middle and Catherine and Daud walked through.

As they passed somebody blew a raspberry and another scratched his armpits. Grunt grunt.

'Did you see the way they parted in the middle there?' Daud asked, elated as he always was by the narrow escape. 'They recognised the moral superiority of their foe and retreated. Death to the infidels! Did you see the way my trusty blade went snicker snack through the rabble?'

They hurried down the sleeping Palace Street, from where ecclesiastic Doges had ruled the Anglican firmament for centuries. It was now an antiquity of windowless flint walls, its pavements broken by high-arched lamp-posts at the end of which hung gloomy lanthorns of ancient design. Behind the walls rose the dormitories of the venerable boarding school created out of the cathedral's monastery in Henry VIII's time. Down King's Lane, past the ironmongery and the King George I where a pile of snow once slid off and nearly killed Daud as he was walking past. *Whether an accident or not I cannot say*, was how he liked to finish the story. Left past the boarded-up garage with grease marks running out into the road. Left into Bishop Street. *The church once owned all the houses down these streets*, he told her. *Have I told you that before?*

As he let her into the house, the smell of damp and rotting wood hit him again. Was he always going to live like this? He abandoned her in the living room and rushed off to the toilet. When he came back he found her waiting for him, a look of utter disgust on her face. He stopped by the door watching her. He could hear the sound of the mill, faintly.

'How can you live like this?' she asked, and swung her arm in a small arc through the air.

He came into the room and sat in the brown armchair, folding his arms across his chest. 'You get used to things,' he said.

'Is that it? You just get used to it? Or is it nice to wallow in these failures? How can you believe in anything when your life is this hovel, that job, hooligans shouting at you in the streets? You get used to them too?'

He smiled, and then stood up and went to her. 'You don't even know what a great victory this is. You think getting used to things is failing? Getting used to things is defeating them, taking the poison out of them and allowing them to become nothing more than layers of grime and clouds of dust. You don't know how hard it is to get to that.'

'How the fuck do you know? How do you know what I know? And take that condescending smile off your face,' she shouted.

'All right, all right,' he said. 'But living in dirt doesn't mean you can't believe in things.' She reluctantly allowed herself to be embraced, and she muttered irritably while he encouraged and persuaded her to come upstairs.

12

He woke up late the next morning, not needing to hurry. The sun entered through the moth-eaten curtains, throwing lances of dust into his room. Catherine had left at first light, saying she needed to change in time for early duty. He stayed in bed enjoying the weekend, and watching the shafts of light slant imperceptibly towards him. In the end, it was hunger that drove him down. Downstairs, he glanced towards the front door, expecting nothing. A blue air-mail letter lay just inside the door. He turned hastily away from it, his face grimacing with misery.

After a moment he went back and skirted it carefully, and in the end picked it up and turned it over. He sighed with relief when he saw that it was not from his parents. It was creased and dirty, and smelt of hot, steamy earth and sweaty hands. The name and address of a friend, Karim, were written on the back of the form, and all the remaining space was covered with HAPPY NEW YEAR wishes. In the middle of July. That seemed not unlike Karim, who had probably carried the letter in his shirt pocket since completing it, telling everybody he met that he had written a letter to Daud, then fishing it out with oaths and passion to silence the doubt he had invited by his bragging. Daud sat down at the table to read it, looking forward to it only a little. Karim always managed a joke or two, which in everyday abundance had made him into something of a tiresome clown. But in the end, he knew, Karim's letter would become the same as the others, full of grumbles and blame for his neglect, and ending with some scheme that required Daud to give up his wages or the freedom to live as he saw fit. He opened it irritably, wanting to get the matter over with so he could shower and get on with his life.

31st Dec 1975
Dear Haji,
(O Pilgrim to the Promised Land)

I am sitting inside our office, or to be more precise, which I ever love to be, inside our store room, being entertained by the sound of sawing, planing, sanding and drilling machines. Together with the rhythmic tapping of hammers on nails, all this combines to form a unique masterpiece at the eleventh hour of the year. The prevailing atmosphere has nothing to do with my writing to you. I appreciate that distance makes communication difficult – my voice doesn't reach that far – but I really hope that we don't lose touch. Everybody here asks about you and sends greetings.

Anyway, allow me to deliver my news. I am presently indentured to a cyclops by name Rahman, whose cave this Wood Works is. (There is no Sindbad or Odysseus to rescue any of us! Do you remember those myths and stories you were always so fond of?) I guess you will be surprised to hear that I am concubined to his daughter. You know how these things are done. She promises me love once the knot is tied and I have sworn undying devotion. Lucky me!

You may also be surprised to hear that today I'm celebrating my first *Go West Young Man* anniversary. It's only twenty miles west as you know, but how big that distance really is! We all have to keep reviving these moments, especially the pilgrims among us, lest we discover one day that they have overcome us. As Verlaine has said: *Si ces hiers allaient manger nos beaux demains?* Exactly a year ago today, on a Sunday afternoon that was hot and dry as December always is, myself along with some other freedom-lovers were preparing to act and follow that great genius, Master and Generator of Electricity, the organiser and pilot of our expedition, Captain-General Jabir Ahmed. (I am sure you have a vivid memory of the fantastic performance of *Hamlet* he delivered in the back seat of his father's Austin 1100.) I discovered the identity of the mastermind too late to retreat, just as the sail was being hoisted in fact. But before we could wave fond goodbye to our homeland, for ever verdant and green, we were tackled by a wandering militia, those guardians of our state. It needed a hefty bribe to fix him, the good *varantia*. We had a hazardous journey, during which it became clear that our Hamlet did not know southerly from a hand-saw. Miraculously, we landed on a beach which was only eighty miles from our destination, which was Tanga. It could have been back on the Island of Paradise for all our captain knew. Once we landed the journey was smooth and easy, disturbed only by the Captain-General, who felt it necessary to discourse at length on the unpredictability of the sea. Water's funny stuff, he kept saying. Suffice it to say that we arrived here bored but in one piece. So much for the forced adventure.

What has been happening to you over the last year? Nobody seems to know anything about you. Are you still alive? Your last letter contained one line. It was a lovely line about a water-mill, I think, but it would be nice to have some news, blaza. Or have you simply forgotten us? Anyway, do write and tell me how you're doing, buddy. Are you still studying? I want to hear about all those females who are keeping you busy. Send me a snapshot if you can.

I've been continuing with my studies in evening classes. It's hard work, going from the mill to college most evenings. As you might guess, I'm not doing very well. You don't know how lucky you are over there. Still, nothing ventured and all that, so I am doing what I can over here. I've become very interested in the poetry of the French Symbolists, but as you know it's not easy to get books here. If you see anything along those lines could you send it to me, *ahsante sana*. Refund by pigeon-post.

I miss the conversations we used to have. People just want to gossip about politics here, at the level of who has been caught fiddling government funds and who's been locked up. That is what passes for serious discussion. It is like an obsession, whenever people meet they talk about some new pettiness as if it is the greatest outrage since the destruction of Kilwa.

A lot of the pals from home are here now. Hassan was caught trying to escape with some Goan girls in a *ngarawa*. He said he was taking them fishing. I don't know how he does it (the Goan girls, I mean). Nothing happened to the Goan girls ... that we know of anyway. Hassan found another way of escaping as soon as they released him from prison. He won't say how he did it. Dan is now a rising star in the Gestapo Chekurity. Some people say he was already on the payroll when we were at school. Subash has gone to a university in Boston to do Intentional Chemistry. Don't ask me, that's what his brother said. I met his brother recently here and he told me that our Subash is paid plenty Yankee dollar by the American government. I can't imagine him studying chemistry. He always so much wanted to be a barrister.

Anyway, I'm thinking of applying to Uncle Sam to study nuclear medicine, ha ha.

Did you have a nice Christmas? We celebrate it here now. It was very quiet except Bachu got drunk and started to call our island leader 'ham-neck'. He always used to make up names for people, didn't he? Incidentally, do you remember Amina, Marehemu Rashid's sister? She must have been about twelve when you left. She's now a prostitute. No more room. Write soon and don't forget the snap.

Regards from all the pals.

Yours,

Karim

He put the letter down on the table, his mind racing with Karim's news. It was the thought of Rashid that came first, and the term of respect that Karim had put in front of his name. *Marehemu*. He saw that and felt pain like betrayal at Rashid's name, even before he took in the horror of Amina's fate. He felt as if he had neglected him too, had neglected to mourn his memory and keep its grief fresh in his mind. God's mercy be on you, Rashid. He had never seen his name written with the word of death before it. *Marehemu Bossy*. He tried out the word with the joke name he had used for his friend. It seemed ostentatious, a term he had heard used only with the eminent dead. Not Bossy. *Dear Marehemu, One of our friends from the past has written with all the news from our dear homeland. He tells me your sister is a prostitute … because you were not there to care for her*. He wondered if Bossy's mother still lived, and what privations could have driven them to such an end? Could the neighbours not have helped them out? He tried not to hear the sniggers and laughter of children in the streets as she walked past. *We would have done the same. We would have watched while a neighbour turned beggar and sold his daughter for shark-meat. And we too would have laughed and mocked, and pointed taunting fingers at the girl. Our elders would have quoted the relevant lines from the Book to confirm the righteousness of our cruelty. The elders! All they taught us was how to be meek and docile, how to be obedient and to fetch and carry, and how to show respect. All we learnt was how to ride roughshod over other people's pain. She appears as a footnote, and not a tear shed for her, at the end of a gleeful tallysheet of our past misdeeds. I think of the time there was, and how we ended it all with a careless selfishness. He calls you Marehemu, God's mercy on you. You missed the worst, my Bossy. You missed the worst. Terrible, shameful things have happened to us.*

He folded the letter and pushed it away from him, then sat at the table for a long time, feeling the memory of Rashid warming in his hands like a chilled animal stirring out of stupor. It was not at all that he had forgotten him, but when he thought of him usually it was with fear. Over the years he had learnt to hide from the memory of the love that he felt for Rashid. When England was too cold and hostile, and when loneliness overcame him, he still wept for him, still missed him. But he had thought of him too much, and had wept for him with such grief that in the end he had learnt not to think of him. The thought of Bossy now made him remember how he had given way, as if by his weakness he had betrayed something of their time together.

A long time ago that was, sitting on the barnacled pier, swinging our legs through the air. Princess Margaret Pier in the long shadow of the afternoon, watching the sea beneath us frothing with arms and legs and flashing teeth. A long story I told him, a narrative that was urbane and wise, a fabric of lies, and watched his suspicion turn to enchantment. I told him of a man who stood by the sea, oblivious to pain, awaiting the rains that the season had forecast, and how he peed and his pee was continuous without end. And to see him laugh then was like watching a bird take to the air, like watching a horse cantering down the green hillside. On Princess Margaret Pier I fed him lies that rose easily to the tongue and were too unlikely to be mistaken for wisdom. We watched Ferej eat up the water like a shark, Ferej whose bandy legs made life a torment for him. The water was choppy and bright on the day he won the Schools Championship. Princess Margaret Pier, named after a day in 1956 when the good Princess laid foot on our humble land and honoured it for all time with her gracious touch. We waved flags of welcome at her. We fought over the little flags, and I was forced to wave a Union Jack when others had the red flag of our Protected Sultan. On the other side of the pier were four guns, riveted into the concrete and facing the sea. Ceremonial firecrackers to bid the Princess welcome. The guns boomed their welcome, we waved our flags and the Royal Barge was met by the Plumed Resident. The guns had other uses later.

He rose to go and wash when he felt the beginnings of the morning in December when he lost Rashid. He did not want to think about that day, not again. Even as he fought off the memory he knew it would come … but perhaps not yet.

He was late for work, and arrived smiling tensely, ready for a fight. On the way he had passed Catherine's flat, and had wished he could call to see her, to tell her about Bossy, to rant and blubber about his misery. He wanted to throw himself on her and wallow in the loss of his people and his home, and have her comfort and love him. But he knew she would be at work. He rehearsed instead what he would say to Solomon should he reprimand him for being late.

He strolled into the general theatre, casting poisoned glances at Sister Wesley, *the old hag*. She looked up at him and then at the clock, and ignored him for the rest of the afternoon. A small group of nurses was standing round the surgeon, listening to him explain what he would be doing. When the afternoon's business was in full swing, Daud was sent word that Solomon wanted to see him. He grinned what he hoped was a wolfish grin and left the theatre without waiting for Sister Wesley's permission, thinking even as he did so how petty and irrelevant all this was. He went to the changing room first, stopping and wondering whether it would be best for him to change and leave. His miseries and guilts were none of Solomon's fault, none of his business.

In the end he went in to see him, relishing the prospect of delivering his rehearsed thank-you note to the Ineffable Solomon. The Superintendent twitched his face in his peculiar smile and invited Daud to sit. *Dear Papa Sol*, he began. *Thank you for the last million years of torture, and more besides. They have worked wonders on my character. I just wanted you to know that without the stability and support that you were able to provide me in this sanctuary where the only quality that counts is a battered body, I would've turned out all wrong. It's not your fault but what's that to me.* Daud looked at Solomon's leathery face with disgust, and watched as the Theatre Superintendent took his spectacles off and started to clean them. His eyes were red and swollen, popping out of his face. He looked tired and unhappy, and twitched at Daud again before he put his spectacles back on.

Daud was tense with anger, waiting for Solomon to complain about his lateness, willing him to be crass and overbearing so he could run amok on him. He wanted to tip the desk over the skinny old fuck, rip the work rotas off the walls, tear the Beecham calendar into shreds and stuff them up Solomon's arse. 'Is all well?' Daud asked in the end, unable to ignore the misery in the man's face. 'You look a bit knackered.'

'One of the boys isn't well,' Solomon said, twitching his face again, this time with a kind of gratitude. 'I didn't get much sleep last night. Nor did he, Colin, poor lad. I'll have to go early and I wanted to speak to you before I went.'

Daud was surprised by Solomon's sadness. He thought of him as an archetypal whingeing survivor, the kind who if he was a shopkeeper would have false bottoms to his measures, or if he worked in a hospital would steal rubber tubing and plastic canisters for his wine-making. Since the night he had mentioned his two boys, he had taken to bringing them up in conversation, opening up to Daud in an unexpected way. *Dear Theatre Bully, What does it matter to me? I've got my own problems.*

'I hear that you'll be leaving us,' Solomon said, looking at Daud and waiting for a response. Daud could not restrain a smile. 'It was always obvious that you would. I mean you were patently too intelligent for the job. Frankly, I'm surprised you've stuck it out this long.'

Daud twitched his face in a parody of Solomon's smirk.

'Was it theology you were studying?' Solomon asked. Daud did not answer. He shrugged his shoulders, discouraging Solomon's interest, and watching the dart of surprise on Solomon's face with satisfaction. Get on with it, you old fuck, he thought. He wondered that Solomon should think that a few kind words now would make him melt. After three years of hurling him out into the dirty corridor to wash instruments, and inflicting endless and unavoidable little snicks and cuts on him.

'We'll be sorry to lose you,' Solomon went on, speaking with some disappointment but, Daud guessed, with an inkling of his real feelings. 'Your contribution has been invaluable, and I know the other senior members of staff agree with me. I just wanted to tell you ... show our appreciation and wish you luck. I hope things work out better this time.'

Solomon nodded to emphasise what he had said. Daud laughed softly, making no effort to disguise his mockery, wanting to explain that he did not give a toss, to coin a phrase, for Solomon's appreciation and would rather have his habitual antagonism. *Dear Superintendent, Too little too late, and you can keep it. Your kindness is to warm the cockles of your own wounded heart and nothing to do with me. True, kindness is kindness and gives dignity to our existence, but I know you. Twitch your lips today and some coon joke tomorrow. You've got the wrong coon!*

'Sister Wesley's got too many people in her theatre,' Solomon said after a moment. 'I'd like you to go out into the disposal corridor for the rest of the afternoon, and then clean the theatres at the end of the list and re-stock the anaesthetic rooms if you have time.'

He nodded again and then twitched his lips, dismissing him. Daud glared at him, wishing he had the nerve to make a scene, throw a tantrum and curse the whole poxy establishment to buggery and back. He spent the rest of the afternoon smouldering in the dirty corridor, thinking he would call on Catherine on the way home. He did his best to hide from Karim's letter and the memory of that December day, but once the day staff had gone, he was left on his own with three dirty theatres to clean.

It was a beautiful morning in December, bone-dry and hot. The excitement of the first few weeks of the school holidays had gone, and they were feeling the burden of all that time and freedom hanging on their hands. They had wandered in the museums, gone for long walks on the beach, played endless games of football and cards, stayed up into the early hours of the morning, gone for picnics and cycling trips. They were bored. That morning they were sitting on the sea wall behind the dried-fish warehouses, *Forodha ya Papa*, watching the fishermen clean their boats and the Chinaman on the other side of the creek hanging strips of shark-fin on a line in the backyard of his shop. Little boys were playing between the pillars of the Harbour Police boathouse, as they had done when they were younger. Rashid suggested they borrow a boat and go sailing. He went one way, Daud went the other. He got a boat, Daud didn't. It was always the same. Rashid could not help taking command. He was so suited to it, but he was still sensitive to the name Daud had given him. They treated it as a joke but Daud knew that he tried hard to make sure that the name Bossy was not justified. They talked of friends they could recruit for the trip, but the decision was taken out of their hands. Daud laughed as he remembered Yunis appearing on the sea wall, and how he and Rashid had clambered into the outrigger and cast off, afraid that they might be forced to take him with them. Yunis was nicknamed Wire, because it was obvious that he had some wires disconnected in his head.

Dear Catherine, I wish you were with me so I could sob in your arms, and feel the warmth of your body making the pain softer. I wish you were with me so I could tell you how hard it has been to live another life like this. I could tell you about Wire and how guilty I felt as I watched him standing on Ras Matengo looking our way and smiling in his vague fashion. He was used to people running away from him. You could see he was born mad, and that in his old age he would wander the streets with a beard as long as your arm and eyes that lit up in the dark. Yet we had been friends at one time. I'd been very ill with something, one of those near-fatal bouts that we call fever, and could be anything from a mild flu to cholera, and was taking a long time to recover. By the time I was well, I had lost track of all my friends. They were all doing other things. So Wire and I came to spend a lot of time together. He was going to build a ship and sail it himself. The people at the Shipping Control Office knew him and called him Captain to please him. He could only talk about ships and about India. If you talked to him about anything else his eyes went blank and he stopped listening. Everybody bullied him because they knew he was mad. I saw a little boy of six urinate in his mouth once while he lay asleep under the shade of a tree. Wire stood up and left without saying a word and with a vague smile on his face. The adults watching laughed and patted the boy on the back, predicting that he would be a real man when he grew up. Wire was so helpless, so terrified, that he lathered at the mouth with fear when he had to walk past a group of jeering youths. But under the line of trees by the dockside very few people bothered us. I boasted to him about how well I was doing at school while he listened contentedly, blasting off lentil farts now and again. He lied to me about his father's estates in India.

The estates were important. They were the reason for the ship-building, for the family could not afford the passage back home. Wire had a huge store of incredible stories which he always ascribed to some Indian sage. Did you know that if a man stood by the sea and peed, and did not lose his nerve, that he could pee for ever? Indian sages have proved this. Did you know that a man's soul lived in his throat? That was why to kill a man's soul you had to thròttle him. He had read this in a religious book. His grandfather had kept elephants in India and had once caught his elephant keeper trying to have sex with a bull. Did you know that the old Aga Khan used to have his shit weighed every day, to see how much weight he had lost in the night? He loved talking, most of all about his father's estates in India.

Yes, I know he was mad, my darling. So what was I doing messing around with a nut like that? That was what my parents wanted to know. His father was mad too, if anything he was even more mad. He was supposed to be a shopkeeper but all he ever had in his shop were boxes of rusty nails and showcases with old fishing-hooks and twine. If anybody stopped to shoot the breeze with him or give him a good morning, he asked him for money. He went to the mosque every day, and after the prayers he asked people for money. Whenever a customer appeared at his shop, the barber opposite him, another Indian, would shout out a warning: Watch your pocket, watch your pocket. He's going to ask you for money. Why don't you go back to India, you filthy Bombay scum? Why you come and spoil everything for us? *And everybody laughed, winking at each other behind the barber's back while one Mhindi abused another in the language that they used to abuse both of them.* Bombay scum, shit-scraper, lentil-eater, are ma, curry-eating bloodsucker. *Nothing seemed to touch the old man. He went to the Welfare Office and filled in countless forms and got nothing for it. He laughed and chatted with the clerks, and took no notice when they told him to go back to India. He walked with his fixed smile through abuse and blows, and asked all and sundry for money. He was mad, but with a kind of courage and persistence too. I saw a man in the streets here once just like that, an old man with a carefully trimmed beard and a grimy Salvation Army cap. In one hand he carried a deep, leather hold-all with a bunch of flowers sitting on top. He was only a small man, a little bent, but as he walked he twirled a cane high over his shoulder and the pavements cleared in front of him. On his thin wasted face was a look of stubborn determination. That was how Wire's father looked, thin and small, with a sunken jaw that had no teeth left, but with a blankness in his face that mere words and blows would never be able to reach. In his own way, Wire had something of that look already, so that despite his leathery and flabby appearance, as if he was something that lived under the ground, he had a doggedness that persuaded his tormentors to leave him alone in the end. And you know how he will end up – disappointed and alone, and very crazy.*

I did not think all this as I watched him standing at the water's edge on Ras Matengo. This comes back to me now. I begin to understand a little how crazy the man must have felt in that place. Go back to India, you shit-scraper! And India, profligate enough with its talented sons, let alone its damaged ones, wanted him as little as that place did. Shipwrecked on the island he tried to beg for a return passage, while his son planned to build a ship in which they would all sail away home. In their separate madness, they both wandered the streets, naked and abandoned among strangers.

Rashid laughed at Wire. He was ashamed of Daud's friendship with the idiot boy. He mimicked Wire's mad mannerisms from the boat, and ignored the look of disapproval that Daud gave him. Rashid peeled his shirt off and leant back, stretching in preparation for work. The sun was beating down on his bare chest, shining in his eyes. Bossy was in his element. He lived almost on the water-line, and had gone sailing with his father and the other fishermen from about the time he could walk. Daud knew nothing about boats, and could only be trusted to carry out instructions, a state of affairs which Rashid exploited for as many laughs as he could.

It hurts to talk about you like this, as if what has happened has not happened. I can see you stretching like that in the sun, with the light in your eyes. To the island and back before dinner, you said. I could not understand why you would want me to be your friend. While Rashid was winning prizes in his first year at Sharif College, and being spoken of by the teachers as a future head-boy, Daud was being clouted by the same teachers for not paying attention. Rashid was a champion swimmer, a national record-holder over 440 yards. He was an aggressive and skilful footballer, and a very useful slow left-arm bowler. He was fair-skinned and handsome, and wore a wristwatch with a silver strap. It was given to him by the English Club for taking seven of their wickets for 23 runs. Daud could not understand why such a paragon would want to befriend him.

Sister Wesley had been watching him for some time, peering in through the smoked-glass window in the theatre door. She came in so suddenly that Daud did not have time to rise from the anaesthetist's chair he was occupying, or to lift his chin from the end of the mop on which it was resting. For a moment he panicked, unsure where he was. And even when memory came surging back, the half-cleaned theatre seemed different, brighter and larger than before. The Sister stood just inside the theatre door, watching Daud with dislike. She was a tall woman with short black hair cut in a fringe. She had struck Daud as very dark when he first met her, reminded him a little of the look of some of the women at home, although her complexion and colour were obviously European. She disliked him from the second she clapped eyes on him, lashed him with as much sarcasm as she could decently manage without getting embroiled in a squabble with an orderly. In return, Daud became quietly unco-operative when he was made to work under her. He took a small revenge by starting a rumour that there was a touch of the tar-brush somewhere. He had told Staff Nurse Chattan that Wesley's ma was a Bengali ayah who had married into the family of her employers. He had been gratified to find that a version of the story was very quickly in circulation.

'Having a rest?' she asked him, drawing her words out in a superior accent. 'Well, when you've finished cleaning the theatre, you can go. The chores that remain to be done are a little beyond your qualifications, I think.'

'Yessum,' he said, rising slowly to his feet.

'You can go,' she repeated more loudly, as if taking no chances about being misunderstood. 'You might as well! We'll do our best to manage without your expert assistance.'

'Yessum!' he burst out, shuffling his feet and dropping his eyes. He considered throwing in a cringe as well but feared she might mistake his attitude. 'I go now now, missus!'

'I've told you before, I'm not your missus,' she flared, and left.

'You should be so lucky, you ugly arsehole,' he called after her. She disliked him so much that she would give him two hours off his shift? He ran round the theatre with the damp mop, thinking that it would still be early enough to persuade Catherine to come out for a drink.

13

Catherine lived in a double-fronted house, with a path down the middle of a garden that was filled with rose bushes in resplendent bloom. Two steps led up to the huge front door, which was recessed into the porch. He knew she shared a downstairs flat, and glanced towards the open sash window from which came the sound of a flute. The music did not even stutter when he rang the bell, and he assumed that she lived in the flat with the curtains drawn across the windows.

The woman who opened the door looked at him with interest but did not invite him in. She was tall and a little gangling, with sharp features and flushed, flaring nostrils. There were sharp creases in her uniform, and he guessed she was getting ready for night-duty. Her looseness of limbs and posture softened her appearance, made her seem disarranged and homely, rather than as sour as her etched features suggested. Her little movements had a kind of lasciviousness that seemed unconscious, and as she stood by the door she was not unwelcoming. Yet he was intimidated, fumbling with his words. Her eyes spoke of years of cynicism and boredom. She must have only just got up, he told himself. That was why her eyes were heavy and watery.

'Cathy's not in,' she said.

'Where has she gone?' he asked, distressed by the news, and scotching the memories that had begun to stir to life in his mind. He realised that he had been getting his story ready for her. Uncovering his wounds for her like a beggar.

The woman did not answer immediately but a smile appeared at the corners of her mouth. 'Did she know you were coming?' she asked, frank amusement in her eyes. 'She's gone out with her boyfriend.'

'To the jazz club,' he said at once, without thought, feeling the bottom of his life drop out.

'That's right,' the woman said, looking pleased that he knew about that. 'You've only just missed them. You can catch them up in no time, if you haven't parked too far away.'

'That's right.' He grinned at her and took a step back.

'Shall I tell her you came?' she asked, glancing down the street to see where he had parked his car.

He shrugged as he walked backwards, inviting her to do as she liked. He smote his brow, parodying his anguish. The woman laughed, and Daud grinned as if he had intended the joke for her. She leant forward, waiting to see what he would do next. When he waved from the bottom of the path, she shrugged her shoulders with disappointment, reluctant to see him go.

'Hey, what's your name?' she called out but he just waved without answering. 'I'm Paula,' she shouted to him as he hurried away.

Dear Catherine, It doesn't matter. I guessed all along anyway, and it doesn't surprise me that a damsel as fair as you should have a crop of rich bloods, dashing you about all over the place. They are your own kind of people. To tell the truth, I didn't really know. I wondered, though … I called for you tonight to tell you about a friend. I called him Bossy. It doesn't matter very much any more. One morning in December, when we were both seventeen, I lost him. Today a letter came to bring him back to life. No, I had not forgotten him, but I have learnt to live with his death, his non-existence. To think of him as an accident, a contingent that another contingent overtook. He knew now what he had intended, to hurl himself into her loving arms and sob his tragic history to her. Then she would have gasped at the insupportable misery of his life, and marvelled at the fortitude that held such virulent poison in check. This placid, contented bozo that you see strolling these quiet streets, he would have declared, has seen the glint of the sacrificial blade in its swift rush for his delicate throat. To look on the resolution in his eyes and the unfurrowed calm of his brow, you would hardly guess his torment.

It surprised him that he could keep the pain of her absence separate from the memory of Bossy. He would have expected it all to overflow the same cup, merge into the same noxious brew that would poison and unnerve him. *Dear Bossy, She is the best thing that's happened to me here. I can feel it. I don't think she can, though. How do you mean I should do something about it? This character who's taken her out probably wears jackets and owns things like farms and cars and riding ponies. I don't know what she was doing with me. It was always going to be this way in the end, that she would go back to the comfortable ways she knows. Can you blame her? My house smells and my body reeks of lassitude and self-pity. Do you think I can hide things like that? What do you care about such things? That heartless land has already turned you into dust.*

When he got home he slid into a chair, stretched his legs out before him and shut his eyes. The low hum of the grain factory was mixed with the sound of fast-flowing water running through the sluices of the disused mill nearby. He had not been home long when Karta turned up, hammering on the door as if to wake the dead. Karta's eyes appeared at the letter box like twin glimmers in a tunnel. 'Put your trousers on and let me in, bro,' he called out.

Daud let him in then went upstairs and lay on the bed. He resisted the temptation to read Karim's letter again. He felt no urge to talk to Karta about the letter, or about Bossy. They knew each other without those complicated histories, without alienating details of cruelties and persecutions. After a while he rose and went down. Karta was lounging in a chair, one leg thrown elegantly over the arm. He was toying with a packet of cigarettes, staring at it as if engaged in an inner gazing that preoccupied his sight. Daud saw that he was annoyed, and felt he could understand that Karta should resent the lack of welcome, and the exclusion from his concerns. Suddenly Karta flicked the cigarette packet in a wide arc and watched it land on the table. He smiled with triumph and turned to glance at Daud.

'Where is she? Where is the creature I found you with the other day?' Karta asked. 'There's one question I've been meaning to ask you, you know. How did you manage to lure that creature in here? I mean no offence, bro, but what's a clean-cut bourgeois chick like that doing in your hovel?' He spoke languidly, as if bored and irritated by the question before it had even passed his lips. He stirred in the chair and turned to look at Daud, who did not smile as Karta had expected him to. Karta grinned and raised his arms in mock surrender. 'All right, where is she?'

'At the jazz club,' Daud said, walking to the cupboard for a tin of soup.

'You look ill,' Karta said after a silence. 'Your face is haggard and woe-begone, and you look fucked and knackered, if I may so observe. I presume she's going with somebody else?'

'Yes,' Daud said reluctantly. As he reached into the cupboard he saw that the arm of his jumper was shiny with sweat and grease. It seemed suddenly an emblem of the squalor of his silly life. He pulled the jumper off and tossed it into the brown armchair. He watched with amused interest as Karta shuddered.

'Don't get yourself worked up over nothing,' Karta said casually, making a matter-of-fact observation. 'A woman is always two-faced. You can't trust one bitch of them. Especially these clean-cut English ones. There's only one thing they want from a black man.'

Daud's ears were humming. His leg was throbbing with an inflamed vein. He had gone to the doctor with that bad leg, and had dutifully listened to a lecture about the danger of a thrombosis. The doctor had explained how he was to rest his leg, and Daud had nodded. *I'll let the servants do all the work*, he said. What difference did it make? Maybe one day soon they'd find him dead with an enormous clot stuck fast in his bicuspid valve.

'Is that what you're looking miserable about? Don't let me down, bro! You look long in the tooth like that for one of them two-faced bitches? She looked too neat and uptight for you anyway,' Karta said. 'Let me tell you something, bush-boy, and you listen carefully and drink deep from the fount of wisdom. However much a woman sweet-talks you or gives you the big eye, you remember one thing. Don't trust her an inch. My ma told me that when I was so high, and I haven't found reason to doubt her word on that yet. I've come close, teetered on the brink, but then the words of my ma came flying to my rescue. A woman's a two-faced nothing, remember that, son. You better make that your catechism too. Because when that sweet-talking's done, and the big eye's had its fill, she'll leave you just like that. She'll go find herself another mug like you.'

Daud went into the kitchen, hoping that Karta would switch the TV on, but Karta followed him. He stood at the door watching Daud warm his soup.

'Especially English ones,' Karta said after a moment, speaking with bitterness. 'Let me warn you, young man, they are snakes.'

'What are you talking about? It's this kind of stuff that makes you sound like your mind's full of shit,' Daud said with sudden anger. 'What do you mean two-faced? Who do you think you are, the dude from the Chicago ghetto? The greasy chief of Bongoland quoting the wisdom of Naanam?'

'What!' Karta said, reeling a little from this unexpected assault. 'What are you saying?'

'I'm saying it sounds bad when you talk about women as if they were snakes and lizards. It makes you sound ignorant. Like the baboon laughing at the other baboons' red arses, not realising that his own's a whopper.'

Karta stepped aside to let Daud walk past with his saucepan of soup. 'All right,' he said. 'Keep your pants on. You'll remember what I said one day and you'll say to yourself Uncle Karta was right after all. And you shouldn't make these kinds of racial slurs. What's the Chicago ghetto remark meant to mean?'

Daud sipped his soup from the pan, glancing up to watch Karta from under lowered eyebrows. 'Aren't you going to put that soup in a bowl?' Karta asked, swallowing as he watched Daud's spoon travel from pan to mouth.

'You didn't mind the greasy chief of Bongoland?' Daud asked.

'Not so much,' Karta said, speaking haughtily. 'Bongoland is near the Futa Djallon, just down the road from Freetown. I don't understand about Chicago, though.'

'Because you were talking like a zoot-suited pimp from the ghetto.'

'I mind that,' Karta said and sucked his teeth. 'Anyway, I wasn't talking about women, I was talking about English women. Let me tell you something, that's a completely different matter.'

'What do you know about English women?' Daud asked, relishing his soup all the more because he knew he would offer Karta some.

'More than you think, boy,' Karta said, wagging a finger. He took the pan without protest, without thanks, and drained it. '*They* are snakes. You wouldn't argue with that, would you? Look what's happened to you! When I came round here the other day you were all lovey-dovey, so bad that I felt I'd better get out of the way. This is romance, I said to myself. Now look at you! Bundled out and dumped for some smart guy with a sports car.'

'Never mind what's happened to me,' Daud said, ignoring the sports car. 'What do you know about English women?' Karta sat down at the table, and after a moment dropped his eyes and laughed. Daud was alert now. He had sensed that something was wrong with Karta.

'I know about English women because I fuck one of my tutors. Four weeks ago it started. It's disgusting,' he said, his voice as small as his wounded ego.

Daud waited for him to continue. 'Is that it?' he asked, smiling to see his friend's revolted face. 'Where's the tragedy? It's been known to happen before.'

'Not to me! I like to respect my teachers. She'd been making signals a long time but I ignored her. Funny thing is that sometimes I thought she disliked me. She makes cold, unfriendly remarks ... the way they do when they think you can't answer back. A few weeks ago I asked her for some advice, about the exams. I suppose I was being a good boy, trying to flatter her. She knew. But I thought it wouldn't matter, she'd still be flattered. It's not that you think about these things, you just do them. She invited me to her house. Sunday morning, eleven o'clock. She smiled like that ... I mean she knew what she was doing. I just never thought.'

'You should be so lucky! So? Why do you ... feel bad?' Daud asked.

'She cuts her hair short, and she's old. She just started talking and playing music, and making lunch. And she knew what she was doing. I could see the smile in her eyes.'

'You must have wanted her too, otherwise you'd just have said no and walked out.'

'I had no choice,' Karta cried.

'She tied your legs to the chair and then leapt on you, did she?' Daud asked. 'And you screamed and screamed but nobody heard you.'

'The exams! She could've failed me.'

'Uh-huh,' Daud nodded, unconvinced. 'Anyway, I still don't see the tragedy. You slept with her, so what? Did she steal your brains while you were sleeping?'

'She's ugly! She's ugly and old, my bro. It's disgusting,' Karta said, a look of deep revulsion on his face. Daud watched with astonishment as Karta tried to bring himself under control. Ugly people, he had heard Karta claim, made him physically sick. Sometimes they had been forced to leave a pub because he had seen someone who made him feel ill. Daud had never quite believed this aversion to be real, taking it for another Karta affectation. Then one day they had travelled up to London, to go to Regent's Park Zoo. Karta had been amused and excited by the animals, until they reached the apes. He had stopped laughing and insisted that they leave at once, saying he could not stand how ugly they looked. 'And it's still going on,' Karta said, bringing himself under control. 'She won't stop.'

'Can't you stop?' Daud asked.

'I guess I'm bored. I've got nothing to do now the exams are over.'

'Don't you like being with her at all?' Karta had made such a virtue of his rejection of English women, *the fat scrubbers*, that Daud could understand his resistance to feeling anything for one of them now.

'She lives with somebody, you know. I tell her she must stop but she won't listen. She rings me when he's not there and I go round. I can't help it, I'm a man. I like women but this makes me sick. When she sees me, when I turn up at her door, she smiles with this kind of look. Like a snake. Afterwards ... when we've finished, I think to myself what am I doing here? I don't think the black man was meant to have anything to do with these white women.'

'It hasn't bothered you before. What can they do to you? Crush your gonads? They have poison ducts in their cheeks so when they kiss you they steal your will power and turn you into a furry teddy?'

Karta laughed and slapped his friend's thigh. 'Cut out the crap, bro. You know what really makes me angry? That I'm so nearly ready to leave, and I go and become involved in this. Three more weeks and then I'm gone. Back to the land of the living. You can laugh as much as you like but I don't know how to deal with this woman. I don't trust her. She's just using me.'

'So leave her!'

'There's no point now,' Karta said. 'Just a few more weeks and then I'll be gone. It's just that I can't stand being used like this.'

Daud waited to see if Karta would hear the self-indictment in his own words and then rose to make some tea. In the kitchen, he chuckled to himself at the thought of Karta getting a bit of his own medicine.

'Do you know?' Karta said, following him to the kitchen. 'The first time I slept with her … she was dry. That's never happened to me before.'

'Dry?' Daud said, feeling the beginnings of distaste for the conversation.

'Dry as a bone,' Karta replied, nodding to confirm the incredible. 'I've never had that before. It's English women, isn't it? They're cold inside. She's all right now that I've lubricated her with the natural oils of a black man. Made her feed on the green plasma of the living world. But that's the way it always has to be.' Karta saw the incredulous look on Daud's face and grinned. 'That's why I'm saying that a black man was not meant to have anything to do with these white women. It's not natural. We give them vitality and strength. They give us nothing. They take their pleasure and give us nothing. They just use us. I mean, look at you. Look what happened to you.'

They drank tea in front of the television. After a short while, Daud began to feel pangs of hunger but was deterred from setting any food out for fear of Karta's bottomless maw. There was not much left and it had to last another four days. When his stomach started to grumble for more food, he rose to go to bed. In any case, he was feeling inexplicably tired. 'You carry on watching if you want,' he told Karta. 'Just remember to switch it off before you go.'

Karta looked up from the TV and blew Daud a kiss.

14

Look at me, he said to himself after searching in vain for Catherine in the dining room. The room had been full of clamouring harpies, all secretly pining for his natural oils, but there had been no sign of his chosen incubus. He wondered if he should call on her again on his way home, but he doubted if it would be the right thing to do. She had, after all, been out with her *boyfriend*. If she was bothered she would have sent him word when she found out he had been round. He could be forgiving and magnanimous when called upon, just let her try him. For the moment he would thank God for small mercies and bide his time.

The ward she was working in was near the dining room, and he considered calling in to make his presence felt. *Hello there, Cath, everything cool in here?* Who was he to play the wounded knight? What good would it do him anyway? He did not want her to escape his clutches on such a feeble excuse as his shattered ego. What a nonsense! He would call and see her, or ring her from theatres. When all was mended, she would lean fondly towards him and comfort him. They would laugh at the stupid misunderstandings that had almost come between them, and he would promise never to let his house get dirty again. Who was this boy-friend? What did he know? Daud wanted to make her laugh, talk to her and have her listen to him while he told her about the places he had left behind. He needed her beside him while they walked the lanes as those old pilgrims had done, sure of salvation. But in the end he came back to the thought that if she was bothered about dissuading him from anxiety she would have sent him word.

Look at me, he told himself. *I should be plotting, intriguing, laying traps to ensnare the boyfriend into error so I could sneak in and steal the picnic basket. I could send him a brochure about a holiday in Tunisia. Who could resist that? Then while he's there he could catch a tummy bug and perish painfully when he returned to his country estate.*

He passed a woman in the long tunnel to the new wing. She was wearing ordinary clothes, and although he glanced at her, he passed her by without recognising her at once. It was the eyes that he remembered first, heavy and a little puffy, as if short of sleep. There was something peculiar about the mouth too, as if she was sucking a large sweet.

'Paula!' he cried, turning on his heel.

She seemed pleased to see him. 'You remember my name!' she said. 'I thought you didn't recognise me. So you work here. I knew I'd seen you somewhere when you came round the other day.'

'You look different,' he said, grinning for all he was worth.

'I should think so.' She coloured a little and gave him a slight smile. 'I think those Sisters' uniforms are positively dreadful.'

'I couldn't agree more, although I thought you carried yours off pretty well when I saw you the other night. How's Catherine?' he put in quickly, before she wanted to know where he worked, or where his car was parked. Or what he was doing tonight. He assumed from her flirtatious smile that she took him for something honourable, a physiotherapist at least, or a doctor. Some doctors walked around in rags. Daud had seen them.

'Catherine? I haven't seen her for a couple of days. You know, I'm on night-duty this week and she's on late duty most of the week. She's nice, isn't she?'

'Have you seen her since I called round for her?' Daud asked, suddenly twitching with an excess of hope. *Answer me, you dopy cow! Speak, in the name of your God who is Great!* But he restrained himself from grabbing the lapels of her jacket and shaking her.

'No,' she said, her mouth dropping slightly at first but then opening into a knowing smile.

'So she doesn't know I came?' he asked.

She frowned. 'I asked you if you wanted me to tell her,' she said.

'Could you tell her now?' he said, grinning triumphantly.

'All right,' she said, looking amused as she understood something of the situation. 'You'd better tell me your name this time.'

It came to him later in the afternoon, when he had calmed himself down, that Catherine's ignorance of his visit need not mean anything. She probably would still prefer the boyfriend's blue sports car to his smelly slum. He would give her a day or two, and if he had not heard, he would call on her and work some juju. At the sight of his strength and vitality, which she secretly relished, all her resistance would crumble.

When he got home, he strolled round his grubby rooms to see if there was anything he could do to improve their appearance, something swift and fundamental that would brighten his existence. How could she resist such wholesale conversion? He wrote ideas down on a piece of paper, but they seemed feeble whichever way he looked at them.

Finally he settled for a less ambitious transformation and sat down at the table to work out the colours he would re-paint the walls. His heart leapt up at the knock on the door, but he knew it could not be her. And when he heard the letter box being rattled he knew it could only be Karta. He wondered what he had ever liked about him.

'What's on television?' Karta asked as he settled himself down.

He could picture Karta in a few years' time, he thought. A *technocrat* in his government, running his department with style. He would buy pages of advertising for his government in international newspapers, and invite the world's tourists to come and rejoice and revel in the new *village* a dozen miles down the coast from the squalor of the city. Built for the OAU ministerial conference, it can now be turned to beach-huts and chalets, to swell the wallets of the government's loot-hungry owners. And in the meantime he could see him haranguing an indifferent world with mind-boggling rhetorical hypocrisies while the people waited in vain for the sacks of aid rice to reach them.

As he watched him, surprised by his own bitterness but feeling no remorse, Daud saw Karta cock a leg over the chair and lean back, pouting with irritation and bad temper. 'You'd better warn this pink-skinned geriatric neighbour of yours not to stare at me whenever I come round here. I'm serious … that decrepit old cripple next door. Whenever I knock on the door he appears there at the window. And he needn't think his age gives him any points with me. They don't fool me one minute these old buggers. Fifty years ago he'd have shot me dead without a pang of conscience.'

'What's the matter with you?' Daud asked, surprised by the anger even as he noted with satisfaction that Karta had at last seen the fearsome potential of the retired wog-slayers. 'Have you been with your tutor again?'

'No,' he said, rising to switch on the television. 'I've been stuck at home, bored to death.'

Another knock on the door announced Lloyd's arrival, and Daud knew that he may as well write the rest of his evening off. Lloyd grinned at him and patted him on the shoulder as he walked past. Daud followed him into the house, cursing both Karta and him, and knowing that in his present mood Karta would behave like a baby with a dirty nappy. Lloyd was standing by the table, laying on it a gift of a pound of apples.

'Can you get your ugly English arse out of my sight?' Karta demanded. 'You're distracting my viewing. I'm sitting in a chair watching a programme and you come and put your smelly behind in my face, farting your suet puddings and carrots at me. Come on, fuck off out of my way.'

'So-rry,' Lloyd said but none the less moved aside. 'I see the Paramount Chief is in a bit of a sulk.'

Karta stared at him with loathing, keeping his eyes on him until he turned four-square to face him. 'If you don't watch yourself, I'll make your arse run tonight,' Karta said, wagging a stiff forefinger at Lloyd.

Lloyd bowed as if they had only been exchanging courtesies and turned his back on Karta. He fished a book out of his jacket pocket and put it down beside the bag of apples. He glanced at Daud to see if he had noticed his gift, and smiled to see he had done so. Daud remained silent while Lloyd picked up the paper on which he had been writing his colour schemes and repairs.

'What's this?' Lloyd asked, grinning as he waved the paper at Daud. 'Kitchen: light blue walls. Ceiling: white. What's this?'

Daud felt Karta turn to look at him, and after a moment saw him rise and take the paper from Lloyd. 'It's the girl,' he said, slapping his thigh with delight. 'You've gone back to that girl, haven't you? Let me tell you something. That one will get you to marry her! I can feel it!'

'Don't be stupid,' Daud said, looking calmly back at both of them but feeling an utter fool.

'Who is it? Who's doing this to you?' Lloyd asked, laughing and snatching the paper back. 'Wash clothes on Wednesday night. Twenty-five press-ups every morning. Clean the oven. What is this?'

'Let me tell you,' Karta continued, grinning and laughing, and leaning forward to leer in Daud's face. 'She's got her hooks into you, young man. I bet she keeps her legs crossed until you pop the question. I can tell her type a mile off. Too clean! You'll be keeping beer in cans soon, in the fridge door. No more pubbing, darling. You'll have to stay in and do your accounts and work out your monthly budget.'

'And planning baby!' Lloyd added with high glee.

Karta turned to him as if surprised that he was still there. In the sudden silence, their dislike of each other was like a charge in the air. Lloyd lifted his head, stiffening it with challenge. Karta ran disdainful eyes over him, and glared as Lloyd picked up an apple from the bag and held it in front of him like a talisman that would save him from evil. He bit noisily into it, belched, then took another bite, opposing Karta's loathing with his own boorishness. Daud kept his head down.

'You're disgusting,' Karta shouted, shaking with fury. 'You're an ugly, disgusting English pig.'

'You're going too far,' Lloyd shouted back, his face pale with anger. He threw the mauled apple on the table and stood facing Karta, his hands on the point of bunching into fists. The paper slipped out of his grasp and fluttered to the floor. Daud could see his fear, could hear the nervousness in his breathing. Karta shrugged his shoulders at Daud, asking him to see that it was not his fault. He went back to his chair and returned to watching television. Lloyd too sat down, pulling a chair out and sitting at the table to finish eating his apple.

Daud went out to the kitchen to make some tea. The window was open, and from outside he heard what sounded like a football being bounced on concrete, a dead, demoralising sound. Perhaps a boy strolling home from the playing fields in the quicksilver gloom of the late summer evening. It reminded him of being a child, bouncing a ball on his way home at dusk, lonely and frightened by aches whose meaning he could not understand. He leant out to hear more clearly. Birds flashed across his sight in a streak of black, so quickly that he was uncertain if he had seen anything at all. He did not want to return inside yet. It was the young boy who had unexpectedly recovered from fever that he remembered from the sound of the bouncing ball. Too weak to play with other boys yet, too ill even to return to school, ignored by everybody except Wire. The mad boy had befriended him because he was lonely too, had circled and cringed expecting to be rejected and abused. And on that morning in December he had run away from him while Bossy laughed at his mad mannerisms.

Dear Catherine, You should've seen us then as we pushed off into the sea! Not this whipped creature that skulks in mouldy slums. You should've seen my Bossy! The sea was blue and calm under the morning light, the sun hot on our shoulders. The sail on the outrigger caught the breeze and we slipped over the sea with the hiss of an oiled keel cutting through water. Bossy started to sing, imitating the Kenyan singer Yasin. He sang very badly and only did it to provoke laughter. And we laughed with the raucous pleasure of being young and being alive, lifting our chins and bellowing at the sky. I remember he stood up and looked back towards land. Then he turned round to me and said didn't it look beautiful from here. It was good to be out on the sea. It was like getting away from a suffocating room and running free in an open field, breathing in lungfuls of clean air. The water was cool, as you might imagine water to be, not like the lukewarm water out of a tap. It was the town that looked unreal. That famous water-front, with its white-washed houses and minarets, was like a quaint model in a builder's office, clean and ordered, belying from that distance the chaos and the filth of the narrow alleyways. Visitors spoke of the charm of our narrow streets and steeply rising houses, and the pungent smell of spices in the air. They first saw us from the sea, from a distance that encouraged such self-delusion. From there it did not matter that the windows charmingly shuttered looked out of rooms that were congested with people, and enclosed women who were hidden from the lustful gaze of men. There were no smelly alleys to walk through, no slippery ditches to cross, no fanatical elders to humiliate you. From the sea, the town seemed the luscious heart of paradise. Come nearer and you have to turn a blind eye to the slimy gutters and the house walls that have been turned into open-air urinals. Come nearer so we can see whether you are dark or fair, friend or foe.

But Rashid did not leave me to enjoy paradise for long. He was leaning against the side of the boat, one arm on the tiller and the other trailing in the water. I thought at first that he was just getting bored, so I changed the subject. I stopped talking about the town and asked him about the sea. That irritated him too, and he punched the water with frustration and anger. Poor Bossy, he had become obsessed with his family since his father's death the previous year. He wanted so much to leave but he could not stop thinking about his ma and his sister Amina. Oh Yallah, he would say, what will they do on their own?

The kettle whistled behind him and he turned to make the tea. Karta suddenly appeared at the kitchen door. 'You didn't take any notice, did you?' he said to Daud, dropping his voice so Lloyd would not hear. 'What I said about the girl … I didn't mean anything. You understand, don't you? Take no notice, I was only joking.'

Karta stood in the kitchen for a minute longer, awkward now after the brief intimacy. Daud followed him inside with the tea. When Lloyd saw him come in, he made a space on the table and then began to bustle with the tea, pouring it and passing it round. He passed the apples too, holding the bag open for Karta to take one. Then they all three settled down to watching TV. When the dancing and singing girls came on, Daud made to move.

'There's a thriller after this,' Karta said, putting an arm out to detain him.

Daud evaded the arm with a smile. He sat in the toilet for what seemed a long time, hiding from the boredom of the television. He would have preferred to leave them to it and go upstairs, but the thought of the explanations deterred him. *Dear Catherine, What can this feeble farmer have to offer you? Would you rather have a sports car than my powerful devotion?*

'Just in time!' Karta greeted him on his return. 'I was beginning to think you'd flushed yourself away. That must be some crap you did in there. Englishman, let's switch over to the other side.'

Lloyd looked at him, surprised at how far Karta was prepared to push him. He glared angrily but Karta only laughed and rose to switch stations himself. The sound of gunshot and screeching brakes abruptly filled the air as the commercials finished.

'A thriller!' Lloyd yelled, mocking Karta's enthusiasm.

'Have you got anything against that?' he asked, going back to his chair.

'It's just escapism,' Lloyd said, picking up his book.

Karta burst into raucous and mocking laughter. 'Somebody as idiotic as you should keep his mouth shut. When are you going to learn to do that?'

Make me, Daud predicted.

'That, at least, is something which the laws of this country are sworn to protect,' Lloyd said, bristling with righteousness. 'And it's not a freedom that we'll allow ourselves to be deprived of, even at the risk of displeasing people like you. Yes, you can laugh!'

'You pompous bastard,' Karta said, staring at the television with a grin on his face.

'I may be pompous, but nobody's going to stop me speaking my mind,' Lloyd shouted, his face red with anger.

'All right,' Karta said, waving Lloyd down, his eyes still fixed on the television. 'Not another lecture on the Magna Carta. Your countrymen told me all about that while I was gathering wisdom at their knees.'

'You may've been told about it, but you haven't understood it,' said Lloyd, his voice rising still further with annoyance and dislike. 'Just look at your Africa …'

'Shut up, will you?' shouted Karta, shifting his eyes at last to glare at Lloyd.

'You see, if you don't like what somebody's saying, your answer is to shut them up,' Lloyd shouted back. 'That's how tinpot dictators start. Just like your African ancestors! Just like the Pharaohs!'

'You go on like this and I'll smash your dirty mouth in ...'

Lloyd rose from his chair and faced Karta, his eyes darting with fear and excitement. He looked like a large clumsy animal preparing to defend itself to the death. Karta was silent with surprise. He glanced at Daud, but Daud made no sign. 'You want to fight me,' Karta said. It was half-question, half-incredulity, but none the less he rose to his feet, not wanting to be caught by a sudden lunge. 'All right, come on. This has been coming for a long time. Come on, nasty English bug, I'm going to destroy you. I'm going to beat the fuck out of you and put you in a hospital. For sure!'

Lloyd's mouth fell open a little more. He shifted his weight nervously and clenched his hands into tighter fists. He lowered his head and looked to Karta to be on the point of charging him. A single, loud shot came from the television, followed by hysterical screaming. Karta could not restrain a grin at the sudden melodrama on the screen. He sat down again, leant back and crossed his legs. Lloyd made no move but a heavy sigh of relief escaped him before he had time to stop it.

'Yes, you were lucky then, English bed bug,' Karta said, wagging a warning finger. 'Next time you feel like having a fight, go find somebody your own size, eh? Somebody as wet and doughy as you. Because if you try me again, I'll break your fucking neck.'

Lloyd stood unresolved for a moment and then turned and switched the set off. The sudden silence was eerie. Karta raised his eyebrows to the ceiling and then glanced at Daud, waiting for him to say something. Still Daud made no sign, wanting them to get on with it and get it finished. Karta rose to his feet and pointed at the television.

'Put it back on,' he said, calm and grim. 'If you don't put it back on, I'll beat the hell out of you.'

Lloyd ground his teeth with nervousness but managed not to climb down. 'You always have to have your own way, don't you?' he said, his voice trembling. He coughed to hide the weakness in his voice, but his whole body was shaking now and sweat was spreading in damp flushes over his face and arms. He seemed to Daud to be on the verge of climbing down, if Karta would let him. His fists slowly unclenched while he waited for Karta to make the next move. Karta suddenly stepped forward and landed sharp, stinging slaps on either side of Lloyd's face. He had stepped back out of reach before Lloyd realised what had happened. Karta pointed again at the television. Lloyd glanced at Daud, then looked around him with quick nervous movements. His eyes fell on a piece of copper gas pipe, leaning against the wall behind the table. Daud had put it there in case of a repetition of an incident, months back, when three thugs posing as carol singers had tried to force their way into the house. With a sharp gasp, Lloyd moved forward and picked up the pipe. He held it out in front of him, smiling triumphantly at his new strength. His arms were still shaking and his grip on the pipe was wobbly and weak. He saw Karta grinning with amusement and took a step forward, grunting and swiping the air with the pipe. Lloyd leant forward, poised to swing the metal bar again. Standing with his feet wide apart, he swaggered a little, as if all his life he had been a vicious and canny street-fighter. He made another feinting swipe at Karta and grinned to see him jump back a step.

'Not laughing any more now?' Lloyd chuckled. 'I thought you people were supposed to laugh all the time.'

'I should've beaten the shit out of you, you English swine, a long time ago,' Karta said.

'All right, better late than never. I'm only a dough boy, so just step in and murder me! Come on, you fucking baboon!' Lloyd shouted, relishing every word. 'Whose arse was it you were going to beat the fuck out of? Come on, you black bastard! You fucking nig-nog! Here I am! Come and kill me!' Lloyd spread his arms wide open, keeping the pipe in his right hand. As it swung through the air, it missed the naked light bulb by inches, making Lloyd glance at the bulb before grasping the pipe with both hands again. Karta bared his gums with irritation, knowing he should have rushed him then. 'You're an arrogant black shit,' Lloyd shouted, shifting his weight from foot to foot, trying to work himself into a frenzy. His face was in constant motion, grimacing and clenching into knots, his lips blubbering between words. Small spots of white froth were beginning to form at the corners of his mouth. 'I'd love to crack your beautiful skull open, you fucking monkey. Just try me, Sambo! See if I don't stuff this thing up your black arse.'

'You'll die for this,' Karta said softly.

Daud knew that Karta was waiting for Lloyd to finish the abuse and become frightened again.

'You'll die for this,' Lloyd mimicked, laughing at Karta's threat. 'You don't even know how to talk. You see, you're nothing but a … but a savage. You just threaten. That's all you know, Carter Benson-Shitface! A proper slave name …'

Karta moved forward with a growl.

'Christ! Come on! I'll smash your head in. Right now! Just try me. Slavery was a favour to an animal like you, you bastard. You ugly nigger, you baboon!'

Karta looked at Daud. 'Did you hear that? What did I tell you? You scratch an Englishman and you find that kind of animal underneath. You know what he wants now? Strike a blow against Black Sambo and die. You let him in your house and he sits here every night, and now it's black baboon this and nig-nog that.'

'No!' Lloyd shouted at Daud. 'Not you! I didn't mean you!' He tried to say something else but his voice caught in his throat and only vague incoherent sounds came out. When he tried again an arc of spittle flew through the air in front of him. He dropped his eyes in shame. Karta stepped forward and snatched the pipe from his hands. Lloyd's face crumpled into a sob and his eyes brimmed with tears.

'One minute playing Tarzan, next minute playing Jane,' said Karta. He threw the pipe behind him and glanced quickly at Daud to see if he would intervene. He walked forward and hit Lloyd in the stomach, doubling him over with pain. He yanked him straight and smiled at him, gloating over the bloated tear-stained face. He hit Lloyd again and again, as hard as he could, following him round the room as he barged into furniture and crashed into Daud. In the end Lloyd toppled to the floor, slobbering with fear and pain, his face covered with blood. 'Get up!' Karta said through gritted teeth, standing over Lloyd with bunched fists. 'That was for my slave grandpapa,' he said, watching the weals rise on Lloyd's face. 'Now this is for me.' He turned and picked up the metal pipe. Lloyd looked at him and screamed for Daud. Karta swung the bar and landed a crushing blow on Lloyd's shoulder. Lloyd screamed, and called again for Daud. Karta glanced round to see if Daud would stop them. When he did not, he swung the bar again, aiming for Lloyd's buttocks. Lloyd was sobbing frenziedly now, abandoned and in agony.

'You'll kill him,' Daud said.

Karta picked Lloyd up and pushed him against the wall. 'The days of the black baboon are over,' he told him. 'Now get out of here!'

'Leave him!' Daud said. 'If you've finished your business just leave him.'

Karta waited a moment for Daud to explain himself. Daud stood up in silence, waiting for him to go. In that small room they were standing close together, and Daud saw Karta's triumph turning to surprise.

'You've had your fight, now leave him!' Daud said angrily.

Karta stared at Daud with disbelief. He spun round and buried a last blow into Lloyd's midriff. Lloyd groaned through his sobbing and slid down the wall again. Karta gave Daud a bitter look and gathered his things to go. Daud waited until he heard Karta's footsteps on the pavement fade into the gathering summer darkness. Then he helped Lloyd to the kitchen and cleaned him up a little under the tap. When he had washed the worst of the blood off, he persuaded him into a chair and made him a drink.

'I'm sorry,' Lloyd said when he had recovered a little.

'When you feel better ... when you can walk properly, you'd better go home and get some rest.'

As Lloyd lay recovering in a chair, Daud rearranged the furniture. He found his list of repairs and folded it carefully into his shirt pocket. It seemed an age ago now, but it was still only nine o'clock. He saw that Lloyd had dozed off. He thought he would leave him for a while, although he desperately wanted him to go. He would give him half an hour and then wake him up. The fight had surprised him with its bitterness. He felt some disgust now at his silence but he was determined to let them indulge their loathing of each other. So often he had intervened to prevent a fight and beatings. He had not really expected them to fight, he realised, had not understood how near the surface their bitter dislike was. Not for a moment had he expected Lloyd to triumph, but Karta's ferocity had been unexpected. Because of a few monkey taunts from a frightened man? To beat a man senseless with a metal bar for such stuff?

He woke Lloyd up after half an hour. He wanted him to go and had restrained himself several times already. He wanted to be by himself, to write crazy letters in his head and drive himself mad with loneliness.

Lloyd came reluctantly to his senses, groaning and panting as the pain returned. 'I'm sorry,' Lloyd said, clinging to Daud's arm.

'You'd better go.' Daud shook his arm free, gently, but none the less rejecting Lloyd's appeal. Lloyd's brow felt hot to Daud's hand, as if a fever was coming on him. Daud helped him into his jacket and walked ahead of him to the door. 'Will you be able to walk home or shall I come with you?'

Lloyd shook his head and then wobbled against the wall. Daud steadied him and wondered if he should really take him to the hospital. Some of Karta's blows looked as if they had done real damage. After all the shouting and groaning earlier, he did not want his neighbours telling the police about a battered man they had seen staggering out of his house.

'I'm sorry about the things I said,' Lloyd said, clutching Daud's arm again.

Daud nodded. 'Yes, I know but you'd better go home now,' he said, holding the door open for him. 'Do you think you can walk all right? Shall I take you to the hospital?'

Lloyd shook his head and walked away.

15

He switched the lights off as he passed into the tunnel that led up to his bedroom. The stairs smelt of rancid and dusty carpets, the smell of cheap rented rooms. He felt his way up, anticipating in his nostrils the odour of sweat that always lingered in his room however much he aired it. He lay down on the bed, and as he rolled over he felt a sinew snap inside his nostrils and his nose beginning to run. He put a finger across his nostrils while he felt for a handkerchief. He could feel his whole hand getting warm and wet, and even as he took it away from his face he knew that it would be covered with blood.

He lay quietly and let the blood flow out of him. What the hell, there's plenty more where that came from, he thought, feeling tough and hard-bitten. He smiled to think how these things all happened at once: like mosquitoes, misfortunes always came in battalions. After a while he shuffled to the edge of the bed and felt around on the floor, looking for the shirt he wore in bed when nights were chilly. He used it to mop his face, then covered himself with it, breathing in its familiar musk. Some of the blood had run down his neck on to one of the pillows. He wiped himself and threw the stained pillow off before lying down again.

It had happened to him once before. They were queuing for tickets for a Gossage match between Kenya and

Uganda. It must have been the excitement, or the crush of people. One minute he was standing in the line talking to his friends, the next everyone was backing away from him with horror, pointing at his bleeding face. Bossy had dragged him to the high bank on the side and bought him an ice-cold tamarind juice. Then they had pushed their way back to their place in the queue with Bossy as the trail-blazer, shouting and abusing the people who objected to his jostling progress.

He was such a little father, Daud thought. *He overdid it sometimes, and came close to being overbearing. It was like he was playing a role, bustling with the unnecessary kindness that he wished for from his own father. At his father's death he mourned him correctly but refused to perform the anguish of the grief-stricken son. He had refused to shed the shocking tears of male mourning, which alone can testify to the grief beyond endurance at the death of a parent. During the funeral ceremonies in the Msikiti Mdogo, he calmly carried out the duties of the bereaved, as if he was marking the passing of a distant relation. He stood by a pillar in the mosque while mourners came to offer him their condolences. An old man went to him, overcome with grief and shaking with silent sobs. He held Rashid's hand for a long time, saying something to him and shaking his head with grief. Rashid had been unresponsive, almost bored, staring at the old man with the steady gaze of cynical disbelief. The old man had walked away disappointed, still shaking his head, and wondering what had happened to young people to make them so unfeeling. He looked like a fisherman, and perhaps had been a special friend of Rashid's father, had owed him something. Rashid had turned away without a second glance, waiting to shake the hand of the next mourner. The other mourners simply observed the form, gripping Rashid's hand and whispering words of comfort. They were restrained out of politeness, perhaps, when their hearts would have burst with grief. It would have been unseemly to show greater grief than the bereaved, the owner of the corpse.*

How I wished through the prayers that he would shed a few tears, if not for himself then for those who cared and trembled at his father's death. Not because they mourned the passing of a paragon, but because they too shuddered at the thought of the journey on which he had embarked. But Rashid's face was hard and stubborn, with a stillness that promised not to yield. How can a sixteen-year-old go to his father's funeral with a dry face? Afterwards he said that the old man who had shaken his hand was nothing but a layabout who used to come scrounging at their house, cringing for handouts and leftovers that they could ill afford themselves. And he had not cried for his father because he had felt nothing, he said. He had wanted to feel sad, to feel the arms of neighbours holding him by the elbows while he sobbed, but instead of sadness he had felt only an irritating responsibility. The burden of his family's poverty would now be entirely on his shoulders. He said his father had been cruel to all of them, beating them and abusing them for no reason, as the whim took him. He had tried to stop Rashid from going to school, saying he would only learn the religion of the nasrani. Instead he had apprenticed him to a shopkeeper when he was six years old, in the time-honoured way. The shopkeeper was an old man, and in his senility gave full rein to his lechery. He had made Rashid share his sick bed, had fondled him and tried to persuade him to open his legs to the objects he wanted to introduce into his anus. Rashid had refused, sobbing and fighting the old pervert off. The man locked him in a darkened store room for two days, coming to the door at times to whisper endearments and blandishments. Rashid had spoken of this time without embarrassment, listening to my exclamations of horror with patience, as if he was simply waiting for me to finish. He used to think me so innocent.

His father had come for him on the Friday afternoon to take him to the mosque for Juma'a prayers, and had found him lying in filth, weak with hunger and fatigue. He had taken a stick to the old man at once, but Rashid had never forgiven him the terror of that week. So he said that he was really quite pleased that the old bastard was dead even if it made him sound unfeeling. I said it did. It made him sound as if he lacked compassion, as if his father did not deserve forgiveness. I said you can't hold that kind of thing against a dead man, not after all this time has passed. Who should he hold it against then, he asked me, playing the smiling, tolerant big brother? Sometimes I don't know why I like you, I shouted at him, stung by his manner. You should pray for him. A dead man, especially a father, needs our prayers. Honour your fathers after me, God has told us. But Rashid only smiled and shook his head. He said prayers would not do the old fucker any good at all. The angels of Hell would've been rubbing their hands with glee at the prospect of his arrival, he said. I told him it was wrong to talk of his father like that. He thought I did not understand because my own father was kind and cared for us. And he is kind, I said, but he can get very mean if you ask him for a shilling to go to the cinema. It was meant as a joke, and Rashid smiled briefly, but I felt sudden pangs of guilt at my disloyalty. Anyway, I said quickly, not wanting to think about the way I had slandered my father, it still didn't seem right to want your father to go to Hell. That was no joke, consuming fires and endless tortures. He was silent for a long while, as who would not be at the thought of that limitless pain. But I knew that he was just refusing to answer, letting me have my way.

It was not really true that his father's death suddenly brought this responsibility on him. He worried all the time about his mother and little Amina. Whenever we talked about leaving and about the future, our plans always foundered on the fear of what would happen to his family. That was what annoyed him that day on the boat, although at first I thought it was boredom with my conversation about the town.

'What will they do?' he asked after his long silence. 'It frightens me just to think about it. That's God's truth! I feel like I'm doing something terrible even thinking about it. Some nights I can't sleep once I start … Ma hasn't said anything but I know she worries. But what is there here? What can I do here?'

'You won't be gone for ever,' I said, trying to reassure him and myself. Suddenly the sail snapped in the breeze and made the boat stagger. Bossy brought it back under control easily, and looked at the sail to check that there had been no damage. He frowned at it, slightly irritated by its wilfulness.

'What was that?' I asked him.

'The beginning of Kaskazi,' he said, smiling at my terror. 'The musim. It will get like this for a few days before it steadies. You're so ignorant. It comes every year in December and you've never even noticed. The tides get higher, the winds fresher and the sea a little choppier … and then it settles into the musim. Don't worry about it.'

'I'm not worried about it,' I said. 'Anyway, it's not as if you'll be gone for ever. You'll be back to take care of them.'

'You're too trusting,' he said, looking away.

I disliked that in him, the way he turned away when he thought I was saying something naive. I too could see the signs of the times, could see the dangers that threatened us. I just did not understand how imminent they were.

'Things are going to happen here now that Independence has come. I've heard some terrible talk,' he said. 'And anyway, Ma's getting old ...'

'You mean riots and things like that?' I asked, alarmed as always by the familiar predictions of violence.

'I don't know,' he said, shrugging with feigned indifference. 'But suppose something happens while I'm away.'

'What do you mean?' I asked, wanting him to say it.

He raised his eyes to heaven, praying for patience. 'Killings! There are going to be killings here! Look at the way things are. The Arabs and the Indians own all the land and all the businesses. The blacks are the skivvies and the labourers. You and I, a bit of this and a bit of that, doing well out of it. How long do you think that's going to last? Don't fool yourself like all these nationalists. One of these days, these people that we've been making slaves of for centuries will rise up and cut the throats of their oppressors. Then the Indians will go back to India and the Arabs will go back to Arabia, and what will you and I do?'

'What will we do?'

'We'll get slaughtered,' he said. 'Who'll care that we feel we belong here more than they do? They will tell us that this is Africa, and it belongs to them, however much longer we've been here than them. There are people still alive who were born into slavery, whose parents were torn away from their land and brought here in chains. What will we do? We'll get slaughtered.'

I could feel tears stinging my eyes as I listened to him talk, not out of fear for myself but for our land and our people. Bossy flashed warning eyes at me, telling me to bear up and not to be pathetic, then smacked my thigh as a kind of reassurance. He leant forward and took both my hands in his. 'What's the use of me going away for five or six years to become a forestry officer or something only to come back and find that my mother's dead and my sister's a whore?'

Daud sat up on one elbow, his head cocked to one side. He had suddenly realised that the sound of footsteps had stopped under his window. Lloyd had come back to walk up and down his pavement. He waited, but the silence stretched out for so long that he began to wonder if he had imagined the sound in the first place. It was still early and his bedroom light was on, inviting Lloyd to knock. He could imagine him returning just to avoid having to give explanations to his parents. Daud grimaced when the knock came, but his body was already poised to rise from the bed.

Catherine was standing on the pavement. He stared dumbly for a second and then sighed with relief. He opened the door wide to let her in, grinning at the unexpected pleasure. She smiled at the welcome and made an embarrassed face. As she started to move forward, she saw the blood on his chest and the blood-stained rag in his hand. He had forgotten about that. She looked into his face with a frown.

'Nose bleed,' he said.

On her face was a look of mock horror, she who daily lathered stumps of amputated legs with disinfectant. She came into the house and embraced him. 'Does it hurt?' she asked, whispering as she leant against him.

'Not a bit,' he said, thrilling at her voice as it rumbled through his body.

'You're so brave!' she said.

He pushed her gently away in the end, afraid that the blood would stain her clothes. She sat down at the table, sighing with tiredness.

'Have you just come off duty?' he asked.

She nodded. 'Paula left me a note. She said you came round one night while I was out. Is everything all right? Are you all right?'

She sighed, as if she wished herself playing a different scene. A less complicated one, he guessed. From the way she glanced at him he assumed that he was expected to be mature and reassuring, and not scream curses and abuse about boyfriends. 'All right?' he asked, on the point of clapping his palms together in great good health. 'Sure I'm all right. I'm fine! Apart from all this blood. Let me make you some tea.'

'I don't want any tea,' she said, frowning. 'Why did you come to see me? Has something happened?'

Her sharpness confused him at first. Perhaps she was just tired, he thought. Or she was irritated that he had gone round after she had discouraged him from calling on her during the week. He saw her eyes going back to the spatters of blood on his chest. 'I came to see you because I wanted to talk to you. I wanted to see you,' he said.

'What about?' she asked.

'Why are you so annoyed?' he asked, smiling because she expected him to act hurt. That was why she was bristling, he guessed, annoyed that she could be thought a cheat. 'I just came to see you. I had a letter from someone at home and it brought back a lot of things. I thought if you were free you might come out for a drink … and maybe we could talk.'

She sighed, then nodded. 'Tell me,' she said. He saw that she was beginning to lose the struggle to control herself.

'I didn't know things were complicated for you,' he said.

'What did you come to tell me?' she asked as tears began to run out of her eyes. 'Oh, why do women have to be so pathetic!' She brushed the tears from her face and sniffed furiously, trying to bring herself under control. He hurried to her and knelt beside her. Her head dropped on his shoulder, and her voice came muffled through his body. He made some tea anyway, and drank her cup as well as his while he waited for her to come back from the bathroom.

'I'm sorry I wasn't there,' she said when she came back.

'Who is he?' he asked, not wanting to be kept waiting with something that would not hurt quite so much as it should.

She sighed and sat at the table facing him. 'Don't you want to tell me about your letter? I never let you talk. I'm always so full of dramas of my own.' He said nothing, waiting with a sick half-smile for what she would say. 'His name's Malcolm. I've been seeing him for about six or seven months now. I was going to tell you.'

'You didn't mention him. I had no idea …'

'I was going to tell you. I wasn't sure when,' she said and laughed.

'Why are you laughing?'

'He was coming round for me tonight,' she said. 'We'd arranged to go out for a drink. To the Black Dog probably. We often go there. I didn't tell you that either. We're going away together at the beginning of August, driving around France and camping.' She looked blankly at him, inviting him to say his worst, already cringing from his contempt.

'Does he have a blue sports car?' he asked, wanting the truth in its full ugliness.

'A white Mini,' she said, frowning.

'Is he a farmer?' he asked, beginning to smile. 'I imagined him a rich young farmer driving a blue sports car when you mentioned the Yacht Club.'

'I only went there once,' she said. Her frown deepened but he assumed that was only surprise. He could already see a sparkle of amusement in the very depths of her eyes. 'He's a doctor at the hospital. And he's young and rich, and attractive. Every young nurse's dream. And he chose me out of all the others. How could I resist him?' She spoke again after a long silence. 'Say something,' she said.

'They've dropped Close and Edrich. They made them stand there and take that battering last time out and then just dropped them. It's the work of that Boer. What does he understand about the spirit of Khartoum? The Fourth Test starts this week,' he explained when he saw the incomprehension on her face. 'Will he still be waiting at your house? Do you want to go to him?'

She leant towards him and took his hand. When she spoke, after a long moment, she was irritated, annoyed with her own indecisiveness. 'I don't know,' she said. 'Everything's happened so quickly.'

He nodded, encouraged by her confusion.

'What do you want me to do?' she asked, asking to be persuaded.

'Stay,' he said. 'He'll come back tomorrow. Stay now.'

'Yes,' she said, nodding.

In the distance we saw a steamer, he told her. *Coming from the town. Even from that far away it seemed old and clumsy. We watched it approach but it seemed to be going across us, heading north. As it drew near, we saw the women ranged along the sides. They were too distant for us to recognise them but it was obvious from their dress that they were the daughters of the rich. Rashid chuckled softly as the engine hiccuped and the women moved from the side in a panic. There were some men on the boat and they stood out in their velvet blue waistcoats and dark-green metal-rimmed sun-glasses. They waved to us from their ancient perambulator, and we cupped our hands to our ears to hear what they were shouting to us. Behind them was a small group of ragamuffins who would serve the sweet-meat and coffee. The women were still wearing their buibui even so far away from land. Out for the day with muscular chaperons and camera-clicking siblings.*

We sailed serenely on, rarely speaking, seeking the shadow of the sail in turn to get away from the sun. Eventually Rashid began to sing again, mixing Kiswahili with English songs. He managed one verse of 'Rule Britannia' before I silenced him with a gourdful of sea water.

At the island. Improvised crouch in the bush for temporary lordosis with bent knees, Bossy claimed, playing the dictionary game that we loved. He had looked up the words and had them ready for such a visit to the bush. Grunting and heaving, he managed to achieve a state of bliss sooner than I. Hasty dunking on the treacherously sand-banked beach to wash the crumbs away and depart for the crumbling fortress of a bygone empire.

'Bygone by name,' Bossy declaimed, quivering with insincere emotions. 'We are pathetic victims of neo-colonialism, as we will be for a long time. The day will yet arrive when the barbarian master-race will once again depart its fog-bound northern islands to come and repossess its destiny by these shores.'

We recalled the romantic Royal Navy officer, who had etched his name into history by an unprovoked and entirely one-sided shelling of our town with the famous waterfront. Exhausted by this courageous act, he had sought to soothe his shattered nerves by going rambling on the green, off-shore island that was unmarked on his map. It was the same island on which we now found ourselves, but he had been the first European to stumble on it, discovering it. Well-guarded by his marines, he roamed its gentle hills. Its potential as a prison immediately struck him. He considered himself a bit of an archaeologist, and his brief studies on the island convinced him that the site had been used immemorially as a place of confinement. Later, he wrote a very brief monograph on the subject, which was published by the Universities Mission for Central Africa and attracted attention in the reading rooms of the Royal Geographical Society.

Over the remains of the naval officer's dream, Bossy read the Psalm of Life, lingered meaningfully over 'dust to dust returneth' and sang another verse of 'Rule Britannia' with an emotional choke. Some few yards right of the mound round which we had been standing was a sturdy pole or stake, firmly fixed to the ground and reaching a height of seven feet two inches. Bossy speculated that this was a post to which offenders were attached before punishment. He did not seem aware of Blunt's discoveries in the area. In demagogical style, right hand clasping the heart, left hand resting lightly on the stake, he elaborated. Deadwood remnants of the crude implements used to punish trivial offenders against the autocratic rule of the Viceroy of a northern island crown. He refused to be more specific, but was willing to speculate that it might have been part of the British hordes that briefly occupied many parts of Africa. Moving quickly right and left again, and on one occasion lying supine for several seconds, he attempted to demonstrate how the punishment post or totem might have been part of an important barbarian ritual. At the word of command, which he insisted I utter, the salvo blew his cheeks apart. 'That will teach the wog bugger to pay his taxes next time,' he concluded.

I begged to differ. I conceded that the stake was clearly deadwood remnant but I inclined to the view that it was more reminiscent of the pillar-post thatchwood style of the Indonesians. This had the merit of according with Blunt's discoveries. On once water-covered plains, now the dry plateau beloved by big-game hunters, a musical lyre was found by the British Archaeological Expedition to the East Coast of Africa in 1929, under the leadership of Blunt KCMG, to clinch the theory of a massive Indonesian invasion of Africa. The instrument was clearly not indigenous. None of the Stone Age natives found in occupation of the plateau at that time were capable of the manufacture of an artefact of such complexity. Fragments of skull found by Blunt KCMG at the lip of the gully on this same island suggest human life before the beginning of time, as counted from the eighth millennium BC. *Before that do not apply.*

We found Blunt Gully with ease, and Bossy crouched again, nearly choking from the smell. I made some enquiries about his diet and delivered him a brief warning on the laxity of his standards of hygiene. I quoted directly from my mother's regular pronouncements on the matter.

In a grove of palms choked with weeds and wild tomatoes, we discovered an underground town. We paused to study the extent of the settlement and the occupations of the settlers. Our intention was to capture a small handful of the beasts, to torture and dissect them at our ease. We were not welcome and hurried away from fierce mandibles until, weakened by fatigue and hunger, we collapsed under a mango tree. Pungent leaf-mould and rotting humus and ripe mangoes oozing contentedly on the ground. We named this place Mango Park. Bossy bigboots was voted upstairs to wheedle bounty for the starving vanguard of a civilising race. Mangoes on the ground in torpid contentment, oozing their dysentery under the clouds of flies. The Captain returned with phosphates in his eyes, the bounty of a discordant piebald crow. We sank to our knees in humiliating penance and fought for mangoes with the flies. God was on our side.

Bossy brushed the dirt off his booty while hygiene rang through my skull. I held Hunger in Abeyance and warned him that by Avarice he was undone. 'O Mummy in my heart,' I prayed, 'if I ever needed you it is now. Tell me truly, O Fount of Hygiene, will I sooner die of Hunger or of Dysentery? O Wiper of my Arse, I have heeded your word through Thick and Thin, generally speaking, but now a Text sirens through my guts to throw Caution to the winds. Could it be the Serpent, viper vile, that so flatters me to eat against your Word?' To a thicket I slunk and guiltily Rash gorged of the Forbidden Fruit. Earth trembled from her Entrails, but I took no thought, content to eat my fill.

I knelt down waiting for the thunder to strike while Bossy looked on in pagan amazement. 'I have seen the error of my ways,' I whispered. 'I have sinned when knowing that I was sinning. I have no right to ask of you that you show mercy when all that I have done invites your anger. Forgive me, forgive me just one time, Mother Hygiene. I have sinned.' Mother Hygiene restrained her hand. We left that pernicious grove, myself restrained and chastened, Bossy exultant and full.

To the waterfall. It seemed then that there ought to have been a windmill as a sign of progress and evidence of an ancient Indonesian culture. Feet in the pool at the base of the miniature waterfall, kicking the water in adolescent delight.

We drank the water at our feet, walked to the slimy rocks mid-pool, half-submerged like rising crustaceans covered with slime. We posed for a photo to show the folks back home, hand on hip. This rock we named Bygone My Arse.

As we sat under that rippling fall, we gazed at what the old voyagers must have seen. In this same place an Indonesian Sultan could have stood, with the power of the human gaze to tear holes through nature's incomprehensible veil. Bear thee up, Bossy, and trust the power of thy unflinching gaze. How many men stood where you and I then stood and saw nothing of what we saw? We were God's chosen, and I say this with all possible humility. It was our destiny. We sat by the brimming pool and saw world without end in our humble reflections, in foolish daydream pretence. The words of dead past masters were ringing anvils in our ears to confirm the destiny of our race, to stiffen our self-esteem in times of trial. Not for us the frenzy of self-affirmation and worldliness. Our task was greater than all of us.

Soon it was time to leave the haven of that waterfall encampment for the final leg of our journey. Bossy took the lead while I patrolled the rear, for the thought of raiders from the underground town we had disturbed earlier still troubled us. As I watched our Captain hack his way through the thickets, I wondered again at the destiny that the Almighty had arranged for us. But, come what may, I knew we had done our share in fulfilling the burden of our race.

When we got to the beach where we had left our outrigger, we went in for a swim. A ritual ablution, Bossy suggested, and proceeded to thrash around in the water like a demented priest. He screamed strange words at the sky, holding his arms aloft in a curiously vulnerable gesture. Having cleansed his soul, he stroked gently away from the beach while I stood waist-deep in water washing the grime off my body. For no special reason Bossy increased the pace of his strokes and started to sprint away.

'Don't show off,' I shouted.

He waved, a large grin resting lightly on the water. He turned towards the beach, treading water for a few moments, then swam furiously inshore. I shouted out to him again, telling him not to show off, but he could not possibly have heard me. He hauled himself out of the water, a contented self-satisfied grin on his face.

'Did you enjoy that? I'm impressed,' I said. 'Perhaps one day you'll grow up and realise that it's childish to show off.'

He threw himself on the beach, still grinning. We sat in the sun for a little, not speaking. Suddenly he chuckled. 'I can swim to the town quicker than you can sail the boat there,' he said, his face radiant. 'Take a bet on it if you don't believe me.'

'I believe you,' I said. He often boasted like that so I took no notice. When we had pushed the boat back in the water, I jumped in first and helped Bossy in after me. We caught the breeze immediately, and as soon as the sail was secure and our progress was steady, Bossy said goodbye and jumped overboard.

'See you in town,' he shouted, grinning in the water.

I shouted to him not to be stupid but he was already on his way. I stood in the boat calling to him, yelling his name with anxiety and growing anger. Suddenly a fierce squall filled out the sail and I struggled for the tiller. The fierceness of the storm was unexpected. The sail was ballooning out ahead of itself, moving the boat across the island and away from the direction of the town. I tried to manoeuvre the tiller and nearly overturned. I sat horrified while the boat sped away with me like a frenzied animal. I thought of lowering the sail but as soon as I let go of the tiller, the sail flapped savagely and I had to grab the tiller to steady the boat again. I cursed the fool and his showing off. He would have known what to do. We were still going alongside the island, and I could see me being blown out to sea and dying a violent death at the jaws of a shark. I tried to calm myself. Don't panic, don't panic. I tried to imagine myself standing firm at the tiller, grimly bearing up, face turned to the freedom of the seas. We were beginning to leave the island behind, still heading away from the town. Then just as suddenly as it had started, the wind died away. I rushed for the sail and lowered it.

I could not find him. I called for him, yelled out for him, screamed for him. I tried to turn the boat round to go back to the island, but as soon as I put up the sail the breeze filled it out and took me in the opposite direction. I didn't know what to do.

You left me, Bossy. I knew then that you'd left me. You played your games once too often. You left me all too soon. Hardly time to wave and say fond farewells. I knew as I stood there calling out to you, calling you back, that you'd gone. Bossy, what happened to you? O Bossy my Bossy, I sat in that boat hugging my knees to my chest, not knowing what to do, knowing that I had failed you. I sat in that boat frightened to death that you might be in trouble and there was nothing I could do to help you. The boat was too big for me, the water too deep for me, and you were nowhere in sight, Bossy. I called for you and all the time I was moving away from you. Bossy O Bossy my Bossy, you wanted to make me feel a fool while you swam to land and I felt a fool, but where did you go, Bossy? You left me. You left me and I was lost, Bossy. I did all that I could but I could not turn that boat back to you.

You would have admired its power, Bossy, you would have admired its power even while you laughed at me you would have admired its power. What else is there to say? I tried all I could.

Then I thought that maybe I was just being a fool, that you were safe and well and on your way to town. Then I thought I would never make it back to town myself and I was angry at what you had done. 'Childish bastard! Suppose I'm late back!' I stood up in the boat and called you names and all the time I knew you had gone. I think of you even now and I still cry for you. I think of you in times of need and I still cry for you. What else is there to say? I managed to reach land. I don't know how. The wind and the tide took me round the northern headland and dragged me on to land.

You missed the worst, Bossy.

It was night when I landed. I knew it was somewhere near Mbweni because it was still light when I started coming in towards land and I had recognised the Hindu crematorium on the cliff, surrounded by the shadows of the vegetation all around it. It was dark when I reached land. I walked along the beach, mile after mile it seemed, worrying if the boat was safe where I had left it. I was hurrying to find out if you had come in. I did not get past the golf course. I was beaten by men with sticks and stones. They told me the day had come. They told me this was the day when all Arabs would get theirs. There must have been six or seven of them. I could see the road into town across the golf course, the street-lamps lighting it up as broad as day. I cannot describe the pain. They hit me with sticks first. I thought only the first few would hurt but incredibly the more they hit me the more unbearable the pain … Eventually they held me up, held my head up and made me look at the man standing in front of me. He said something but I was past understanding. He took deliberate aim with his stick, swinging it easily from side to side like a golfer practising a stroke. I closed my eyes, concentrating on the pain in my bones and on the panic-stricken howls thickly flooding my ears. I felt every ounce of that man's hatred on my skull.

I thought I was dead. I woke up on the beach. Perhaps they had dragged me there to drown me. Grit and sand were caked with blood down one side of me. When I tried to sit up I felt blood sliming down my face and dripping down on my arm. I heard the sound of gunfire in the air. At first I did not recognise it, it sounded like children playing with pop-guns. A car streaked at speed along the road towards the town. I struggled along the beach, stopping to wash the salt of the sea into my wounds. I was too afraid to go on the road and ask for help. I knew I could get home by following the beach all the way round to the other side of town. I got as far as Shangani before I was stopped by a large group of very wild-looking men with pangas and guns. Where did they get guns? I was too weak to run. They said I was an askari from the barracks and they were going to shoot me. They said they had overrun the barracks and the Prime Minister had surrendered and they had beaten the fuck out of him. The day had come, they said. The Sultan had already run away to the ship off the harbour, they said, and if they were to get hold of him they would whip his cloth off and fuck his arse before stuffing it full of dynamite. All the dirty arse-fuckers would be dead before the night was through. They told me I deserved to die with the rest of them. Mtu mbaya! They said where did you get those cuts from if you weren't at the barracks? Kill him! They said kill the bastard! They said there'd be none of us left by the time they'd finished and what was I shaking like that for? They said this fellow is a khanithi. Fuck him before you put a bullet in him. They said we've got no time, kill him now before the others get to the rich houses. They said if we don't hurry all the best stuff will be gone and all the good women will be ruined. They said don't waste a bullet on him. Here, let me do him with my steel. Here, they said, hold your head up … but I was too tired and weak and they beat me and urinated on me and left me lying senseless on the beach.

16

Catherine rocked him from side to side while he wept like a wounded child. She was the one who was really the child, she thought, having found it so hard to let him see tears on her face. He seemed oblivious to her, sobbing with small, bitter gasps like a man gulping the last breaths of air before his life ended, baby man railing against an indifferent universe. When he had managed to stop, he lay silently beside her in the dark, saying nothing for a long time. She felt him beginning to doze off and gradually drifted off to sleep herself. When she came to, it was light and he was sitting up beside her, waiting for her to wake up. It was she who spoke first, her mind turning to the boy in the sea.

'Did you find him?' she asked. 'Tell me how you found him.'

He did not reply, but he turned to look at her, to show he had heard. It struck him how lovely she looked, her body glowing with health, with a kind of radiance. He, on the other hand, felt tired and ill. She looked bright and clean, when he felt grimy and full of aches.

'It's so hard to credit,' she said, resting on an elbow and pressing forward a little to lean against him. 'To connect the things you hear with real people. You see someone and you think of him as a man, or a woman, or just another person to handle with care. It never occurs to you what history he brings, or what tragedies are tearing him apart. Perhaps even that thought presumes too much. Why should there be anything? You see people like that, it's not that you don't. All messed up and torn apart. But you know them. They have scarred faces and eccentric stares, and carry an air of misery about them.'

'And you imagine them living in dingy rooms performing unspeakable cruelties on themselves and on their loved ones,' he finished for her. She made to protest but he stopped her, putting up a hand and smiling. 'What about your histories and your tragedies?'

'But they're so bland they hardly seem real,' she said.

He was suspicious, but did not feel that he wanted to convince her that her life did not lack tragedy. *Tragedy is in the eye of the beholder*, he might have started if he had been in a letter-writing mood. Instead he slid back into bed and shuffled up against her, groaning with contentment as she responded to him.

'What happened to you?' she asked after a while. 'After the …'

He waited for her to complete the question, but she did not. 'I tried to get home. Running and hiding … in that small place! I was captured … detained before I got home. It wouldn't have made any difference. My parents were already in detention. Everybody was rounded up … some people never came out of those camps but for most of us it was just humiliation and abuse. The two men who captured me tied me up and made me watch while they raped an Indian girl.'

'Oh no, I don't want to hear,' she said, turning away from him.

'It's all right. I wasn't going to tell you.' *Two men with guns in their hands, one holding a young girl while the other clubbed her mother with the butt of his rifle, the mother rolling silently on the ground, unable to avoid the blows.*

'Tell me,' she said, her face still turned away.

'Why do you want to know?'

'Tell me!' she shouted, whipping round and punching him furiously on the chest.

'All you could hear was the thud of the rifle butt striking the woman on her head and chest. The young girl, maybe fourteen, was trying to free her wrist. I just turned a corner and came upon them. I don't know why I didn't run. I couldn't believe that a man could do that. The woman was in her death throes, and the man was following her movements, taking careful aim each time before delivering his blow. Then he laughed and shared the joke with the other man. The girl screamed when she saw me, crying for help. The man looked up from his work with glaring eyes, a picture of primeval guilt, Adam eating off the tree, a weasel plundering an egg-nest. Then I ran, but it was too late. The alley was too long. They were shooting behind me but I didn't really think they'd hit me. I remember shouting Bang Bang, *ebo* missed. It's what we used to say as children when we played cops and robbers. But the gunfire was so frightening that I ran into a handcart. I panicked, I just didn't see it.

'They took me back to where the two women still were, the girl kneeling beside her mother. There must have been people watching behind closed shutters. They tied me up with the mother's sari and then raped the young girl. She must've known the moment would come, and when it did she stood in front of the men, her arms pressed to her side. Long tresses of hair and dark glowing eyes. They threw her on the ground and raped her one after the other. The girl's sobbing would catch as a new pain took her breath away, and then she would howl with agony. They were not gentle with her.'

He sighed and was silent. 'They were very angry when they saw I was crying,' he said. 'There were people watching, I know there were. They left them there, the girl spread out on the road with a trickle of blood pulsing out of her and her mother lying nearby.'

Catherine lay with her face buried in his arm, her head turned downwards, not looking at him. 'Did you find out about Bossy? Tell me how you found him,' she said at last.

He shook his head. 'There were too many bodies.'

'No.' She looked at him and grimaced with disgust. 'You must have found him. What do you mean too many bodies? You did look for him, didn't you? His mother must've looked for him. What did she do? She must've looked for him.'

'Do? What do you mean, do? Thousands were held in the camps for days. There were killings going on, wiping the slate clean, putting the record straight. For three days there was an orgy, and squalor and humiliation you could not imagine in your wildest dreams. They let us out into a curfew, into empty streets. There were signs of looting everywhere but no signs of fighting. There were no burnt-out houses or fragments of doors that had to be battered down. Nobody had stood up and said you can't do this to us. We'd allowed ourselves to be treated like contemptible bloodless parasites, to be brushed off as if we truly did not belong there.'

'But Bossy! What happened to Bossy?' she asked, insisting now, wanting to know, as if this was important to her.

'By the time we were allowed to look for our dead, many of them were beyond recognition. Those that could still be found. We looked for him. We looked where we could ... and asked where we dared.'

'What did his mother do?' she asked.

He shrugged. 'She prayed. There was no news, nothing that we knew for sure to be true. There was a rumour that a body had been washed up by the golf course. A body that had been in the water for several days, bloated and mutilated by the waves. On its wrist was a watch with a silver strap. There were so many other stories at the time. A naked body washed up on a beach, that was all there was of him. When she went to ask she was told no body had been washed up by the golf course, and if she had any sense she would get lost and stop asking so many questions about bodies. We hardly knew what was true. And our own end seemed so near that one more death, one more threat did not seem to matter such a great deal.'

She looked at him with a kind of horror, disbelieving him. 'What's happened to her?' she asked.

'She's probably dead,' he said, hating himself for his cynicism but not wanting to fall to pieces again. 'And if she's still alive she's probably sick with shame at the way our lives have turned out. They are dead or dying out there and I'm here, struggling from day to day as if there's some purpose to this endeavour, as if there is any point being here. She used to say I would marry Amina one day. It means nothing, just a way of paying a boy a compliment and embarrassing him a little. Take your betrothed a drink of water, she used to say to Amina and laugh to see me so flustered. Now she's probably dead and Amina is a prostitute. Bossy's dead who should have been there to guard them, and I'm here, wondering what could credibly make any of this worth the bother.'

He looked at her and thought that perhaps she was beginning to become part of the answer. He smiled at her, ruefully acknowledging the melodrama of his despairing talk. They made love with slow care, relishing the pleasure they took in each other. Later, when he rose to go to work, she rose with him. She touched him as he poured himself some tea, leaning against him, made sleepy by fatigue. She sat at the table with him while he ate his bread and butter, dozing a little but not wanting to leave him.

'I'd better go,' he said, lifting up her wrist to check her watch. 'Will you be here later?' he asked.

She shook her head slowly. 'I don't know.'

He nodded, then leant forward and kissed her. He had thought she would say that. He thought he would have done the same thing too, if this Malcolm was half-way decent. 'You're making a terrible mistake,' he said.

She shrugged, grinning at his style of wooing. 'I don't know,' she answered. 'I have to see him, talk it out with him. Right now I'm going back to bed. And you'd better get going to work or you'll be late.'

He was, and Solomon was popping in and out of the changing room to check his arrival. 'What kind of time do you call this?' he asked, his eyes sharp with checked anger. 'There's a panic on in here, son. Two Staffs are sick and you turn up at this time. Get your finger out, will you? ENT Theatre with Sister Shelton.'

'Big day tomorrow,' Daud called out as Solomon was about to disappear out of the changing-room door.

Solomon came back, looking even more irritated than before. 'What?' he asked. 'What did you say?'

'Big day tomorrow,' Daud said, taking his time. 'The first day of the Test Match!'

Solomon looked as if he would burst. 'Get the fuck in there,' he yelled and almost ran out of the room.

Sister Wilhelmina Shelton was gowned and waiting for the first case when he strolled into the theatre. She unclasped her gloved hands and put them symbolically akimbo, allowing them to hover over her hips without touching her gown. 'I don't know what you think you're playing at, my boy. Is this some kind of church social you're turning up for? Dr Rao's been waiting to start his list but he has to wait for you, Your Majesty, to wake up out of your sleep.'

Daud bowed deeply to the Sister, and gave Dr Rao merely a perfunctory genuflection. 'I didn't need to wake up out of my sleep since I wasn't in it,' he said to the Sister. 'I didn't sleep at all last night.'

She threw her head back and laughed. She liked to think of him as a restless young wolf, and was always tempting him to tell lies about his adventures. 'All right, I'll let you off from a real hard time if you tell us what happened,' she said.

'Big day tomorrow,' Daud said as the first patient was wheeled in. Dr Rao was a lover of the game as well, and after the patient had been positioned, the microscope brought up, the doctor comfortably seated on his operating stool and the anaesthetist had dropped off to sleep, they settled to a busy but fulfilling morning of cricket talk. The afternoon passed reasonably enough as well, and Daud congratulated himself on having spent such a pleasant day when he might have been miserable.

He hurried home. He told himself not to expect anything. *Face the facts, boy. She's got herself a young, attractive doctor who's an Englishman son of an Englishman. He's rich. And his daddy's rich. In a couple of weeks' time they go driving across France. Next year they go flying to Florence. She couldn't go wrong even if he turns out to be a wife-beater as well. Now look the other way and see what she's got as competition against that. Say it how you will, it comes to the same thing. A foreigner with a whole chapter and verse of dreadful scars. A sleazy customer, past his best, paint running off him. He lives in a mouldy slum and doesn't have a penny. His only friends are a couple of idiots who hate each other. For a living he cleans floors in a hospital, and could just as easily have been cleaning car park toilets. Even his father hates him! So face the facts and prepare yourself to take this like a man instead of blubbering all over the place like you ain't got no black pride.* But still he hurried home.

She had left him her telephone number. That was all. Her telephone number! He wandered round the house looking for other signs of her. He found some hair on his pillow but little else. None the less the house was full of her, and having satisfied himself that her smell filled the air, he sat down to rest and almost immediately fell asleep. When he woke up, he made some food and settled down to eat. It was dark now, past ten. He wondered if it was time to try again to write to his father. He had not mentioned his parents when he told Catherine about Bossy, but he had thought of them. How frantic they had been when he did not turn up that night, gunfire and wild rumours filling the night air. How pleased they had been when he arrived at the detention camp. His father came to look for him, having heard from someone that he had arrived. By then the fever had come over him and he had been taken to the infants' school where the wounded were dumped. No one attended to them, and if no relative came to remove the seriously wounded, they lay there in their waste and filth. The school rooms were filled with the smell of rotting flesh and vomit. Over the carnage hovered flies in disgusting numbers, bloating themselves to contentment on the filth. His father found him and carried him out, making small encouraging noises while he silently wept. '*Haya haya*, my son. There there, *mwanangu*.' His mother tore strips of her dress to wipe and bandage the cuts. She said that she was happy now, that there was nothing they could do to her. She had her family together. When he came to tell them about Bossy, they hardly listened. There were so many dead that day.

He would write to him. It was just that he knew his father would not reply. They had saved their money for years, keeping it safe in the rafters under the galvanised roof, thinking that one day it would come in useful. In the good years, as business prospered, they put more away. In the bad years, when the harvests were poor, they tightened their belts. His father was a school teacher but he had bought himself a piece of land with a bequest from a relative. For years he did both, teaching school and working the land for vegetables and eggs. Then Daud had taken the money to go and study. Daud knew he had not been grudged the money. It was him they grudged losing, seeing him running away, perhaps never to return. The money was nothing. Then he came to England and really found out that it was nothing, hardly enough to allow him to survive for a few months. He had hung on for more than a year before everything became too much and he fell to pieces. They thought he had lived it up with the money, their hard-earned savings, and that that was why he had failed. He would write to them, but he did not think they would want to hear now.

He went out to look for a phone box and try out Catherine's number. Another woman answered the phone and told him to wait. He had to hold on for a long time. Two men had already walked past and glared into the phone box. A dog urinated against the side while its owner, an old woman whose sons must certainly have roamed the globe slaughtering Muslims, glared at Daud with utter loathing.

'Where've you been?' he asked when she came to the phone, unable to keep the terror the old woman had made him feel out of his voice.

'Oh, hello. How nice to hear from you! I'm fine, thank you. And you?' she asked, speaking with the forced cheerfulness demanded by an unexpected call from a long-abandoned friend or relative.

'Like that, is it? Is the hero there?'

'Yes,' she said. 'It *has* been a lovely day. We could do with some more of them, couldn't we? Although it's been a lovely summer so far, hasn't it? So, what have you been up to?'

'Shit! I risk life and limb to come out in the middle of the night to ring you. I stand here, exposed and vulnerable while murderers and witches stroll past, feasting their eyes on my luscious body, weaving their fantasies round it and making my skin crawl. You keep me waiting for hours while you pluck up the courage to tear yourself away from your lover boy ... don't try to deny it ... and this is all the welcome I get? Will I see you tonight?'

'Oh no,' she said laughing. 'Nothing like that. I wish I could say it was.'

'Why not? Can't you get rid of him?'

'I don't think so. Oh, but I'm really pleased that you did manage it. Did your mum like it? I bet she did!' she said.

'My mum? I don't have a mum, I have a ma. How can you even remember what you last said? He probably knows exactly what you're doing, and is only waiting for you to get off the phone before ...'

'I don't think so. But thank you for the thought. I think I'll just send her a card.'

'Are you trying to tell me to piss off?' he asked after a moment of silence.

'Not at all.'

'Will I see you tomorrow?' he asked.

'I don't know.'

'This is a stupid conversation,' he said. 'Is he standing beside you or something?'

She laughed. 'Well, more or less! But you know how difficult it is to remember dates. I'm really sorry.'

'What kind of creep would do that?'

'Oh no, it's always nice to hear from you. I won't forget! I'll send her a card tomorrow. I'm sure it'll get there in time. No, of course I didn't mind. I keep meaning to call you but somehow ...'

'I know what you mean,' he said.

'But it's always nice to hear from you.'

'Thank you, dear,' he said.

'Bye bye then. And I won't forget about the card. Bye.'

He paced his silent living room and tried to chase away the thought of her with the grubby-fingered farmer. He wondered if he had been too easy on her. Should he have thrown a telephone tantrum and insisted on turning up at her door? And although he told himself not to expect her, he stayed up late, straining for her steps on the pavement and fearing the clop of Lloyd's feet. He gave up in the end, feeling his early excitement turn to irritation and resentment. He knew she would not give up her farmer, but he wanted her to come to him a few more times. There was a limit to the abuse he would put up with, though. She should not leave her telephone number if she did not want him to call. There were plenty more where she came from. He felt, despite his bluster, that there was nothing he could do, that he was at her mercy. If she felt like coming to him again he would welcome her. He thought she would come, perhaps a few more times, before the squalor of the arrangement depressed her and drove her where hard-headed good sense demanded she should go.

As he took two steps and turned he tried to shift his mind from her, but as he moved forward again so his thoughts found her as before, chasing away the images that had appeared while his back was turned. When would Karta come back, he wondered? He needed someone to talk to, someone who would take his mind away from her. Karta's hurt that his brave deeds against the white oppressor had been found fault with would only last for a week at most, Daud guessed. Perhaps he should go round to Karta's digs and smooth his coxcomb. He was glad, though, that Karta was not around to advise him, because he thought he could guess what his advice would have been. *Ditch the bitch!*

In another place he would have been a candidate for a good whipping by now, perhaps even a blade through the gut or worse. With his own people he could imagine what he had done being thought quite improper. A nice girl with her doctor boyfriend being messed about by a foreign boy who cleaned lavatories. A few brothers would have got a little act together and chased the rat away. He could hear the righteous self-congratulations of the heroes responsible for this deed of communal responsibility. *These English boys are the scum of their own people, street-sweepers and sons of prostitutes. Boys from good families don't behave like that. They think they can come here and treat our women like whores. They have no respect, no manners. But we gave him a small instalment today. If he wants a whore he should go pay for one, not corrupt a decent woman.*

Poor Amina, no one was going to speak of her as a decent woman. When he was let out of detention and had gone to Bossy's house to see if any word had come, it was little Amina, only six years old, who had opened the door to him, squinting in the strong sunlight. He had followed her into the dark and shuttered house, giving up his hand to her and allowing her to lead him to where her mother sat cross-legged by the back door. They had squatted together and sobbed for their grotesque bereavement. The mother's sobbing had soon turned to howls and groans for the death and torture of her son, and both Daud and Amina had stepped back to watch with horror as she lamented the dead.

Even as he told himself not to wait for Catherine, he found himself tensing for the sound of her approach. When he went to bed he found frequent subterfuges to cock an ear for the sound of her hurrying step. He tried to distract himself with the thought of the Test Match, inventing huge scores for his heroes and pathetic collapses for the England team. West Indies 580 for 2, England in reply 21 for 9. Tony Greig, 0 first ball, was last seen grovelling in the dressing room, trying to avoid the wrath and contempt of his team. In the end Daud buried his head under the sheets, disgusted with himself. He woke up feeling sore and thick-headed, and left the house surprised by the dejection he felt and by the way he had allowed his desire for her to enfeeble him. He began to feel that the worst was over, that knowledge of his pathetic behaviour was the beginning of the refusal to play that game. So utterly did he dislike the way he had been the previous night that he resolved to have nothing more to do with Catherine. He would avoid her, tear up the telephone number she had left him.

At work he found himself in Sister Wilhelmina Shelton's team again, a fate to be devoutly wished for on Test Match days. Sister Shelton made no concession to the holy calling of healing where cricket was concerned, and brought a transistor radio into the theatre to listen to the ball-by-ball commentary on the day's play. The boys did not let her down, putting up 437 runs for 9 by the end of play, with centuries for both Fredericks and Greenidge. The consultant was a paid-up member of the MCC, and he cast many reproachful glances at the radio as play progressed. The Sister had no mercy, and could be heard muttering things like *Make that man grovel!* to encourage the slaughter. Daud had tried to teach her to call him a rascal, but she had failed to see the point, and insisted on calling him that man.

He went to call on Karta after work, going directly there. Karta lived in a large Victorian building, owned by the university and rented out to postgraduate students. Daud had no idea how large the house really was, but he guessed there were at least a dozen people living in it. The house was in one of the leafy, residential streets near the university that spoke both of prosperity and the cultivation of a relaxed scruffiness. You wouldn't catch anybody picking up dog turds down this street, he thought. The little pile of turds would be casually skirted until the Council sweeper came by and scraped it away.

But Karta was not in. The man who opened the door came back to tell Daud that Karta had gone away. For a day or two, he thought. Did Daud want to leave word for him? They had a notice board. Or he could ring him the next day if he wanted to take the number.

'No, don't trouble,' Daud said. He would have liked to ask the man his name, and get him to talk about his work, his *research*. Anything so he did not have to return to the house just yet. He thanked the man and left, smiling ruefully to himself as he reflected that he had been in England for too long, and had learnt the reticent bad manners of the natives. He thought also how much he envied Karta these civilised trappings, a desirable residence and intelligent company. Yet

Karta always spoke of the students he shared with as if they were contemptible half-wits. Daud wondered how much Karta's absence had to do with the fight with Lloyd.

There was always Lloyd. He kept inviting Daud to go round and meet his parents. What better time than now, after the beating that Karta had administered? Daud could arrive as the messenger of a gospel of brotherhood and tolerance. He knew, from what Lloyd had told him, that the father was inclined to believe in jungle bunnies and coons. He would not have been amused by the sight of his injured son, abused and assaulted by a Jungle Jim run amok. Daud could preach co-existence to him with unctuous hypocrisy, the way the victorious always did to the defeated. But the victory, if it was that, had not been his, and the Lloyd clan could hang on to their cruel delusions for a little longer. In the end he went back to Bishop Street, with only the cricket highlights to look forward to, although 437 for 9 was a lavish enough feast.

Catherine came at around ten. She grinned at him as if her arrival was a conspiracy they had both shared. He let her in but would not allow her to pass until she had submitted to a long embrace. She was still wearing her uniform, and about her was the smell of hospital wards and disinfectant.

'How's the farmer?' he asked, although he disliked the anxiety his question implied the instant the words were out of his mouth.

'He knows about you,' she said, sitting at the table, then leaning back to stretch her tired body. 'I told him last night. I didn't think it was right not to. He surprised me too. He was so upset, wanted to know who you were, what you did. It was strange, not what I expected at all. He pleaded that I shouldn't leave, when I thought he would get angry and storm off.'

He said nothing, hardly dared breathe. His mouth felt dry. He waited for her to continue, and she looked at him with a kind of complacent happiness, pleased with herself.

'I wanted him to stop asking me questions and go away, so I could come back here. But he wouldn't go, especially after you rang. He knew it was you. He called me all kinds of names,' she said and shrugged. 'He insisted on knowing your name. When he found out ... He said he could not understand how I could touch you. How I could sleep with you! He kept calling you all these things, nigger, wog, that sort of thing. It was almost funny in the end. He wouldn't go, kept on pleading. Until early morning he was still there. It was so unexpected. I wouldn't have believed it. I didn't think he would feel like that. I thought I was the one who should feel flattered. He'd chosen me. He took me out to all these places.

'We go round as a little group, you know. All the men are doctors, and all the women are nurses. Some of the older women have been passed from one man to another, although that's not what we call it. Like Paula. The lucky ones marry their doctors and whisk them away. That's what I was into.' She looked at him, unsmiling and inviting his censure. 'I felt squalid, and too weak to do anything about it. Like the brazen girl at school who pretends that she likes being pushed into the English store and mauled by the boys. I felt I should know better, but I did nothing. I hated it so much when I came here. But I thought I had to stick it out. I was afraid they would think me weak at home if I didn't. That's when I moved out of the nurses' home to where I am now. I thought I would have fun, anyway. Going out, having a man. Whenever I caught those looks from the other nurses I pretended they were just envious, but I knew it was really the same contempt I felt for women like Paula. It never occurred to me that Malcolm felt any different really. He didn't treat me as if he did. He took me out, bought me drinks, slept with me.'

'Don't keep saying it like that,' he said.

'But he did! That's how he made me feel.' She looked at him with assurance, prepared to explain, to persuade. 'It was such a relief when I began to tell him. Then you rang, and that made me feel good. He wouldn't go. I knew he wouldn't go until I slept with him. So in the end ... I did, so he would go.' She looked at him again, waiting to see if he had anything to say. He said nothing, but in the end a sudden grin of elation escaped him. It was the contemptuous way she spoke of sleeping with him that filled him with joy. *On your bike, farmer boy.*

'He'll be back,' Daud warned, adding a dash of fear in his voice to hasten his rival's transformation into a demon.

'Yes, I know,' she said, not sounding annoyed enough for Daud's liking. 'He told me. He said he wouldn't give up just like that. He was there tonight. I rang home before I left work, and he was there waiting. He's got no right to do that. He doesn't own me. Do you know last night he asked me to marry him? I told him not to be ridiculous. He just could not bear the idea of me going away. I was like a toy he was losing.' Daud was surprised by the offer of marriage. She was elated by her escape, and the discovery of the ascendancy over the doctor and was dismissive of him. Perhaps later she would see the matter differently. Daud kept quiet, happy to hear his rejected rival abused. 'I think you'd better stay here until things calm down,' he said, injecting as much horror and shock in his voice as he dared. 'You don't know what an enraged doctor is capable of.'

'Of course I'm staying here,' she said with a sigh. Then she flashed a small grin and shut her eyes.

17

He dreamt that night that Lloyd had joined a regiment of Hussars and had ridden over Sister Williams's fence in his gleaming uniform, snatched a bottle of sherry out of her hand and refused to leave unless she agreed to let him ravish her. Daud found this image of Lloyd so difficult to credit that he woke up with a headache. To his further consternation, Catherine began to talk a little guiltily about her doctor. Daud had much preferred the abuses for which she had condemned him, even though they were painful to contemplate. Her doubts about whether she had treated him shabbily had an ominous ring.

'Shabbily!' he urged her. 'This man thinks you're a diseased woman. He thinks you're some kind of sex freak because you want to be with me rather than his pink-skinned self. He thinks I'm a diabolical monster! How can you treat someone like that shabbily? Nothing is too shabby for a horror like that!' There was more, but he did not want to win the doctor any unnecessary sympathy by running amok. He gritted his teeth and listened as Catherine tried to rehabilitate the man's character. It was what Daud had been afraid of, that the offer would seduce her into taking the doctor's affection seriously again.

'I keep thinking of what he must be feeling. I had no idea how involved he was. Marriage! I mean you don't offer marriage just like that, do you? Imagine that you loved someone enough to want to marry him, and just when you think that all's well, it turns out there's somebody else. I'm not really that bothered about what he said—'

'Well I am!' he interrupted, launching a swift counter-offensive. 'That's how it begins. You may think that he said all those nasty things because he was disappointed. Ah, poor doctor, he was only a little upset. That may seem to you to be a good reason for him calling people like me a nigger monster, but not to me. Next week he'll turn a blind eye to some poor black woman's disease. And a month after he'll gloat over an underfed little piccaninny that's been beaten to death by its mother, crazed and hapless on drugs and despair. All because he's upset, when normally he likes nothing better than to kiss little coon babies' buttocks. Words like that don't come out of the blue. They come out of what we think.'

'Aren't you exaggerating?' she asked, grimacing with distaste.

'Do you think so? He probably does that already.'

'What do you take him for?' she shouted, glaring at him. 'Anyway, it was about me ... I meant I'm not bothered what he said about *me*.'

'Well I am. You may not mind that he treats you as he wishes ... Look at the way he used you. Even on the night when you were telling him to go, he wanted his bit of flesh first.'

She laughed. He was annoyed with himself for having brought that up. It made him sound petty but he could not imagine that she would find any defence for such a brutish act of vengeance. 'So what?' she asked, looking at him with a mixture of defiance and anger. 'What does that make me then? It was hardly that great an imposition. I've been sleeping with him for months, and I've been sleeping with you, and there were others before both of you. What do you take me for? A little virgin dairy maid taken advantage of by a wicked squire?'

He made no reply. He imagined that in this scene he was the naive and idealistic lover. Why did they all take him to be so naive? Bossy, and Karta, and now her. They sat in an uncomfortable silence, turning back to cups of coffee that had grown cold. 'Do you think he was serious about marriage then?' he asked, trying to expunge any mockery from his tone, and posing the question, he assured himself, entirely out of academic curiosity.

'You don't think so?' she asked, keeping her voice level but unable in the end to stop herself smiling. 'I don't know. I don't think so really. It was completely unexpected. I suppose that was what he thought I wanted. Perhaps he didn't mean it, but intended it to buy him a small delay. Then in a month or two he'd have left me … or something like that.'

'I don't think he meant it,' he said with finality.

'I don't think he did either. I was looking at the way I'd behaved because I was beginning to feel that I'd behaved badly. Then you get so angry, and make him into some kind of monster. Anyway, you'd better go to work. I think you're going to be late.'

The thought of Solomon rampaging round the changing rooms, checking the clocks and looking for him, made Daud laugh. 'Will you come here after work? Or go back to the flat?' he asked.

She was silent for a long moment. 'You won't misunderstand me, will you?' she said. 'I have to go back to the flat. Be by myself for a while, and think things out. And I really fancy a bath.'

'If he … comes? Will you be all right?'

She gave him a brief look, followed by a pitying smile. He was lucky, he thought, to escape without another lecture on his innocence. 'I'll have to deal with it,' she said. 'I'll have to know how to deal with him.'

He shrugged and stood up to leave. 'Good luck.'

'You're a bloody bully,' she said angrily. 'I have to sort it out with him. I can't just leave it like this. It makes me feel bad enough as it is. And I need a little more time … rushing from one thing to another won't do any good, will it?'

He nodded. 'You're right,' he said reluctantly. 'You'd better take your time.'

She looked suspicious, thinking he was being sarcastic.

'I guess I'm afraid he might persuade you back,' he said and stopped.

'You afraid?' she asked, and he was unreasonably pleased by her incredulous tone.

'It's pay day today,' he said. 'I'll get some food for tomorrow and cook a lavish dinner. Will you come?'

He ran most of the way to work but still arrived twenty minutes late. He changed as quickly as he could and went to Solomon's office, expecting to have to cringe in front of the Ineffable Locksman. *May I address your wise self? Do tell me if I'm rushing you too much. These are interesting days in my life. I begin to feel unusually light. I feel I can take to the air, at times I feel invincible. You've been warned!* Solomon merely glanced up and twitched his lips. Daud hastily retreated, wondering what event had occurred to deprive him of his scolding. At least, he consoled himself, he had not been denied the disposal corridor. He discovered the reason for Solomon's good temper in the sluice area, where three trolleys of dirty instruments and mountains of bloody linen awaited his attention. The night staff had been working flat out and had had no time to clean up. Daud had already seen the frightening size of the morning lists. With the addition of the emergency trolleys, he would be kept amused for most of the morning. He gave Solomon a small round of applause, appreciating the subtler qualities of this morning's malice.

Dear Clive Lloyd, You're on your own! I can't be with you this morning while you take on the England cricket team. My services are required in the interests of surgery and humanity. Have no mercy on Tony Greig! Crush him! Tony Greig went on to make 89 not out before close of play, taking England to 238 for 5. This was better than the 90 all out Daud had predicted. Aside from the number of runs the Boer made, he made them with style and a bit of dash. And he was still there, intent on getting even more! Also the wage packet Mrs Coop had given him was slimmer than he had anticipated. A mistake, she assured him, which would be put right in his next pay, a whole long week away. He went home with a sinking feeling that he would find something smelly had been pushed through his letter box. He found a letter from Piano Keys, regretfully demanding rent. In something of a high dudgeon he fetched pen and paper and arrayed them on the table, composing a fierce reply in his mind as he prepared himself a sandwich. *Dear Piano Keys, You do not deserve the tolerance with which I treat you. You shame the sobriquet that I have borrowed for you. After all, you're nothing more than a slum landlord.*

When he came to it, he wrote a letter to Catherine instead. He told her how he had left his home, about the forged passport, the bribes, the bogus health certificates. He described the suspicion of the Immigration officials at the airport, the terror of the machine-gun turret on top of the airport control tower, the long walk across the tarmac to the steaming aircraft. He told her how he had expected a bullet to end that endless journey. He was young then, he explained, and inclined to be melodramatic. *Catherine*. He liked to say the name to himself. He saw her with her brown hair streaked with gold, sitting waiting for him to arrive. He saw her as she had been in his house, roused to anger by the filth in which he lived, lying beside him like a gift from the gods.

By the time she came the following day, he had cooked the meal and was waiting for her. When he opened the door to her she smiled.

'Did he come?' he asked.

She nodded. 'It's over.'

They sat in the darkening living room, the dirty plates in front of them, the television blaring from next door. 'You must be tired,' he said, dropping what he hoped were heavy hints. They took their coffee upstairs, lying on the bed to be near each other.

'You ran away,' she said after reading his letter. 'All that danger to come to this? Is that what makes you sad?'

'I don't think so. Maybe sometimes it does seem like a lot of wasted effort. All the labours you put to survival are in aid of this? As if you had a choice. But no, it's not that. It's being a stranger. That is what's so crushing. The community you live in carries on in its complicated way, and it is entirely indifferent to you. It requires nothing from you, and in return you are a complete irrelevance to it. You are free. But you're also without any function. Do what you like, it makes no difference. You see, sometimes it's tempting to think of yourself as in some kind of exile. Exile means there is no choice. There's a purpose or a principle behind what you do. But really the matter is much less lofty than that. The principles, if they survive the crushing of the spirit, turn out to be mean, self-deluding little ambitions. I want to be an accountant. That kind of thing. Perhaps the real ambition is to escape. Not to escape the particular, the threat to life and fulfilment, but to escape as a kind of drama that gives meaning to life. As you say, this is what you run to, this is what you escape to. Instead of soaring with like-minded idealists, you are grubbing among the lumber of your little life-raft, trying to remember the reasons for this shipwreck.'

She said nothing, watching as he shrank into his desolation. She felt she understood something of his loneliness but did not want to seem impatient. After a moment he started to talk again. He told her of the furtive farewell he took of his parents, whispering behind the front door, before he set off on his own for the taxi park.

'Can you go back?' she asked at last, when he would say no more.

He shook his head, then shrugged. He told her of the weight of his father's arm on his shoulder as he said goodbye. Then he had gone rushing out of the house, too full of anxieties to worry about what his parents felt. 'Now I think how cruel it was, leaving them like that. At the time I thought they were fussing. It *didn't* feel like I would never see them again. It didn't feel that way at all. I think how I must've hurt them acting like that. And the trouble is that I can't just meet them and make it all better. You know, buy them a bunch of flowers and say sorry. They remain like that, standing behind that door whispering their goodbyes, feeling bitter at my impatience. That's how I remember them. And that's how they'll remember me.'

He stopped and gave her a startled look. He had not thought of raising that picture of them, had not fully imagined it himself. He would be burdened with that image of them for ever.

'I have a feeling that you'll be meeting them sooner than you think,' she said.

He nodded, accepting the comfort, and feeling that perhaps he was going on. As they lay dozing in the dark, he surfaced now and then with a snippet of something funny that had happened in his childhood. The last thing she remembered was his halting monotone as he talked about the Test Match, predicting a miserable Saturday for England.

To his great annoyance, England survived the Saturday comfortably and the hated Boer reached 116 before he was removed. Daud became quite petulant once the score passed 350. Catherine persuaded him to come out for a stroll instead of sitting in the house on such a lovely afternoon.

'I might as well,' he said, on the verge of saying something cruel about the beloved West Indies team. He took her to the common and showed her the huge bank of nettles which he found so terrifying. They sat in the grove of ash and birch trees, playing at being lovers. He quivered a little when a dog came in sight, but her presence and the joyful way that she dealt with the monster reassured him. None of the boys playing in the park came to throw stones at them, or call them names. After a while, he began to feel safe and he lay on the grass beside her, shutting his eyes.

'This is the warmest summer I remember,' she said.

They met Lloyd on their way home. He was so delighted to see them that Daud knew he could not just shake him off. He could not reject so much affection. He came back to the house with them, and Daud invited him in.

'I thought I'd better stay away for a while. After all that business. You know what he's like,' Lloyd said, addressing the last remark at Catherine. 'Karta! Have you met Karta yet?'

'Yes,' she said brightly.

Lloyd struggled to smile. His whole manner spoke so much of strain and anxiety that Daud could not be certain if the smile was to do with what she had said at all.

'He hasn't been round much,' Daud said gloomily, discouraging Catherine's cheerfulness.

'You must come and meet my parents. Both of you! I've been asking him for months but he won't come,' Lloyd said, enlisting Catherine's support. 'You must come! They're really keen to meet you. Come tomorrow, come for Sunday dinner.'

'No,' Daud said at once, even though the remark was addressed to Catherine and she was smiling politely as if feeling herself forced to accept the hospitality. He saw her face cringe a little, and saw her look away.

'Come for tea,' Lloyd said, the plea in his voice unmistakable now.

She glanced at Daud, daring him to refuse, and he nodded. Lloyd sighed softly and then smiled at Daud. He did not stay long after that, hurrying to leave once he knew that they were planning to go to the cinema that evening. He waited for Daud to see him to the door, and then stood on the pavement, looking past Daud into the house. 'I'm sorry about all those things I said,' he said. 'It's him. He makes me feel like that.'

Daud said nothing, but he nodded because he could not bear the look of misery on Lloyd's face. Large and formless as he was, with that pasty look, he was like a lump of dough, Daud thought. There was nothing he could do for him. He had only felt Lloyd as a burden, and after the baboons and nig-nogs outburst with Karta, there was little more to be said. Go find yourself another golliwog, he thought.

She was annoyed with him when he went back, but he shrugged off her criticism. He wanted nothing to do with their squabbles, he told her. He could not understand why Lloyd should have pleaded for them to accept. Daud wondered if that was because of Catherine, because she was so obviously English. The other invitations had been lightly tossed at him, and never pursued. The thought had struck him when Lloyd first asked. He asked *her*, in that pleading voice. Now as he thought about it, he wondered if he would have acquired greater respectability because of Catherine. An *au pair* with a heavy accent would have suggested cheap sex and nightly orgies perhaps, and he would have appeared as a kind of tormented Florialis to Lloyd's parents, a fornicating black baboon. Not if he turned up with Catherine, though.

The thought of going to meet them spoilt his Sunday, he insisted. He had heard enough about Lloyd's parents to imagine what it would be like to spend an afternoon with them. The father would be a large, muscular gent with curly fair hair. He would possess a huge paw with which he would attempt to crush Daud's hand, no doubt imagining that it was really his gonads he was turning into jelly. *She* would be skinny and nervous, having spent a lifetime under the tyranny of this hulk. Lloyd had told him that his parents never said anything of any significance, so he could imagine them fixing him with long, baleful stares, while they sat silently gulping tea.

Lloyd invited them into the house shyly, almost humbly. His greetings and his questions tumbled over each other, revealing his delight that they had come. 'Come and meet my parents,' he said in a conspiratorial whisper.

Daud was astonished by the affluence of the house. The outside gave no indication of the richness of the carpets and of the furnishings, the luxury of the papered walls and the polished banister. Yet Lloyd had chosen to leave this comfort to come and spend his evenings at Daud's dirty hovel. It was disappointing to discover that the appetite could tire of such luxury and seek instead the disagreeable discomforts of his kind of squalor. Lloyd probably felt guilty about the carpets, he thought, or had a secret ambition to undertake abject tasks.

They were met at the door of the living room by a short, stumpy-looking man. His squat, meaty head was grizzled and lined even under the closely cropped grey hair. His eyes passed quickly over Daud and settled on Catherine. He stepped forward and took her hand, smiling at her with a brashness that was not going to be denied. 'You must be Lloyd's friend,' he said to Daud, still holding on to her hand. 'Come in, come in, come in.'

He propelled Daud into the living room, giving him a firm push in the back. Daud found himself faced by a slim, dark-haired woman, striding towards him with obvious delight. She shook his hand with unexpected force, saying something welcoming to him. The handshake reminded him of his first Englishman. He had been only a boy then, rewarded for his diligent pursuit of excellence by a school prize that was to be presented to him by the Director of Education. There was some disagreement among his teachers about whether the Englishman's name was Mr Hens or Mr Hams or Mr Hands. After this brief meeting, Daud knew he could only be Mr Hands. He had learnt his lesson from that, and now shook hands with Englishmen with circumspection and force. It was high time, he reflected, that he applied this simple survival skill to his encounters with English women as well. She motioned him into a chair, and he sank into it with muttered gratitude.

'I'm Mrs Marsh,' she said, speaking gently and watching him warily, as if she expected him to despise her. 'And this is Mr Marsh. Lloyd, of course, you know.'

'How do you do,' said Mr Marsh loudly, enunciating each syllable. He guided Catherine to the sofa and sat beside her. She had repossessed her hand but it was clear already that matters would not be that easy. He leant towards her as he spoke. 'And what do they call you, my dear?' he asked.

'Her name's Catherine, Dad,' Lloyd called out, standing awkwardly by the door and watching his father.

'What? Why are you standing there?' snapped Mr Marsh.

'Come and sit down, Lloyd. Come and sit by your friend,' Mrs Marsh advised, settling herself nearby.

'And what do you do with yourself, Catherine?' Mr Marsh asked.

'She's a nurse, Dad. Don't you remember Lloyd telling us,' Mrs Marsh cheerfully reminded him, not appearing to notice how his hand came to land on Catherine's thigh. 'And Dudley works at the hospital too.'

'Daud. My name is Daud,' he said, looking on as Catherine removed Mr Marsh's hand from her thigh.

'Oh, I'm sorry,' she said. 'How silly of me! English people are terrible with names, aren't they?'

Her wariness surprised him, but when he became used to it he saw it as a kind of nervous alertness. She leant back in her chair, taking herself out of the picture. When she saw him watching her she smiled. It was a friendly, surprised smile: *Oh, you are interested in me.*

'What country are you from?' she asked.

When he was in the mood, he enjoyed this question. He would have a captive audience to whom he could recite a fantastic and fabricated history with complete freedom. Sometimes he mined for gold in the Ruwenzori, working a stake in the city of *She. Oh yes, it exists all right*. At times he was a princeling, a provincial khan, fated to inherit his father's twenty wives. On occasions he claimed descent from Bajun pirates, and could describe in detail the initiation rites of his people, or whip off his shirt to demonstrate the scars left on him. He was distracted, though, by Catherine's plight, and attended to her in case she needed help.

'Tanzania,' he said.

'Oh, how nice! I bet it's a wonderful country. What comes from there? It must be lovely and warm,' Mrs Marsh said with a vivacity that was clearly false, that was an attempt to disguise her nervousness. None the less Daud thought he detected an undercurrent of enthusiasm and warmth in her voice.

'Have you been to Africa?' he asked, misled by the tone with which she spoke.

'Oh no,' she said with a disappointed voice. 'But Dad … Mr Marsh has.'

'Tanzania! That's one of these socialist one-party democracies, isn't it?' Mr Marsh asked, turning slightly to face Daud.

It was a pity the grizzly fart had started with such a good one, Daud thought. What can you say about socialist, one-party democracies? They were an abomination, anathema, thinly disguised dictatorships, intended to allow the abuse of freedom within the state, the resort of the intolerant and the chronically authoritarian. He could not think of a single good thing that he could say to defend socialist, one-party democracies. For national unity he read national bullying. Their enthusiasts described them as traditional forms of government. Whose traditions? If some greasy King had managed to gain ascendancy over his own people, and molested and harassed them for some bizarre ambition he harboured, was that a reason to follow in his bloody footsteps? No, there was nothing to be done with socialist, one-party democracies. He was glad that Mr Marsh had turned his attention to him, though, and given Catherine a rest. Daud smiled at the squat bugger, hoping he would come charging out with something else that he could crash right out of the ground for six.

'Yes, Andrew was in Africa during the War, and he even had some African friends,' Mrs Marsh told Daud. He caught the nervous, sympathetic look again. She was afraid he might have understood the anger in Mr Marsh's remark, he thought.

'What was the name of the place where you were, Dad?' Lloyd asked.

'The White Man's Grave,' Mr Marsh said, smiling at Daud. 'I can remember what it used to be called, although God knows what it's called now. There was a time when you could look at a map and recognise the places. Now it's Tanzania, Ruritania, Krakatoa or any other pretentious name they can dream up. It was a different Africa in those days,' Mr Marsh said, turning back to Catherine and leering at her. 'It was probably the only time in its history when Africa had a bit of order.'

'Oh, Dad.' Lloyd glanced at Daud to let him know that Mr Marsh could not really be serious.

'Well, ask him,' he said, talking to Catherine, but pointing at Daud. 'Nothing but starvation and chaos. Ask him! Ask your friend why he doesn't go back there.'

Mrs Marsh sighed. 'Oh, Andrew, it's not as simple as that,' she said.

'I don't mean any offence,' Mr Marsh said, looking at his wife. 'I don't believe in all that colour bar nonsense, you know that. And I hope what I'm saying will be taken in the spirit it's meant.'

'Of course, Dad,' Lloyd said in the embarrassing silence.

'I have nothing against you personally,' Mr Marsh said, turning to Daud. 'After all we invited you to our house. But there are just too many of your people here now, and we don't want the chaos of all those places to be brought to us here. We've done enough for your people already.'

Daud listened patiently to their display of insular meanness and arrogance. Catherine made a face, asking if he wanted to leave. He shook his head. Lloyd was sitting silently nearby, and Daud wondered why he had wanted him to come and see this. In the end Mrs Marsh rose to get the tea, and called Catherine to help her. By this time Catherine was fuming with anger at Mr Marsh's fumbles, and as she left the room she glanced at him with loathing.

'You should've thought of all this before,' Daud said. 'Before you set off on your civilising mission.' He did not have to do this, he told himself. He was just performing a social duty, educating the world at large in the benefits of cultural exchanges. To be as blissfully unaware of his ridiculousness as this man was a quality only builders of empires possessed. It was the same with those Chinese and Roman Kings who had disregarded the most obvious hints of their impending destruction. They had pranced and preened, and could not believe what pathetically vulnerable figures they cut in front of their barbarian enemies. They were so convinced of their superiority that they could not take the danger seriously.

Mr Marsh looked at Daud for a moment, as if wondering whether to reply. He turned to Lloyd and talked to him about the shop instead. Mrs Marsh came back in with a tray of tea things while Catherine followed with the cakes and biscuits. She came to sit on the floor beside Daud, avoiding Mr Marsh and refusing his most fervent pleas that she should return to the sofa.

'She wants to be by her young man, Andrew,' Mrs Marsh said sharply, silencing the bully.

'It must cause you problems sometimes,' he said, looking at Catherine. 'Do people say things to you about him ... Dudley? I think it's worst of all for the children. Something seems to happen to the children when you mix the blood. They seem to take on only the worst qualities of both races. It isn't fair to them really.'

Daud shook his head sharply, as if to clear it of hallucination. He glanced at Catherine, telling her it was time to leave.

'Oh, has Lloyd told you about joining the Army?' Mrs Marsh asked, looking stricken and ashamed.

'I've been telling him for years that that's what he should do,' Mr Marsh said. 'Make a man out of him.'

Daud glanced at Lloyd. His head was lowered but as he sensed Daud's scrutiny, he looked up. He shrugged his shoulders and smiled, a rueful admission of defeat. Daud looked away, not wanting to add to his misery. Mr Marsh was talking about regiments and medicals, but Daud had heard enough. He guessed that this was the reason for the invitation to tea. Lloyd had wanted him to know but did not want to have to tell him himself. Perhaps also, although Daud was less certain of this, Lloyd had wanted to show him that he had had no choice.

They made little ceremony about leaving, rising to go after another exchange of glances. Mr Marsh attached himself to Catherine again, holding her hand as they stood by the door, and then following her down the front steps.

'Don't get hurt,' Daud said, shaking hands with Lloyd.

'Not like the other day! Did he tell you about how he fell off the bus? Silly boy,' said Mrs Marsh.

Mr Marsh shouted out some pleasantry as they began to walk away, but Daud did not hear it. He thought Lloyd would walk with them down the road, but his mother had her arm on his shoulder and he stayed with her.

18

'It was the woman I felt sorry for,' Catherine said, making a disgusted face. 'And Lloyd … having that man for a father.'

'I told you we shouldn't go,' he crowed. 'It was a nice house, though. No mice in the walls and no mould in the cupboard.'

'I don't know how you could've just sat there, listening to those obnoxious things,' she said. 'We should've left as soon as he started.'

He shrugged. 'I was imagining that Bossy and I had come upon bugger Marsh in the fastness of Prison Island. He might have been shipwrecked, certainly immured in a fortress of stakes, muttering to himself and looking for somebody to bully. Like Robinson Crusoe. While I was listening to him, I imagined Bossy and me interrogating him. He probably would've been difficult and we would have been forced to get rough with him, beat him up a little, pull his long, wispy beard. That kind of thing …'

That night he had another dream. He saw himself walking the streets, turning to look at whatever pleased him. Opposite the cathedral gates he saw a man waving a banner announcing the end of the world. His grey hair was shiny with dirt, tired eyes open but unseeing. Then the eyes fixed on Daud, the face took his father's shape and turned wicked. Instantaneously, Daud found himself in Bishop Street, reading a letter from his mother. He saw her speaking the words as she laboriously wrote them out. She was sitting beside his father's bed, waving the flies away. An Indian doctor, crooning love songs to her, was writing a prescription. The radio was blaring music. Try as he might he could not see his father's face, just a shape covered with flies. It became important to see him, and he became frantic as he tried to fight his way to him before he died.

He woke up in tears, his heart soaring with dread. He curled up in her arms while she comforted him, rebuking him for the pain he caused himself. 'I fear news of his death,' he said. 'There's no avoiding him going, but I know that when he goes he will still be angry with me. I keep dreaming of his death.'

She stayed the rest of the week with him. When they had the same duty, they walked to work together, cutting across the common. The days continued warm and dry, starting talk of drought and crisis. The grass on the common was turning golden and bare patches were beginning to appear. One evening she came back from work and went and stood outside, looking at the rock-strewn garden. She started to clean it up, talking of planting flowers or perhaps some vegetables. He was reluctant at first, inclined to scoff and mock, but then his mind was fired by the idea of fresh hot peppers and homegrown lettuce, perhaps even some okra. After a few hours of moving boulders and broken paving-stones they gave up. They showered and went out for a curry. He kept her abreast of developments in the Test Match, and it was to her that he admitted, holding her hand and swearing her to secrecy, that perhaps Tony Greig was not quite such a creep as he had at first thought. Although that in itself was not saying such a great deal

… England still lost, as was only right and proper, but the Boer had come out of the match with fair scores.

Karta turned up on the Thursday evening. He looked depressed when Daud opened the door to him, and a little shame-faced. He patted Daud's arm perfunctorily as he walked past, a contrast with the brazen embraces he had taken to performing in recent weeks. Daud sensed Karta's disappointment that Catherine was there, it was something about the length of time it took for him to greet her. And then he stared at her, as if rather than say hello he would have preferred to make a pass at her. She was on her hands and knees scrubbing the living-room lino, where Daud too had been before he rose to let Karta in. Daud's arms were wet with water and suds, and he rolled his shirt-sleeves up both to draw attention to his working state and to clown a threat for Karta to watch his manners. Karta smiled knowingly and exchanged a look with Daud. *The English have got you*, his look said.

'We're nearly finished,' Daud said, dropping down beside her. He did not enjoy the ostentatious, silent way that Karta convulsed with laughter. Karta leant against the wall for a while, his eyes constantly returning to the figure of Catherine on the floor. In the end, growing tired of standing, he attempted to leap over the wet patches to reach the chairs stacked in a corner.

'Get your filthy boots off the floor,' Daud screamed.

Karta stepped back, startled. He shook his head sadly at his friend's deterioration. 'Well, I'll see you sometime then. I'm going to France for a few days … with a friend,' he said. Daud guessed that the friend was the tutor, and that Karta had come to talk.

'We're nearly finished,' he said in a more conciliatory tone.

It was too late, and Karta left, muttering his misery. Daud could not suppress a chuckle. She too looked up and grinned. *You were a bit off with him, I thought*, she said. He dropped his rag and rushed towards her, calling *Catherine Catherine*. She squealed with surprise but was not quick enough to escape his grasping hands. She fell into the soapy mess on the floor, shrieking as the cold water soaked her shirt. *You fucking idiot*, she said, trying to hit him with bunched fists. He wrapped his arms tightly around her and stole a passionate kiss. They abandoned the mess on the floor and struggled up the narrow stairway, throwing shirts off on the way.

In the evenings they went for slow strolls through the town or to the pub. They explored the medieval alleyways and the quiet, faded streets. One afternoon they hired a boat and drifted lazily under the old arches and bridges. He showed her an orchard which came down to the water's edge and was surrounded on three sides with high walls. He told her the story of the woman who had lived there, a daughter of a rich landowner who fell in love with a vagrant boy whom her father had taken in out of pity. *He was a difficult boy, moody and violent. The servants used to beat him for his dark looks. The master regretted his kindness and constantly spoke of casting the boy out. The daughter was the only one who treated him with kindness. The parents warned her, in the end threatened her, but she would not stop. There was talk of bewitchment and black magic. To save himself the youth turned vagrant again and ran, but first he lured the daughter into the orchard and slaughtered her, mutilating her sex to show his contempt for her. Years later, his body was found there on the river bank, where he had returned to die*. She asked him to explain what the story meant, but he said he did not know.

They tied up their boat beneath an overhanging oak and had their picnic. An old man came out of one of the riverside houses and shuffled to the outside toilet. He glanced at them and then turned to look again. As if he did not trust his eyes, he returned to the house for his spectacles and came to look again. Catherine blew him a kiss.

At first she railed against the second glances they sometimes got, making abusive gestures at people who stopped to look at them. She turned on a man who had walked past them and muttered *The beauty and the beast*, calling him a fuck-head. The man got very angry and turned to Daud for explanation and apology. *You shouldn't have called her a beast*, Daud said.

On the Sunday evening she went to a call box to ring her mother. She had arranged to go home for a few days and wanted to check the details with her. She came running back after a few minutes saying a man had tried to force his way into the booth. He had managed to get an arm in and kept trying to reach her, saying *I want to fuck you, I want to fuck you*. When she threatened to call the police he blew a raspberry at her and wandered away. Daud went back to the call box with her, sitting on a concrete plant tub while she made her call. He postulated a class of derangement that could be called the telephone box syndrome. He had been spat at, threatened, pissed on for being in a call box. He had assumed that his assailants were simply made envious, turned mad, by his dark good looks, but perhaps the matter was more complex than that. Catherine looked stern and affronted as she spoke to her mother, but he knew from his own experience that she would be quivering inside.

He looked forward to the week on his own, relishing her return. He planned several surprises for her, but as he considered them in detail, they appeared less attractive, and rather too much work. When Karta came round on Thursday evening, fresh from his French tour, Daud was pleased to see him. He had found himself missing her, wishing she was here or he was there. Karta looked round the room with a friendly, mocking grin.

'So how has it been down here in Verona?' he asked. 'I assume that Juliet is not with you … You take my word for it, you're going to marry that one. Remember that when you've lost your freedom! Uncle Karta warned you! As for me … That smells good, my bro. *What* are you cooking?'

Daud shrugged. 'I've eaten,' he said. 'There's some left. Go and help yourself if you want.'

'As for me, I maintain my philosophy,' Karta continued when he had loaded his plate and returned to the living room. 'Don't trust a woman! Fuck her and leave her! You know I went to France with Helen. She paid for everything, man. Everything. I've been living with her these last two weeks, and she can't get enough. But … she'll have to get used to it. The time's almost here, my bro, and then I'm away from this fucking place.'

'What happened to the man she used to live with?' Daud asked.

'That pathetic man? I tell you this country's fucked and gone. He has left to spend two weeks with his mother in Scotland. You think I'd leave my woman on her own to go and stay with my mother. He's coming back tomorrow.'

'Oh, I see, so while he's been away you've been …'

'Yeah!' Karta said, grinning at Daud.

'Do you like her?' Daud asked and saw Karta cringe a little before he laughed.

'I'm telling you she's just a two-faced white bitch I'm screwing until it's time for me to go home. If it wasn't me she'd find herself another student to do it with. You know this man she lives with, this potter or painter or whatever, she talks about him all the time. I think that's sick! She can't even be loyal enough to him not to … reveal everything about him.'

'Maybe she feels guilty,' Daud said.

Karta scoffed. 'They're just dirty people. They don't know the limits of decency. When he comes back she'll probably tell him all about me. Anyway, I don't want to talk about her.' His mood had changed from the cockiness of his first entry when he had seemed pleased with himself. Now he was agitated, shaking his head a little as if evading a pain.

'So they're all waiting for you at home. Everything set up for the returning hero, eh?' Daud said. 'I confess I feel bitter with envy.'

Karta laughed. 'It's fantastic! I've already been offered a job.'

'What job?' Daud asked.

Karta shrugged, opening his arms to demonstrate his ignorance and his indifference. 'Government department … I don't know what kind of work. I don't have the kind of expertise that's needed out there. They sent me here to do some shit-arse course whose only function is to keep a couple of lecturers in jobs … and other things. The British Council pays for it, so who cares?'

'Don't you care?'

'The Ministry of Trade and Commerce will suit me,' Karta said and then laughed to see the face that Daud made. 'You get more benefits in a department like that.'

'You mean bribes?'

'I surely do,' said Karta, grinning. 'I've got to get something for this year. And anyway, dash is part of our culture. What do you think I am? A crusader?'

Daud sighed heavily, suddenly and involuntarily, making Karta wait expectantly. He shook his head, telling Karta that he had nothing to say.

'You don't think I'm serious, do you? Actually, it'll probably be a job at the Education Ministry,' Karta said, smiling at his friend. 'There are no big bribes there, that's for true. But I get a house, a car loan and a big salary … and the esteem and gratitude of my community.'

'You sound like you're turning religious,' Daud said, not quite believing him.

Karta laughed. 'You must come and visit, come for a holiday. I'll introduce you to some hot Freetown belles … Talking of which, where's your beautiful damsel? I hope she'll be back in time for my farewell party,' Karta said, lighting a cigarette. 'Only the best are invited. We'll slaughter a goat and cook some *jolof*. None of your baboon meat and carrots … And talking of baboons, have you seen anything of that English monkey? He won't forget Uncle Karta too soon I shouldn't think. Did you hear what that swine was saying that night?' He sucked his teeth and flicked some ash on his dirty plate.

They went out for a drink, Karta doing all the buying because Daud had run out of money. Karta talked about his journey, about the homecoming he expected and the presents he had bought. He asked Daud if he would come and help him on the day of the party, just to get the place ready and that kind of thing. They parted outside the pub. Karta laid a hand on Daud's shoulder, and there was a heaviness about it as if this was their last meeting. 'It was good to see you again, bro,' Karta said. 'You're looking good. Give her my love. Tell her she's good for you, and that Uncle Karta is always free when she gets tired of you.'

She won't get tired of me.

When she came on Sunday she was carrying a suitcase and a bag of supplies. 'I told them all about you,' she said, pleased with herself. 'I told myself to keep quiet, but I couldn't. They were a bit rattled at first. We argued and fought, and in the end sulked at each other. But every time they thought we had finished I started again. It was almost funny, but I wasn't going to give up. You were on my mind all the time, and whenever I opened my mouth your name came out. In the end they groaned every time I mentioned you. I even got the atlas out to show them where you came from. Soon they'll want to meet you. Just give them time.'

'What about the doctor? Didn't they ask about him?'

She shrugged. 'They asked. Daddy thought I was mad giving up a doctor for a floor cleaner, but I told him you weren't any ordinary floor cleaner.'

'Was he convinced?' he asked.

She shrugged again. 'And at night, when I was in bed I tried to imagine that you were there beside me. I wanted to hurry here, to be with you, to make you smile and tell you all the things I'd been thinking about.'

He smiled, drinking in her words as if they were the sweetest poetry. He took her case up to his room while she unpacked the supplies her parents had pressed on her. He envied her the happiness she found in her parents, the way she could win them round with warmth.

19

The university accommodation officer had described the tall, narrow tenement that Karta lived in as a period terrace, which had meant nothing to Karta, who would have accepted almost anything to escape the hall of residence. At the back of the house was the beginning of the university wood and Karta claimed that he sometimes heard scratching and cracking noises coming from the wood. *Perhaps a tribe of Englishmen live in there*, Daud suggested.

Daud had agreed to go there in the afternoon to help move the furniture and get the place ready for the party. It was the Saturday of the Oval Test Match, and Michael Holding would be ripping the innards out of the England team, God willing. He resented missing the match to go and help move a couple of pieces of furniture that Karta could quite easily have moved by himself, but he guessed that he was being tested. He tried a few opening flourishes on the beauty of Holding's athletic lope but Karta cringed and grimaced with such loathing and disgust that Daud felt shame for having exposed the cricketer to so much indignity.

It seemed to Daud that there were scores of students living in the house. Karta complained about them constantly, but Daud was filled with curiosity. They looked grubby and unconcerned, as if their thoughts were elsewhere, on higher things. He could not resist associating their superior indifference with an intellectual contempt for petty details. He was ashamed of his naivety and did not tell Karta how glamorous their student lives seemed to him.

For his party, Karta had taken over the living room where the television held pride of place. 'You see this television,' Karta told him as they manhandled it out of the room. 'I have fought bitter battles over this damned thing. Whenever I want to watch anything the rest of them groan and complain. They find my tastes somewhat plebeian. Do you understand what that word means? All they ever want to see are *serious* programmes about the starving millions of India. Sometimes the word goes round that some smug American shit-face, or some inarticulate Italian, is going to predict the end of the world. You should see the turds. They all crowd in with their friends and sit waiting for some overfed monkey to tell them how the world is running out of food or water or something. They sit smoking their stupid joints, listening to these half-baked theories and feeling that they're really getting to grips with the problems that face mankind. I tell them that I pay my blasted share of the rental and I'm going to get my share of viewing.'

'And?' Daud asked, feeling that he was required to prompt.

'They outvote me, the bastards. I say to them that democracy is not in my culture, that they're destroying my identity ...'

It was obvious that something was troubling Karta, and he gave Daud pensive looks as if he was considering saying something. At last he spoke. 'I'll tell you the truth, my bro. I have a big problem on my mind. You know that tutor, Helen? She's coming tonight. I couldn't very well not invite her, could I? What I need tonight is somebody like that Dutch Rosa. The word lust was invented for her! Sticky Dutch Rosa! A night with her would be one way of saying goodbye to this dump, don't you say, my bro?'

Karta had created a legend around Rosa, since the time he had taken her to a party in London, to show her off among some countrymen, only to discover later that she had knocked off the host in the bedroom during the course of the evening.

'What I'd do for another night with Rosa, man. Instead … I invited the potter or whatever he is as well. She can't have much to complain about, can she? I'll be leaving here tomorrow afternoon and then I can shake her off for good. I'm just annoyed that it should spoil my party like this.'

'What are you talking about?' Daud asked, surprised at the complications Karta was clearly in the midst of. 'I thought you were just having a sordid little affair with this woman. Has it become more serious than that?'

'I don't know how to stop her,' Karta said, a hint of fear in his voice.

A very plump girl appeared from the kitchen and stood watching them with a smile on her face. 'I've done the sausages, Karta,' she said, her cheeks glistening with good-will. She had huge buttocks and large lumps on her chest, the kind of woman that bushmen like them were supposed to adore, Daud thought.

'Angela, you're an angel!' Karta said, imitating her fawning manner. 'I should take you back with me as my housemaid or something. There are some cheeses and bread in those bags if you'd like to put them out.'

Angela looked pleased with these new instructions and grinned at Karta before returning to the kitchen. 'She's a shit,' Karta said, dropping his voice. 'Most of the time I've been here she's been spying on me and spreading rumours. She says I steal her food from the fridge. I wouldn't touch the noxious crap if you paid me. Then she does this … It doesn't surprise me, though. They like to put you in their debt by such kind gestures. Too much for their puny hearts to hate you without convincing themselves they'd been decent to you first.'

They moved most of the furniture into the dining room and lifted the kitchen table, covered with a table-cloth that looked as if it was a bedsheet, into the living room. Angela was at their heels and suggested that they give the room a quick hoover. Karta succeeded in looking lost enough for her to offer to do it. After they had brought the hi-fi down from Karta's room and stacked the records underneath the table, they wandered round the downstairs room, looking at their handiwork. Karta declared himself satisfied with the results.

'I don't know what to wear,' he announced. Angela looked at him with a ready smile. More work for Angela, Daud thought, looking forward to catching an hour or so of the destruction of the Boer's men. 'I want to look stunning for my final appearance, don't I? I have an all-white outfit …'

'Great!' Angela said, clapping her podgy hands. Karta gave her a warm smile, observing her bloated body with pity rather than with his usual disgust.

'No,' he said, shaking his head and glancing at Daud for corroboration. 'It would be too conspicuous. Some radical will read a deep psychological hang-up in my choice of colour and start quoting Fanon at me.'

Daud left them debating velvet brown trousers and a white silk shirt. He declined the invitation to go upstairs and observe this costume *in situ* and rushed home to catch what was left of Saturday's play. To his utter disgust, he found England still alive at 304 for 5. Amiss, his pipe clamped in his teeth, was still there at 176. He had hoped to find England abjectly hanging on to a wicket or two; instead they were flourishing. He knew this was because he had not been there to encourage and offer advice as the game progressed.

Catherine arrived with her suitcase, the last of her things that she still needed to move from the flat. Her friends had asked her to go in the end. They had tried friendly persuasion to gather her back into the fold, saying not a word against him, but lauding the fun of belonging to the medical harem. They ostracised her, sent her to Coventry and then just waited for her to go. She talked bravely of confronting Piano Keys and forcing him to do the repairs and pay for the decorating. *He's nothing but a slum landlord. I don't know what you're scared of.* Daud agreed with her, and waited for the day of action.

'You're not watching cricket again, are you?' she asked, huffing and puffing as she manoeuvred the suitcase into the middle of the room. He glanced at her with a look of pain and betrayal. 'It's all right, I'm only teasing,' she said, grinning. 'But you could at least say hello. Do you know I heard today that they're rationing water in the West Country? Apparently this is the driest summer since … I don't know when.'

He helped her carry her suitcase upstairs, and then stayed with her while she unpacked. He lay on the bed and watched her with a hungry look. 'I'm not paying any rent until the windows are fixed,' she said, ignoring his exaggerated invitation. 'And the bathroom's been made decent.' In the end she walked too near him and he lunged for her. She pushed him off with a practised and merciless shove. He waited patiently, and when the opportunity came for a second attempt he made no mistake. She lay down beside him and then made a face of pain, as if stopping herself from crying.

'What is it?' he asked. 'Did that lot say something to you before you left?'

'Only Paula,' she said. 'And it doesn't matter anyway.'

'What did she say?'

She brought her face nearer, kissing him between her words. 'She said that the reason I was moving in with you is your huge black penis, and when you've finished with me nobody will want to touch me. It's stupid!'

'Have I?' he asked.

'What?' she asked, beginning to grin.

'A huge black penis.'

She hooted with derisive laughter, and made a gesture with her fingers denoting a minuscule object. He was insulted. His manly pride was roused.

He talked a lot on the way to Karta's house, and she wondered if he was nervous. The house looked enormous to her, and from the rubbish round the steps that led up to the front door, she guessed that it would be none too clean. The door was opened by a very plump girl whom Daud introduced as Angela. When they walked into the house she saw that most of the people there were English. That came as such sudden relief that she was surprised at herself. She realised that she had dreaded being surrounded by black men who would despise her, and tell her that she belonged to a cruel and heartless race, as Daud in his bitter moods sometimes did. It had been a shock to discover the hostility in him, the indiscriminate anger. She glanced at him and saw him looking at her, waiting for her to say something. The music was very loud, and she shook her head and shrugged with a gesture of defeat. He said something to her and started to walk away. When she did not follow he came back for her, grinning shyly as he took her arm. They went into the living room, and there the noise was unbearable. They forced their way through the shuffling couples to where the hi-fi was. Daud bent down to scrutinise the machinery and then turned the volume down.

'What are you trying to do, bro?' Karta shouted behind him. 'You're going to ruin my party with your bourgeois anxieties. How do I look?' he asked Daud but glanced at Catherine.

'You look wonderful!' she said.

He bowed to her and then raised his eyebrows at Daud, waiting for him to pay homage. Daud looked at him for a long time. Karta beamed, turning a little this way and that, like a model. 'You look like a pimp,' Daud said at last. Karta threw his head back and laughed. *Showing the world how an African laughs with all his sawl*, Daud thought.

There were glasses and bottles of wine in the kitchen. It was quieter in there and a group had formed round a short black man of about forty or so. He was wearing a brown felt hat with the brim turned up on one side. A leather chin strap bit into the plump flesh of his cheeks. It was the type of hat beloved by big-game hunters and white settlers. In one hand he carried a swagger stick, and used it now and then to make his point. He was talking morosely, seriously. He glanced in their direction as they appeared, then grinned with pleasure and started to walk towards them.

'Hello, Sam,' Daud said as the man came nearer. Sam accepted Daud's hand eagerly, barely sparing a glance for her. He moved forward and wrapped one arm round Daud's shoulder, resting his head on Daud's chest.

'How are you, brother?' he asked. His voice was soft but rich with a deep misery. 'We're still carrying on the struggle, man.'

'Yes,' Daud said in a strangely small voice. It made Catherine wonder if it was dislike or guilt that she heard in it. When she saw the fastidious manner in which he disengaged himself from Sam's embrace, she knew it was at least partly dislike. Sam turned to her and she smiled. After a moment he smiled back.

'We don't want to lose all our brothers,' he said, turning back to Daud. 'We've seen it happen to the best among us. Keep the faith!'

He turned again to Catherine and smiled at her. There was something premeditated in the smile, she thought, as if he had known she would be there and he had waited for her to come nearer so he could deliver his warning to Daud. He came closer to her and she saw that his face was covered with oily little spots. She thought him revolting, and was afraid that he would want to shake hands with her. He leant towards her and laid his head on her shoulder, an inch or two above her left breast. She felt the heat of his breathing on her, and stepped back calmly, glaring at him. Daud and the little man exchanged silent looks, Sam smiling with eyes full of malice. In the end Daud turned and touched her on the arm, and she glanced in his face to see what the signal meant. Did he want her to smash Sam's repulsive face into a pulp, to stab his eyes out with the heel of her shoe? They could skewer the ugly bastard over a slow fire and sing freedom songs to him.

'A revolutionary blow, Sam,' Daud said.

'Our boys are dying out there,' Sam said plaintively. 'They are killing our children in the streets. Twenty-seven were killed yesterday in Cape Town, and today they've locked up everybody again. We don't want to lose all our brothers.'

Daud touched Catherine's arm again and started to move away.

'Wait!' Sam said, standing in Daud's way. 'I didn't mean anything against her.' He held Daud's arm and raised his face in appeal, his smile looking suddenly vulnerable and anxious. Daud stood still, and Catherine could feel by his hand on her that he would hit him. She waited, wanting him to shred his face in rage. 'It was nothing against her. I'm just telling you that these people are killing us. I didn't mean her any harm. I did not mean to offend you,' he said, turning to her, his eyes watering. 'You know I'm from South Africa. I've been in exile here for seven years now. Every day I think NO, I can't take any more. It would be better to die. I haven't seen my wife for seven years. I haven't seen my children ... Perhaps they're already dead.'

Suddenly Sam began to cry. 'They're killing our children in the streets now,' he sobbed. 'They have finished humiliating the parents, now they are destroying our children.' A woman came from the group and put her arm round Sam's shoulder, looking to take him away. She was in her thirties, her hair bedraggled and grey, her skin blotched with patches of red. Sam leant against her and followed where he was taken.

'He was a bit drunk, that's all,' Daud said. 'She'll look after him. He gets suicidal with all the booze.'

'Who's she?' Catherine asked.

'Mary. He lives with her. They even have two neglected, dirty little children that nobody cares for. He always turns up at parties and at the pub. He scrounges drinks and then cries. I think he'll kill himself one day.'

Karta suddenly appeared in the kitchen. 'Where's he? I hear that Zulu is making trouble again. I won't have the bastard ruining my party. I knew I shouldn't have asked him.'

'It's all right,' Daud said. 'Mary's got him.'

'She's here,' Karta said in a whisper. He glanced at Catherine and smiled with embarrassment. 'Helen,' he said in his normal voice. 'Come and meet her.'

They were standing in the hallway. She was a tall, dark-haired woman with a bright smile. Her face was a little round, adding to the impression of joy and mirth. She was on the verge of forty, Daud guessed, with an appearance of maternal patience and wisdom, although Karta had not mentioned children. She looked nothing like the way Karta had painted her. She was wearing large, dark-framed glasses that made her look severe but only in a playful way, as if she was really only dressing up. The man beside her was also tall, big and bloated rather than fat, but he looked strong. Daud smiled to himself, imagining Karta pinned against the wall by that brute. He looked a rugged, tough *hombre*, he thought. Karta was flustered as he introduced them. Daud saw Helen smile, and saw the look of undisguised loathing that the man gave Karta. His heart trembled a little as he began to foresee trouble. The potter's name was Matthew, and as he shook hands with Catherine his eyes went unashamedly to her breasts, and came to rest there. He did not look for a response from her, was neither wary nor cunning. There was not even hunger or interest in his look. In a way, she thought, the man seemed at sea, all at a loss, not because he was afraid or uncertain, but because he was not where he should have been. 'Where's the booze, love?' he asked Catherine.

She pointed over her shoulder, and Matthew smiled briefly before slipping out of the circle to get a drink. Helen smiled too as she watched him go. She turned to Karta and looked at him with undisguised invitation. 'It's a lovely place,' she said. 'I remember living in a house just like this when I started working. It's the smell that's most familiar.'

She glanced at Catherine and Daud, a moment longer than was polite, as if she was placing them in a scheme of things. There was no hostility in her eyes. On the contrary, her interest was warm, wanting to be allowed entry into the intimate aura they carried. When she smiled again, she radiated an easy and unaffected affection. 'I'd love to dance,' she said to Karta. 'If you don't think I'd look too ridiculous dancing to that music at my age.'

Catherine and Daud were still standing in the hallway when Matthew returned with a drink and a plate of food. Pieces of bread dropped out of his mouth as he ate, leaning against the wall. They excused themselves and went out for some air. They stood on the steps outside, leaning against the railings. She leant closer to him, wedging herself between his open legs. When he spoke, she felt his voice rattle the timbers of her body. A group of young people walked past on the road and turned to stare at them. She heard them say things to each other, then heard their stifled sniggers and carelessly suppressed snorts. They were amused at the sight of an English scrubber and her wog student friend, she thought. But he was talking again, his voice lowered so as not to be overheard. Later, when she thought of the night, she remembered the slight chill in the air, the music heaving and groaning behind them, and the sound of his voice rumbling inside her.

They went back inside for more wine. Matthew was still standing on his own in the hallway, although the party was alive now and people were passing him by. A circle of food crumbs had formed around him. He answered their greeting without enthusiasm.

'I hope there's still some wine left in there,' Daud said, making conversation.

'Loads,' he replied, lifting up his glass in a mock toast.

Catherine waited in the hallway while Daud fought his way to the kitchen. She regretted it as soon as he had gone. Matthew leant towards her the instant they were alone. 'Do you sleep with him?' he asked, his eyes on her breasts. 'What contraceptive do you use?'

She looked at him in disbelief and started to move away. He levered himself off the wall as if he would follow her. Beside her appeared a slim black man who asked her to dance. She accepted without hesitation, and only when she was in his arms dancing with him did she begin to reflect on the man who held her. He was peering at her face, smiling as if trying to please. There was desperation in the way he held her, and it made her feel squalid. He grinned unremittingly but without conviction. She wondered, now that she had become alert to such things, what history he had brought with him, what he might be thinking of her.

She felt his arms wrapped around her in that loud, darkened room and she was powerless to resist his embrace. He squeezed her body into his, pressing his pubic bone into the softness of her thigh. A claw-like hand crawled up her back and rested on her exposed neck. She made to free herself but he pressed her head down on his shoulder, wanting her to abandon herself to him. With sudden, disgusted strength she pushed him away. He did not let go but moved back far enough to show her his face. It was a mixture of incomprehension and hurt, but underneath that was a wily look. Then, as if he intended to parody the words, looking her full in the eye and smiling, his eyes gleaming with a kind of anxiety, he whispered *I love you*. She pushed him off, ignoring his look of dumbfoundment. She saw Daud standing at the doorway, and as she stormed towards him she felt the man following her. Daud's attention was elsewhere. She had stood beside him for some seconds before he saw her. The man came striding to Daud, his hand outstretched. *I am sorry, my brother. I did not know she was with you*, he said.

While Daud listened to the man's protestations of ignorance, she looked away, trying not to attend to what was being said. She found the mutual masculine reassurance irritating. Daud should tell him that it was to her he should abject himself, not to him. Nothing would be gained by making a scene, she told herself. As her eyes wandered the room she found it quite easy to allow the sound of the music to drown out the man's voice. Karta and Helen were still dancing. They were clinging to each other, oblivious to all around them, while their bodies swayed and their feet shuffled as a formal acknowledgment of what they were doing. Their mouths were together in a kind of endless kiss, their arms wrapped round each other. Looked at quickly they seemed like one, a grotesque beast without shape or grace.

Catherine glanced behind her, and saw that Matthew was still standing in the hallway. He was talking to a dishevelled-looking couple who seemed to know him well. His plate had been replenished, and the crumbs of food around him had increased. She glanced at the dancers again but they seemed without care, without fear. At last the music stopped, and after a moment Karta disengaged himself to look towards the hi-fi. Helen held on to him as he went to put another record on. Catherine saw that his face was wet with sweat, and in his eyes was a distracted look. Helen seemed the same, flushed and elated, her mouth open. Daud said hello as they walked past them, and Karta glanced round and raised an arm in greeting. She thought he had lost control of himself. She looked over her shoulder again at Matthew but he was still in the hallway, tipping and spitting crumbs of food on the floor.

The party was beginning to break up into groups. Daud wanted to leave but he did not want to seem dull and boring. Voices were raised everywhere they went now, passions were aroused and people were leaning towards each other as if anxious to be closer. They danced in the noisy living room for a while but stood mostly outside, talking and drinking wine.

'Let's go,' Catherine said soon after one. 'I think we've done enough for this party.'

When they said goodbye, Karta held him in a tight embrace for several seconds. *Let's not lose touch*, he said.

'Are you all right? Be careful!' Daud said.

'Yeah yeah,' said Karta.

'I mean … with what's happening in there …'

'I know what you mean,' Karta said quickly. 'It's been good knowing you, bro. Let's make sure we stay in touch.'

Daud looked at Karta in silence and then nodded. 'Be careful!'

20

The streets were silent at that hour. *So civilised*, he said. She asked him about Karta, and he hesitated for a moment and then began to talk about things they had done. His voice was full of pleasure at the memories. He noticed that the gate of St Hilda's Church was open, and because she was with him and he was feeling happy, he did what he would not otherwise have done. 'Let's walk through the church-yard,' he said, holding her arm as she made to walk on. 'We'll come out nearer home.'

'Not on your life,' she said, shaking his hand off. 'Not this time of night!'

'Coward!'

'I don't care. I'm not walking through that graveyard. Do you know that cemetery's been in use since the four-teenth century? There could be all kinds of things crawling about in there.' She could see the idea interested him, and she groaned.

'The fourteenth century! I didn't think you lot buried your dead then. I thought you just put a stake through their hearts and threw them into the nearest cellar. I'll tell you what, I know some spells,' he said, intoxicated by the hour, and perhaps by the cheap red wine that Karta had provided. 'This is foolproof, potent juju I'm talking about! We could go in there and find some Plantagenet knight, bring him back to life and question him. Or we might stumble over a pilgrim who did not make it back and talk over old times with him. Best of all, we could discover an old slaver who thought to escape our vengeance by getting himself buried here. We could raise him and torture him ... All right,' he said in the end, deflated by her look of patient boredom. 'I'll go in for a quick wander, you wait by the wall there.'

She watched him go through the gate, disappearing in the moonshadow for a moment. He stopped on the other side, standing in the moonlight with the dark stone mass of the church behind him. The shadow of the lich-gate roof fell between them like a barrier. He raised his arms in the air, turned his face to the moon and spoke: 'Watch over me in this iniquitous den. Raise dem up, Mother Hygiene, that I may question and torture the poxy monsters. Raise me their knights and maidens, but most of all give me a slaver that I may bend him to my will.'

He lowered his arms and threw her a pleased smile. When he saw that she remained unimpressed, he made a face and began to walk towards the graves. She was tired of the stupid game, she thought. She was a little scared and did not mind admitting it, but more than that, she thought it was ridiculous. He reached the headstones and bent to read the inscriptions. She wished he would hurry, it seemed unnecessarily provocative. It was not even funny any more. Her heart leapt when she saw some movement among the trees at the edge of the churchyard. Gradually and unmistakably an object began to define itself out of the shadows and grew into men. She called out his name, hissing out an urgent whisper instead of shouting her alarm, but he waved her down without turning round.

As they walked towards the crouching figure of Daud, it was obvious that no juju had conjured these beauties. They were the representatives of the times, six of the best that the National Health, Social Security and Child Benefit could produce. While the shock-troops of modern European civilisation thus approached him, the poor warrior from across the sea was crouched among the dead, looking for a symbolic scrap with a long-forgotten ancestor.

They saw him and hesitated only briefly. Did it not occur to them that this could be one of the dead? One of the spirits? It seemed a strangely catastrophic failure of imagination to her. They saw a man crouching in the middle of a graveyard at an early hour of the morning and they never thought to turn and run. She called out his name, urgently now, and saw him turn to face them. But it was too late. He glanced towards her and shrugged. She felt that she had failed him. She should have stopped him going into the graveyard, she thought, as if that would have prevented the pain that would befall him now. He began moving backwards to prevent them ringing him. What could he hope to achieve, raised as he was on rice and fish gruel, against the Manifest Destiny of barbarian rule? They called him *nigger spook*. He tripped on a gravestone and they fell on him, seeking to recapture the old glory by slaying a wog in their own right.

They beat him, calling him names and taunting him with questions that did not need an answer. She heard his voice above the others. *I thank you, Men of England*. He tried to rise, to fight back, but they were too many for him. When she went to him they took no notice of her, handing her off with a preoccupied *Piss off*. She picked up a long, pointed lump of kerb-stone. *Watch it*, one of them called. *The crazy bitch!* Thin blonde hair flying, one of them knocked the stone out of her hands and punched her full in the mouth, sending her toppling backwards. *You stupid bitch!* he said, standing over her, hands on hips. He kicked her with carefully gathered effort and she threw up in an uncontrollable spasm. They beat him until he lay senseless in the shadow of the church.

After the flower of England had ridden off into the sunrise, she went to him and wept for his mangled body. 'I've broken my arm,' he said proudly when he came to. She found him sitting up when she returned from calling an ambulance, leaning against a headstone and smiling. 'Did you see the way I charged those evil knights? Did you see how they scattered?'

He saw that she massaged her abdomen, wincing as she probed the pain. She told him of the man who had kicked her, described him to Daud as if she expected that he would know him. When he praised her bravery, she made a mocking face at him. 'What a compliment from a great warrior!' she said.

The ambulance men made a joke about reviving the dead. One of them recognised him. Daud asked them if they could put the siren on. *You some kind of royalty?* the ambulance man asked him. The Sister in Casualty insisted that Catherine wait outside but Daud made a fuss. 'She's wounded as well,' he urged. The Sister relented in the end, giving Catherine a long, suspicious look. She felt Catherine's belly and had her X-rayed at the same time as Daud, but she was inclined to pay him her serious attention. While they waited for the X-rays the Sister told Daud about a fancy-dress party in the Sisters' home. She had gone in a grass skirt, dressed up as a hula girl. He passed out when the doctor arrived and started to feel his broken arm.

They allowed Daud to stay in Casualty until Sunday afternoon. Sister Agnes Kirk, the plump old Angel of the Battle of Kut, came to see him while he was asleep. She wiped an imaginary lock of hair off his forehead with tears in her eyes. Catherine told him this when she came to collect him on Sunday afternoon.

'She recognised you. It was strange. She became all flustered and upset. She's really going senile, isn't she? Poor old cow!'

'I must've reminded her of the Mesopotamian campaign,' said Daud, trying to understand the agitation that Sister Kirk's behaviour caused him. Could he have been in Kut during the battle? In some other manifestation? 'What is so senile about that? Why shouldn't the good lady grieve over my injuries?'

Catherine made a face, unimpressed by his heroics. 'What campaign?' she asked, bending down to help him lace up his shoes.

The taxi driver sat morosely behind the wheel while Daud tried to squeeze into the back seat without jarring his wounds. He smiled at Catherine through gritted teeth, making much of his bravery under torture. He winced when she patted him ironically on his good shoulder. She shook her head and sighed. When they got home he refused to sit on the settee, saying it hurt his knee, and she exploded. 'Stop it! Stop making such a fuss about a few bruises.'

By early evening his body throbbed with fever. He went to bed but could not sleep, sweating and turning as he looked for a painless shape. Late at night, after she had dropped off to sleep, he thought of his parents. His heart bled with uncontrollable panic. How he'd failed them! How he'd neglected them! She woke up when he started rambling. *You must stop this*, she said.

He sat down to write a letter after she left for work. It was too late, he thought. How could he explain to them all the things that had happened? How could he describe

England's luminous dusk and say to them that it had not all been pain, after all? He wrote anyway, greetings and abject apologies, asking for forgiveness as he had always thought they wanted him to. He walked to the post office and posted the letter as soon as it was finished. In the afternoon he watched Fredericks and Greenidge torturing the England bowlers, scoring 182 for none in 138 minutes. Greenidge hit the ball as if he intended it personal injury, rising to square-cut it as if it was a loathsome pest.

He told her about the letter when she came home, and she patted his face and grinned, and he grinned back with a kind of pride. He really had done it. Soon enough he was on the cricket, and that wiped the smile off her face. He watched the whole of the final day. With the series already won, and everybody agreeing that the pitch was easy, a draw was the expert prediction, but Daud had a feeling. Holding was the graceful assassin, and no moment was sweeter for Daud than when he yorked Greig for 1. Daud danced round the house, yelping with mocking laughter and whirling his good arm like a demented dervish. When Catherine came home, he ignored her plaintive pleas and insisted on telling her the full story of the day's play. *203 all out. Greig 1. West Indies won by* 231 *runs*. In the end she fell asleep, which he found hurtful.

'How about visiting the cathedral this afternoon?' he asked her on Saturday.

'Why?' she asked, grinning with surprise. 'On second thoughts, never mind why. I'll give you a conducted tour. No moans and groans, okay? You go round obediently and look at all the things I tell you to. No arguments!'

The cathedral grounds were thronged with people, but most of them were standing back, skirting the building, diffident in their admiration. Catherine led him confidently to the main porch and halted him there. He looked up at the stone carvings and the intricate filigree that shielded the saints from the brazen gaze of the pilgrims. He stopped listening to her long before they entered the building, moved by a passion he could not yet name.

In the nave he turned his eyes heavenwards with unashamed incredulity. The pillars will outlast God himself, he thought. He hurried towards the altar, giving the gaudy pulpit the briefest of glances. It had a clumsy grandeur, but neither dignity nor grace, he thought. It seemed to him the work of self-aggrandising priests. He resisted Catherine's insistent tugging and looked with satisfaction at the grubby altar cloth and the heavy tarnished cross that stood on it. They had a more authentic look, he thought. She showed him the transepts, and the memorials to knights and kings. Then, as if keeping the best until last, she took him to the chapel of modern-day saints and martyrs, remembering on this occasion the slaughter of Martin Luther King. He hurried back to the nave and stood under its fluted vaulting, feeling himself soaring at the sight of the incredible grace of the stone and the light. After that he did not want to see more. He wanted to leave.

'This was not meant for God,' he said. 'This was to celebrate the ingenuity of man. We'll come another time. It's incredible. How did a bunch of barbarians in wolf skins build this?'

'I don't like this awed manner you're adopting,' she said, dragging him away. 'Most of it was built by foreigners anyway. Even the stone comes from Caen. It's just a massive Gothic pile standing almost next door to your rot-infested hovel. And it's stupid not to visit it.'

'No no,' he protested. 'It's much more than that.' Ducking and weaving between the crowds in Sun Street and Palace

Street, he tried to explain that what they had seen was more complicated. 'How could feeble barbarian man do all that? What for? Ask yourself that. He was not celebrating the glory of God when he created that. He was showing himself and his time how resourceful and ingenious he was. And that's why all those millions of pilgrims have been coming here for centuries ... Hey, don't walk so fast! They all came filled with faith or sin, but also with another feeling, that they mattered in the scheme of things. And the suffering and pain made that feeling real, gave them strength. Do you see? Why are you walking so fast?'

'Because I'm trying to get out of this fucking crowd!' she shouted.

'Don't you see?' he said when they were back in Bishop Street. 'That's why those pilgrims came, and were so filled with passion, unlike these gawkers who stare with open mouths at everything they see. They came thinking that they were suffering because of who they were, or because of what they had done. Then they saw that incredible vaulting, built by people they didn't know. They must've realised then, must've known that the same faith that had driven them on their pilgrimage had created this stone pile that they had come to worship. It wasn't about God. It was about the resourcefulness to create something huge and beautiful, a monstrous monument to the suffering and pain that we travel thousands of miles to lay at some banal shrine. And it's been going on all the time. Don't you understand? Don't you see?'

She was attentive but sceptical, watching his agitation with a frown of mild disapproval. 'I'll make some tea,' she said.

'Wait,' he begged. 'Let me finish. What links all these pilgrims is the same desire to break out of their limitations, to go beyond what they know ... to change their lives.'

Later, when several cups of tea had dampened his optimistic fervour for continuity, he spoke to her of his own pilgrimage. How he had come, he thought, to beard the prodigies in their lair, to possess their secrets and hotfoot it down the mountain paths to the safety of his people's hidden valley. He had come, carrying a living past, a source of strength and reassurance, but it had taken him so long to understand that what he had brought could no longer reach its sources. Then it had started to seep and ooze and rot. It became a thing, maggoty and deformed, a thing of torture. And he began to think of himself as a battered and bloated body washed up on a beach, naked among strangers. Like Bossy in the end ... The reality was so much more banal. He had come for the same kinds of reasons that had made barbarian wolf-man build that stone monument, part of the same dubious struggle of the human psyche to break out of its neurosis and fears. When he had had a rest, he promised her, he would release the bunched python of his coiled psyche on an unsuspecting world.

Also available by Abdulrazak Gurnah

Afterlives

SHORTLISTED FOR THE ORWELL PRIZE FOR POLITICAL FICTION 2021
LONGLISTED FOR THE WALTER SCOTT PRIZE 2021

Years ago, Ilyas was stolen from his parents by the German colonial troops. Now he returns to his village to find his parents gone, and his sister Afiya given away. Hamza returns at the same time. He has grown up at the right hand of an officer whose protection has marked him for life. He seeks only work and security – and the love of the beautiful Afiya.

As fate knots these young people together, the shadow of a new war on another continent lengthens and darkens, ready to snatch them up and carry them away…

'Riveting and heartbreaking ... A compelling novel, one that gathers close all those who were meant to be forgotten, and refuses their erasure' *Guardian*

'A brilliant and important book for our times, by a wondrous writer' *New Statesman*, Books of the Year

'A tender account of the extraordinariness of ordinary lives … Exquisite' *Evening Standard*

Gravel Heart

For seven-year-old Salim, the pillars upholding his small universe – his indifferent father, his adored uncle, his treasured books, the daily routines of government school and Koran lessons – seem unshakeable. But it is the 1970s, and the winds of change are blowing through Zanzibar: suddenly Salim's father is gone, and the island convulses with violence and corruption in the wake of a revolution.

It will only be years later, making his way through an alien and hostile London, that Salim will begin to understand the shame and exploitation festering at the heart of his family's history.

'The elegance and control of Gurnah's writing, and his understanding of how quietly and slowly and repeatedly a heart can break, make this a deeply rewarding novel' Kamila Shamsie, *Guardian*

'Riveting ... The measured elegance of Gurnah's prose renders his protagonist in a manner almost uncannily real' *New York Times*

'A colourful tale of life in a Zanzibar village, where passions and politics reshape a family... Powerful' *Mail on Sunday*

The Last Gift

Abbas has never told anyone about his past; about what happened before he was a sailor on the high seas, before he met his wife Maryam outside a Boots in Exeter, before they settled into a quiet life in Norwich with their children, Jamal and Hanna. Now, at the age of sixty-three, he suffers a collapse that renders him bedbound and unable to speak about things he thought he would one day have to.

Abbas's illness forces both children home, to the dark silences of their father and the fretful capability of their mother Maryam, who began life as a foundling and has never thought to find herself, until now.

'Gurnah writes with wonderful insight about family relationships and he folds in the layers of history with elegance and warmth' *The Times*

'A story replete with black humour and contemplative politics, told with great generosity' *Times Literary Supplement*

'At a time of forbidding public rhetoric about immigration, Gurnah's sensitive and sympathetic portrayal of his cast feels welcome' *Sunday Times*

Desertion

SHORTLISTED FOR THE COMMONWEALTH WRITERS' PRIZE

Early one morning in 1899, in a small town along the coast from Mombasa, Hassanali sets out for the mosque. But he never gets there, for out of the desert stumbles an ashen and exhausted Englishman who collapses at his feet. That man is Martin Pearce – writer, traveller and something of an Orientalist. After Pearce has recuperated, he visits Hassanali to thank him for his rescue and meets Hassanali's sister Rehana; he is immediately captivated.

In this crumbling town on the edge of civilised life, with the empire on the brink of a new century, a passionate love affair begins that brings two cultures together and which will reverberate through three generations and across continents.

'A careful and heartfelt exploration of the way memory inevitably consoles and disappoints us' *Sunday Times*

'Beautifully written and pleasurable ... The work of a maestro' *Guardian*

'An absorbing novel about abandonment and loss' *Daily Telegraph*

By the Sea

LONGLISTED FOR THE BOOKER PRIZE 2002
SHORTLISTED FOR THE *LOS ANGELES TIMES* BOOK AWARD

On a late November afternoon, Saleh Omar arrives at Gatwick Airport from Zanzibar, a faraway island in the Indian Ocean. With him he has a small bag in which lies his most precious possession – a mahogany box containing incense. He used to own a furniture shop, have a house and be a husband and father. Now he is an asylum seeker from paradise; silence his only protection.

Meanwhile Latif Mahmud, someone intimately connected with Saleh's past, lives quietly alone in his London flat. When Saleh and Latif meet in an English seaside town, a story is unravelled. It is a story of love and betrayal, seduction and possession, and of a people desperately trying to find stability amidst the maelstrom of their times.

'One scarcely dares breathe while reading it for fear of breaking the enchantment' *The Times*

'An epic unravelling of delicately intertwined stories, lush strands of finely wrought narratives that criss-cross the globe ... astonishing and superb' *Observer*

Admiring Silence

He thinks, as he escapes from Zanzibar, that he will probably never return, and yet the dream of studying in England matters above that. Things do not happen quite as he imagined: the school where he teaches is cramped and violent, he forgets how it feels to belong. But there is the beautiful, rebellious Emma, who turns away from her white, middle-class roots to offer him love and bear him a child. And in return he spins stories of his home and keeps her a secret from his family.

Twenty years later, when the barriers at last come down in Zanzibar, he is compelled to go back. What he discovers there, in a story potent with truth, will change the entire vision of his life.

'There is a wonderful sardonic eloquence to this unnamed narrator's voice' *Financial Times*

'I don't think I've ever read a novel that is so convincingly and hauntingly sad about the loss of home' *Independent on Sunday*

'Twisting, many-layered ... Explores themes of race and betrayal with bitterly satirical insight' *Sunday Times*

Paradise

SHORTLISTED FOR THE BOOKER PRIZE 1994
SHORTLISTED FOR THE WHITBREAD AWARD

Born in East Africa, Yusuf has few qualms about the journey he is to make. It never occurs to him to ask why he is accompanying Uncle Aziz or why the trip has been organised so suddenly, and he does not think to ask when he will be returning. But the truth is that his 'uncle' is a rich and powerful merchant and Yusuf has been pawned to him to pay his father's debts.

Paradise is a rich tapestry of myth, dreams and Biblical and Koranic tradition, the story of a young boy's coming of age against the backdrop of an Africa increasingly corrupted by colonialism and violence.

'A poetic and vividly conjured book about Africa and the brooding power of the unknown' *Independent on Sunday*

'Lingering and exquisite' *Guardian*

Dottie

Dottie Badoura Fatma Balfour finds solace amidst the squalor of her childhood by spinning warm tales of affection about her beautiful names. But she knows nothing of their origins, and little of her family history – or the abuse her ancestors suffered as they made their home in Britain.

At seventeen, she takes on the burden of responsibility for her brother and sister and is obsessed with keeping the family together. However, as Sophie drifts away and the confused Hudson is absorbed into the world of crime, Dottie is forced to consider her own needs. Building on her fragmented, tantalising memories, she begins to clear a path through life, gradually gathering the confidence to take risks, to forge friendships and to challenge the labels that have been forced upon her.

'Gurnah is a master storyteller' Aminatta Forna, *Financial Times*

'Astonishing, superb' *Observer*